Blood Sister

Blood Sister

Kenna McKinnon

Dedication

To my children, Diane, Steve, and Ward; and my grandsons Ryan, Brendan, and Aaron. I love you very much.

Acknowledgments

My UK editor, Morgen Bailey, as well as my Michigan beta reader and editor, Judith Hansen, and my publisher Mark of 'Authors for a Cause', were instrumental in helping me polish this work, more particularly Morgen, who is a consummate author and editor herself. My former publisher, Cheryl Tardif, was the first to encourage me to write a mystery starring a schizophrenic private eye. I also want to acknowledge my friend Linda ('Moo Moo') Thomas, who was a preliminary beta reader and cheered me on. My children, as always, are inspirations and the jewels in my author's crown. My parents, Jean and Kenneth MacDonald, instilled in me a love of reading and writing, and I am grateful to them for that.

As schizophrenic myself, any others I met along the way helped to provide me with an appreciation of the illness and the potential we have for success. A special thanks to Austin Mardon, my friend and fellow traveler, who suggested the particular torture and delight of hallucinations and voices which Annie experiences.

Reviews

Reviews for Blood Sister:

'I loved the ending…it didn't spoil the end for me because there'd been so many suspects.' Morgen Bailey, UK, Editor, author of '*The 365-Day Writer's Block Workbooks*', '*The Serial Dater's Shopping List*', etc.

'Blood Sister is a fascinating look into streetwise crime-solving by a young woman dealing with a mental illness. The author, herself schizophrenic, offers an inside peek into the strange world of "voices" and hallucinations in a way that endears us to very likeable young Annie, the detective.' Judith Hansen, Editor, The Eastland News (defunct)

Chapter One

My cell phone woke me early. It was the cops.

"Somebody bashed Doctor William Hubert over the head with a blunt instrument last night. They drilled his brains out of his skull with a surgical tool and piled them in a heap by his bloody skull. We need you, Annie. Hit the street."

The call scared the pajamas off me, and I wanted to wake up Samir, shake him, make him see me, and help with the fear. Even the voices in my head didn't know what to say at first.

My size ten feet hit the floor in a hulk stomp.

My roommate, Samir, was in the next bed, huddled under his grey blankets with no sense of what was happening. His long black body looked lumpy like a dun toad. Samir was my first real boyfriend. Ain't that something? And me twenty-four years old and all, plus this mental problem.

I twirled the circle of cheap yellow metal on my left ring finger. Samir and I'd met in an ESL (English as a Second Language) class I volunteered to help teach a couple years ago on this island. We drifted together, two outcasts just able to afford this half-way house, and sharing for financial reasons. Only way Social Services would let us stay here together, in the same boarding room, was if they thought we were married. No questions asked.

The Powolskis were like a foster family to us.

Then the voices in my head started screaming. I covered my ears with my hands. *Be careful. You didn't listen to the phone call close enough. Stupid. It's way over your head. It'll take you more than hard work to solve this case, Iron Head. It'll take brains and guts and you don't have that.*

"Son of a brownie," I said in response. "Go away."

You're a homely girl, with kinky bleached-white hair and buck teeth. Good thing my personality more than made up for it. Yeah, at five foot nine I was a force to be reckoned with.

I yawned, trying to get air into my lungs. *It's your heart, stupid, you're gonna die!* No, it wasn't my heart, I was only twenty-four years old and solid as Twenty Mule Team. My psych in Campbell River told me that anxiety made me short of breath and I'd yawn.

I thought of the phone call a few minutes before. They need you, Annie. The Doc's dead as a salt cod. Grisly murder. Get on it. So I pulled on my jeans and shirt, and shook Samir.

Chapter Two

"Kids," Mrs. Powolski called up from the kitchen. "Breakfast's on, and the rent cheques are due."

Samir and I paid the rent with my Justice Department's salary and his pension. I had a little money put away, too. His pension was a Canada Pension Plan draw for the severely handicapped—although Samir was only 21 years old, he could still get a pension 'cause of his bad legs.

Samir isn't handicapped in my opinion. He got a disability, like me, but that ain't handicapped unless you let it be.

"I got work to do today, right away!" I called downstairs. "I'll pay my share when I get home."

Guess you're wondering what I do for a living, for the Justice Department. I'm not a cleaner and I don't work in a kitchen. I work part-time but it's a good job. After all, I got the G.E.D.—the General Equivalency Diploma, I earned my high school the hard way, at Central High in Vancouver, and also what the street people know as the Canadian Hard Knocks University. If it weren't for Constable Tom arresting me for shoplifting last year, and the court giving me a second chance, I don't know where I'd be.

I did Community Service work for Lorne O'Halloran, Private Investigator, for six months and after that, they hired me, casual like, to work on Serendipity Island for the Justice Department—I was that good. I also know a lot of the people on the street, comes in handy, and I don't mind saying the pay is good, and I enjoy my work.

I still report to Lorne, that was one of the stips in my contract. They thought I wouldn't work as well for anyone else but good ol' Lorne O'Halloran, Private Eye and slot machine enthusiast. That's when my voices took over, though.

The Island was just perfect for me to live and work on since my mom died, after we left Vancouver. Serendipity was big for a place in the Gulf Islands, with a flourishing population in the amount of twelve hundred sturdy souls; five street people that I knowed of; and a drug and alcohol problem amongst the general population. There was also an Indian nation down near the lighthouse on Modge Bay, near the float house Mom had left me. I couldn't live there permanent because of the court case fourteen months ago when the judge said I had to live in a group home with the Powolskis.

"What, rent due again? Blasted werewolves and vampires and landlords." The grey toad in the next bed wriggled and morphed into my handsome dark companion of six months. Samir rubbed his eyes, which appeared bloodshot.

I pulled at the Canadian flag pinned to the window and squinted out at the yard. Only the old yeller dog was there, chained to a post in the middle of the yard, and he wasn't sleeping either.

Sometimes I saw the sun rising in the west, not the east, like a huge speckled orange and the sky was lit with fire. Those were the times God spoke to me. Or the Devil beckoned.

Samir said I hallucinate and hear voices because I'm a nut case and a private eye should not be a nut case. But I thought the voices and visions helped me a lot, they cleared my mind the visions did, and the voices made me think out of the cage. I knew the voices and the visions came from my own ego and sometimes from deep down under my subconscious. So in a way, I was talking to myself, and my unconscious mind was a powerful force. Jung would say that.

Chapter Three

Samir had his jeans on already and an oversize nightshirt. He hobbled to the john. First thing I woulda done had I been his mom, was to get that boy some physiotherapy after the soldiers broke his legs. Or at least seen a doctor. Guess doctors and physios were scarce back there in the Sudan. Still—I woulda tried.

Now he was twenty-one and they'd have to break his bones again to splint them proper, some bone doctor in Campbell River or maybe off in Vancouver at some fancy clinic.

Samir grunted something in return. I didn't hear what. A blue butterfly, five feet long, hovered over the bathroom door. It was beautiful. Thank you, visions, and then Mrs. Powolski called again.

The toilet flushed. I could hear African curses from the next room. The cursing grew louder and my voices jittered in reply. I started to count the spots on the wall.

"I tripped on dem damn jeans."

"Watch where you pull them down then, angel pie."

"Legs are no freckin' good. I should just kill myself. Good morning." I could hear the shower start up.

I let the flag curtain drop. "Okay," I said when he was out of the shower. "So how are you going to kill yourself this time?"

Samir's smile flashed white-silver quick in his dark face. "Don't know. I'll think of something, Annie."

"Why'd you take a shower this time of the morning? Mostly you wait till after brekky."

"None of your business, angel pie." He hugged me.

"You smell so good. You sure you're all right? You slept like a stone all night."

I thought I should take my meds then, half of them at least, time to tippy-toe down to the kitchen and quiet the murmur of my voices for a couple of hours.

Samir pulled a shirt over his tall, lean frame. "How do you think I should do it?"

I didn't answer.

He stooped to tie his muddy Nikes. He looked real good.

"Coming?" I brushed a big piece of lint off my flannel shirt.

"Sure." He grabbed his cane. "Ready when you are, Tin Pan Annie."

I was afraid he would kill himself some day and I couldn't stop him. My voices got real quiet. I was thinking they were happy.

If only those darn voices would disappear. My doctor says I'm OCD, too, that's Obsessive-Compulsive Disorder for those of you not educated in psych talk. It means I ruminate a lot and I count. I count just about everything, on my fingers, under the table if I can.

"Time to go downstairs for breakfast," I said to Samir, who hobbled after me down the carpeted steps. "Time to meet the day."

"Oh, shit," he mumbled and thumped his cane. "Time to greet the Powolskis and watch them feed their goddarn animals before our muzzles are in the trough."

"Mrs. Powolski is a good cook."

"I want to kill myself."

"This can be arranged."

"Ha, ha. Very funny, Annie. I mean it this time."

"You've got a hangover, Samir. You'll get over it." I started whistling as we went downstairs. He groaned as we reached the bottom step.

Chapter Four

Outside on the dun-colored lawn, dry leaves twisted and soared. The yeller dog bayed from out back. Coffee was on and bacon crackled in the pan. Mrs. Powolski stirred the greasy strips and cracked some eggs. Her heavyweight husband sat with thumbs hooked in his suspenders.

"Mornin', kids."

I smiled. "Give me my meds, please, Mrs. P." She was supposed to keep an eye on us, and that included giving me my pills. Group home rules. I hated that.

Samir lurched into the room and sat on one of the truly vintage chairs that amazingly would hold Mr. Powolski's weight.

"Have to go out early this morning," I said. "I feel so good and I got work."

"Dress warm," Mrs. Powolski said. "You'll catch your death of cold."

"That's good." Samir threw back his head and laughed. "Can I go, too? I'd like to catch my death."

"He wants to kill himself," I explained.

To finish my morning rituals, I counted to twenty on my fingers, twice, under the table before tackling breakfast.

"Somebody's done in," Mr. Powolski boomed. "Somebody kicked the bucket. Else you wouldn't be so happy, missy. I heard your cell phone ring early this morning. Can only mean bad news for somebody."

"It means our private eye here has work." Samir licked his fingers. "More bacon, please."

"Yeah, I got a phone call early this morning from the cops' office," I said. "You're right, angel pie Samir, I got work."

"I knew about it early like," he said.

I can't help it, my analytic mind like goes into high gear and I just put things together that nobody else might think of, and I can't help it if maybe friends get all mixed up with foes.

He can't be trusted. He just sleeps in the same room with you because he wants the rent from Social Services, not your lousy body, babes, nobody would want that. He must have been talking to the coroner last night, they're in cahoots, just like the Justice Department's office, they know everything you do.

I started counting on my fingers again. Sure, I could trust Samir. He was the only person I could trust in this little hell-hole of a town. *Why do you say that, you little witch? You know you love it here. It's just like you, small-minded and dirty.*

"I ain't small," I said to the voices. "I'm big boned and I'm tall."

"What?" Mrs. Powolski beamed.

"I'm what they call an Amazon," I said. I checked my cell phone to see if there were any more calls, and went upstairs to shower. Samir was there before me and out the door before I had my shoes on. He was always quick in his movements. Fluid-like, here and then gone.

Lordy, Samir was one good-looking Sudanese man. If we had babies they'd be cuter than me.

Chapter Five

Samir was down at the Serendipity Hotel, already having his first argument of the morning, when my Vespa scooter and I put-putted down the street past the old white building, past the sign that said, *Flapjacks and steaks, all you can eat Tuesdays.* I noticed they'd torn up the sidewalks again and fresh asphalt smoked in the cold morning air. I was heck bent for velvet to Lorne O'Halloran's place, Private Investigator. He was my boss since I stole that swag and got sent to community service and probation under his supervision.

I'd met Samir and his Sudanese pals in an English as a Second Language class I'd volunteered to teach. It was serendipity, hee, hee. Then the court sent me to the Powolski's group home and Samir was there. Since my mom had died and left me her float house I was real ticked they wouldn't let me stay at the float house, but I had steeple sized hopes that I'd be let off soon, maybe eventually get a pardon from Erna at the Justice Department in Victoria. My probation was over and all, now I got paid to work for Lorne 'cause I was such a dang good Private Eye.

I parked the scooter and rocketed up the stairs, two at a time, to Lorne's office. He didn't seem surprised to see me. "The doctor," he said. "You heard." He rearranged some papers on his desk.

"Yeah. Tell me about it," I said. Lorne took a gulp of black coffee and crushed out a cigar in an ashtray shaped like a horseshoe. *Edmonton, Alberta* was etched into the metal semicircle. Lorne's face was round, too. He was round, all around. Lorne was fat and bald and loud. He reminded me of Mr. Powolski.

"The Doc's dead as a crushed beetle. You got the call? Somebody's pretty sick, I'd say. Security, or maybe it was the caretaker, found the door open and called the cops. Doc was on the floor, no locks broken. The Justice Department in Victoria gave the case to us, said they needed somebody the street people trust. Constable Tom and the sergeant were working all night on this."

"Ugh. I can think of one or two I know, if they were real high on somethin', but we don't have no psychos in this town besides me, far as I know. Would have to take a psycho to do that. This is a sick, sick case, you're right. Just a minute while I heave up my greasy eggs and bacon."

I didn't puke, of course, but this case sure made me feel sick, thinking of Doc's slimy brains all over the floor and the hole in his cranium, who'd do that.

Doc wasn't my friend but I knew him. Everyone knew Doc, the high-end pill pusher, and even he didn't deserve this. I pulled my sturdy body up even straighter and smiled. On the other hand, it was work for Lorne and me. I had the stamina of a Peterbilt truck and loved to get my lily-white hands dirty. But a surgical drill into the skull? Gruesome.

Even my voices were quiet, probably shocked that somebody else had thought of this before they did. Wouldn't put it past them to suggest it, but they never had. I shuddered and counted the freckles on the back of Lorne's hands. Now what?

"The impossible just takes a little longer. We've got the case, Annie. Victoria called, like I said, and they specifically asked for you."

"The Doc's clients were drug addicts and crystal meth freaks, trying to come down and get clean. Could be any one of them after more methadone."

"Yeah. Any one of the five street people. Or we're supposed to think that. So it's up to us, we've got to go out there and find out who did it." Serendipity Island was fairly big in area for a Gulf island, had a small town nestled into its crags and mountains and shores.

"It's up to me, you mean." I picked my teeth with the edge of a fingernail and sighed. "Where do I start? Could be any one of them boys living on the street and looking for his next fix, short on cash, Doc wouldn't give him any more methadone, hit the Doc over the head with—what?"

"Could be any kind of blunt instrument to knock him out first, then the drill."

I thought. Hard. The voices whispered in my head, *Stupid. You'll never figure this out. Why'd you think you could do this job in the first place?* I talked out loud in order to drown them out, tried not to let on I'd heard them.

"Doc had all kinds of instruments could be used to bean him. He was an old guy, Doc was, fat as a rasher of dollar store bacon, and would've gone down like a polled ox."

"None of the instruments are missing. All accounted for, his nurse says, including the bloody drill, and she says she left late yesterday and Doc was closing up."

"Really?" I sat up. This might not be so hard after all.

"No," Lorne said, reading my mind. "It wasn't the nurse who killed her employer. Firewall Eddie in Security says he saw her go home before ten, and the caretaker backs him up. The coroner says time of death was just before midnight."

"She came back?" I would cover all bases. "Does Eddie have an alibi?"

"I know what you're thinking," Lorne said, lighting another stogie. "Firewall Eddie has keys."

"Yeah."

"He has an alibi. The caretaker was there with him that night at the time of death, which forensic establishes at within a few minutes of midnight."

Both friends of mine. I breathed a sigh of relief. This was no job for the weak of heart, but better to be strangers or acquaintances than good friends with the suspects. My emotions never got in the way, but I was a *human* Amazon after all. I smiled.

Chapter Six

"I think we should visit the scene of the crime," Lorne grunted. "Would give you an idea of what we're up against."

We went in his van, stashed my Vespa in the back. Didn't take long to get to Doc Hubert's building. Anything was only ten minutes away in this town.

We took an elevator to the second floor. Lorne had a key to the door. He pushed it open. The cops had left fluorescent tape to mark off the murder scene and chalk marks on the floor. Somebody had tried to clean up the blood. There were stains on the floor, though, and across the top and sides of the counter where the drill still gleamed and dripped.

"Cops will be back later," Lorne said. "I've got clearance. You're okay, Annie, you're with me."

"Thanks," I muttered, thinking hard and counting beneath my breath. Fortunately, the body had been taken away, leaving a body-sized stain on the carpet. A few feet away there was a wet mark with a few red noodles curling about like somebody's leftover dinner.

"Brains?" I said. I was curious. I had never seen brains. "Why'd they leave the murder weapon here?"

"They're waiting for the RCMP to come and take over." Royal Canadian Mounted Police, that meant we were in the big time, out of Constable Tom and the Sergeant's league.

I looked around the room. "What time does the nurse usually get to work?"

"You ever see his nurse? Small like a wren. She wouldn't have had the strength to clobber ol' Doc, even if he wasn't expecting it. She'd have the knowledge to drain his brain, though, you're right about that."

"He was a big man," I agreed. "Would have to be knocked out first. Somebody must have been pretty darn angry or crazy, though, to do what they did."

"Clue number one," I said, counting under my breath. "Someone gets in through a locked door and the keys are missing."

"It was Doc's custom to lock the doors before he left and tidy up, lock the methadone away, pull the drapes, check all the doors and set the alarm, then go home. Anyone could nail the time Doc left every night, regular like clockwork," Lorne said.

With one hand, I counted on my fingers, under the table where he couldn't see. "Crikey. I never thought about the alarm. Why didn't it go off?"

"Because he was there when the boogeyman came in. His habit was not to set the alarm until he left the building empty," he said. "There were no signs of a forced entry. We know he always kept the keys in his desk drawer."

"Unfortunately, everyone knew that," I said. "Doc's been a fixture in this town for a hundred years. His habits were common knowledge. Too bad for him, as it turned out. Pore guy."

"I think we've established that he knew the intruder," Lorne said. He frowned at my chewed fingernails, or I thought he did.

"No accounting for taste. It does look as though he was waiting for someone."

The coffee pot in the corner was full and still on. I walked over and switched it off, passing the drill as I did. I shuddered.

The private eye snorted. "We have to do better than this, Annie. The Justice Department is after my hide."

"Only because you're running for mayor this election."

"I have a damn good chance of getting the position, too. Those guys are jealous. I have a good rep with the medical staff and clinics here, am well known in the community."

I'd heard this before. It was best to suck up to my boss. "I could be talking to the next mayor, Lorne."

The corners of his mouth turned up. "If we solve this case for the Department, I'm sure the city will be very grateful. The Doc was a fixture here for over twenty years. He gave generously to every campaign and he was well known. He'll be missed. I could be a natural, riding on the heels of a successful arrest and conviction."

Correction. If *I* solved this case. "Him or her. Ka-bam. Somebody pole-axed him then gimleted his skull."

"Had to be somebody strong," Lorne agreed.

"Ol' Doc wasn't a featherweight."

"Yeah. A friend? Or a drug addict he was trying to help?" Lorne's nicotine stained fingers riffled through the Rolodex at the side of the mail cubbyholes.

I looked through the cupboards. There had to be an appointment book.

My voices howled. *Who keeps a paper track anymore, Annie Tin Pan Alley? Look harder. You don't try hard enough. This is the twenty-first century.*

"He kept his clients private. Your job's to go out on the street and scoop up the perpetrator," Lorne said. He waddled to the other end of the room and helped himself to some tepid coffee from a stained mug.

"Me? I risk my life for some high-end drug pusher?"

Lorne slammed his coffee mug on the desk. "You get paid to follow orders. And you get paid to go out on the street."

"Yes, boss." I looked around. A pink rhino floated in a corner behind the filing cabinet. I blinked my eyes and the rhino disappeared. A pile of papers morphed into a snake, making me smile.

"You schizoid gumshoe, get outa here." Lorne raised his voice. He sounded like the voice I called The Screamer.

No need to call us names, my voices whispered. *You know it's true.*

"I know it's true," I said out loud.

"You're lucky to have a job." Lorne unwrapped a Cuban cigar and bit off the end. "You hear voices," he said. "You friggin' nut case."

"Yeah," I said. He was right. I was a schizophrenic gumshoe. My voices were quiet again. Sometimes it was hard to tell what was real and what wasn't.

"You're a good worker." Lorne's voice was softer. "Now get to it, Annie. I'm sorry."

"Time to get to work," I agreed with Lorne, and took the stairs two at a time, going down. He would take the elevator. Sure, he was sorry he'd ragged me about my voices. I knew he needed me in his down-at-the-heels but respected Private Investigator business. My boss was real good at using people, hadn't read a legal paper or indictment by himself for fourteen months, far as I knew, just had me type it up and read it to him, then he signed his name.

It seemed to me I was missing something, but it couldn't be important. I shook my head to clear the spiders out of my brain, and stepped into beams of yellow dancing dust motes in the lobby downstairs from Doc's office. It was real pretty. I stood still a time to admire the glory of the dawn streaming through the dirty window panes after last night's rain, then nudged open the door and stepped outside.

It was eight o'clock in the morning. The hotel opened at seven. Samir and his cousin Pepsi would have had their first few games of Chinese checkers together and be well into their second argument by now.

I pulled up beside Pepsi's old blue Mercury and parked the Vespa. I had my suspects in sight already. It was time for a convo with tall, thin, and talkative Pepsi, my main man's cousin and best friend. Pepsi was the substitute caretaker at Doc's clinic and knew Firewall Eddie real well. It meant keys, it meant another suspect. Another friend who could be loony tunes when Doc had pulled the plug on the free methadone. But they backed each other up. That was a relief, in a way, but could I trust either of them? Time would tell the story, I had things to do, and a lot of pressure on me to do them.

Chapter Seven

"It's a quarter after six. I missed you."

That would be Mrs. Powolski talking. She was very fond of me. Samir and I were late for dinner. Again.

"Missed you too, hunny buddy." I gave her a kiss on the cheek.

Mr. Powolski glared at me. Dinner wasn't late for him. He'd eaten already but was just mean enough to wait until we got there so he could glare. Samir's veal cutlets had congealed on the plate. My cutlets with baked potato and cheese sauce made my mouth drool like that dog in the Russian's study we took in grade ten. I was like the dog, and Mrs. Powolski was Pavlov with greasy grey hair and a flowered apron. I grinned, washed my hands and sat down.

"What are *you* smiling about?" Mr. Powolski belched and snapped his suspenders.

"Pavlov," I said, and forked my food into my maw.

"Sounds like one of those Polski names." Mr. Powolski wrinkled his forehead. "You been foolin' around with a Polski, Annie?"

"Course she ain't. She knows the rules," Mrs. Powolski said. "Besides, the girl's hitched to our Samir here."

"Wouldn't put it past her," Mr. Powolski said. "I could use another plate of them cutlets, Meredith."

Samir pushed his dinner across the table. "Here, have mine." Samir's face was flushed and his lips tightened.

"Funny," I said.

"What?" Samir asked.

"Your lips go tight when you're mad or embarrassed, and when you blush, your face turns purple. What are you, mad or embarrassed?"

"You got a loose mouth."

"You know," Mr. Powolski continued, "If you two ain't hitched, this whole arrangement is off. No more sharing rooms."

"Or beds," Mrs. Powolski said.

"Funny," Samir said. I sent him a look.

"None of this is funny." I explained about Pavlov's dog. "I was drooling when I saw the meal," I said. "Reminded me of my science lesson from grade ten."

"You never went no further than grade ten," Samir said.

"Did too. Got my high school diploma."

"Some accomplishment for a young lady like you," Mrs. Powolski observed.

"What do you mean?" I laid down my fork.

"With a disability, I mean."

"My aunt teaches at the university. She's just like me. She's a prof. With bipolar or schizophrenia or something."

"Takes her meds, I bet."

"Yes." *Oh-oh.*

"Not like some people we know."

"I'm pretty good with them now. Only missed once last week. I came downstairs this morning and asked for them."

"They cause weight gain," Samir observed.

"Don't give a sugar snap pea if they do," I said, and pushed back my plate. "I just forget sometimes."

"They'll give you a depot injection if you forget too often," Mrs. Powolski said.

"Funny," I said.

"What?"

"Just like Samir, you're making faces, Mrs. P."

His cane was in a corner, carved out of African mahogany with an ivory grip. Had to be dishonest to get that ivory through Customs. I glanced at Samir. His eyes were wide and innocent-looking, like a child's.

"Am not," Mrs. Powolski said. She chuckled, her whole body rippling in time to the deep ahh-ahh as she wrapped her apron around her large stomach and started rinsing dishes.

"Spic and span," I said. The parrots in their cage by the window squawked. Like my voices.

Chapter Eight

Catch us if you can, the voices whispered. *Dream big, you'll never get to university.* I ignored them and my dreams of greatness. *You're bad and not very smart,* they continued. *You'll never amount to anything. Just like Samir. Your mother was a librarian. You'll never come close to her achievements in life. Your crazy bipolar aunt took early retirement a long time ago. You got nobody now. You can't even look after yourself. You don't deserve any better than Samir.*

"Keep Samir out of this," I whispered. "I was good in drama and now I'm a good Private Eye. Maybe I'll be another Miss Marple or he'll find a job in something he's good at, like the military. Like guns. I have my G.E.D."

"What?" Samir asked.

"Nothing." *Mistake,* roared the voices. *Oh, you're bad and they'll catch you out with it. He doesn't like you.*

"Of course not," I whispered, trying to be cool. "We're not really married."

You'll never get married.

"Shut up," I said. The Powolskis were in the next room watching television. My voices were louder than the blare of the TV.

"What?" Samir asked, pushing me.

"Not you. Them."

"Oh. Your *voices,*" he mocked.

A cat slunk around the corners of the kitchen. Kitty had black, matted fur, green eyes, and mean as a she lion with its tail caught in a meat grinder. Mrs. Powolski was the only one fed that cat. She was the only one could get near it. Most of the day it slept in a special dog's bed in the spare bedroom downstairs, because it was big as a small terrier, and come night, it would let itself out the cat door in the kitchen and be inseminated by all the male cats in the neighborhood. It also ate from garbage cans—I seen it. Sometimes when the moon shone high, she rode the fence outside, yowling at nothing at all.

That cat was clearly crazy. If it ever actually caught one of the parrots and ate it, the cat would be history, though. Mrs. Powolski would see to that. Sometimes I left the door to the birdcage open. Just in case. The birds were too smart for me, though, and definitely too smart for the cat. They stayed put until the riptide was clear.

But the main point here was looking at Samir's cane in the corner. Something blackish and sticky was dried on the bottom of the cane. I tried to put one and one together and remember where Samir had been the night before.

I thought I might pay the nurse a call at her little house near the clinic, and see who might like to see Doc dead, who might have the brains and expertise to use a surgical drill, or the strength to knock him out first.

Nobody you know, jeered the Whisperer. *Time to find out. You'll be surprised, Annie my girl.* If I didn't know the voices were constructs of my ego, I'd have thought they're smarter than me, but how could that be? The voices were Annie. Period. Tormenting me with the jobs I couldn't do right. With ideas that slipped my conscious mind. Maybe they were right—I was stupid and bad.

Chapter Nine

"The doctor didn't have a lot of friends," the wren-like nurse said. We were sitting in her immaculate kitchen with the bulging bookcases overflowing into the next room, and her Jack Russell asleep in the corner.

The nurse's scrubs were wrinkled and looked as though they'd been slept in, but her hair was perfectly styled and her makeup looked good, nice pink lipstick. I noticed she seemed to have a tan. Seemed she took care of herself. I suddenly felt frumpy. I wished I looked that good.

"The doctor was a very misunderstood man. I think he worked too hard and took his work too seriously." She snuffled into the sleeve of her uniform top. Her eyes were watery grey, full of tears, and a bit red and swollen.

"Do you know anyone would want to see him dead?"

A rhetorical question. Who, amongst the Doc's patients, would not want the drugs? Just all of them, that's all.

"The police officers took his books and equipment," she said. "But not before I got the memory stick from his PC."

Wow.

"Very smart," I said. "Do you have it here?"

"I saved them all," she said. "All his clients on there and his contacts."

"His friends?"

"His contacts and friends."

She was a clever fox. "Why did you take the memory stick?" I asked. "Weren't the police looking for it?"

"The police are working under the sergeant's orders, and he's under the thumb of the mayor," she replied. "I don't trust the mayor entirely, Annie." She hadn't answered me.

"Do you trust me?" I tried to look sane. The voices roared and I counted under my breath. *Kill her. It'll be worth it to see her bleed.* I shook my head.

"I don't know," she whispered. "I have to trust someone."

"You loved him," I ventured, reaching out to wipe her eyes with a tissue.

She nodded, snuffling again into her blouse. "Bill was a wonderful person to work with, selfless to the end. Always trying to help the downtrodden and the addict and the homeless, never thinking of himself, working long hours and misunderstood."

"They thought Doc worked in that clinic for the money?" She nodded.

"There was precious little money in a methadone clinic. Everyone thought he was a…a…"

"Pill pusher?" Again she nodded. My voices weren't sympathetic. *It's an act. She hated him. Nobody loves an old man who works too many late nights and is bald and overweight…*

"Shut up," I whispered. Nobody loved me, either. "Sorry, I meant the voices."

The nurse smiled. "I understand your illness," she said. "You don't keep it a secret. Good for you. The doctor might have helped you if you'd come to him."

"He was sympathetic?" *You needed a high-end drug pusher,* roared The Screamer. I counted the wrinkles in the nurse's face.

"He helped a lot of the mentally ill in the community." *I'm sure.*

"He must have been a good man," I agreed. *Liar.* "So who would have wanted to kill him?"

The room was very hot. I pushed back my chair. The curtains were open over the kitchen sink. Anybody could see me sitting here. I glanced out back at a beautifully-kept garden. The nurse liked to work in the soil. A rake and spade leaned against a garden shed. Very bucolic. The garden must be a stress reliever, those antiseptic hands buried in humus and cow dung. I could see she had been turning over the soil fairly recently.

"I'll do what I can to solve the murder. Do you have a picture of him?"

She got up and fumbled in a drawer. "I'm afraid not," she said finally.

"That's all right." *Just fishing.*

"You might try this," the nurse said, and handed me the memory stick. "I want you to have this."

"You don't trust the police?"

"They have a lot of corruption in the force from the top down. The cop on the beat is all right, Annie, but Doc knew a lot he wasn't telling the media."

"He told you?" She nodded.

"I heard he was friends with the mayor. That's pretty much high society and the big guns."

"That's the problem," she whispered. "I'm afraid. Be careful, Annie."

"I'll be careful." I was clearly getting out of my depth here, but I took the memory stick with the Doc's patient list on it, and thanked the nurse. She pressed a business card into my hand when I got up to leave.

"It's an old card," she explained. "I used to work in the Operating Room in Abbottsford. But the cell number is right. Call me if you have any more questions."

Did someone in high places want the Doc dead, and why? When I looked back, the nurse was still sitting there, at her kitchen window, and I noticed she wasn't crying anymore.

I looked at the card she'd given me. Her name was Molly (Margaret) Dewitt, RN and former OR nurse.

Molly, you loved Doc Hubert, didn't you? You must be the only one, from what I hear.

Chapter Ten

My cell phone glowed blue and reflected my horrified face when I got the next call from Lorne. He said the mayor was gone, semen blown clear through his balls and spattered on the wall behind, in his fancy office in City Hall, left alone to bleed to death in agony.

"Thanks, Lorne," I said and mentally put him on my suspect list for Murder Number Two.

Nothing like this ever happened in Serendipity, our little island town just off Vancouver Island and five hours from Vancouver. Serendipity Island had been my refuge all these years from the big cities that had been so cruel to me growing up. The moon soared over our small City Hall, its mediocre arches and pillars shadowed and silver like I thought the Parthenon might be by moonlight. Beautiful, I thought, and the stars, like, punctured the sky and showed through a black and silver curtain. I was glad I worked and lived on our Island, connected to the mainland only by ferry and the Georgia Straits.

The mayor's death left me with maybe two suspects instead of one (that one being Samir). Who'd benefit from the mayor gone? Maybe somebody who was planning on running against him in the next election, and would probably lose. The mayor got a pile more money and prestige than a gumshoe detective, aka private eye, a gumshoe detective with a SIG Pro semi-automatic pistol and a twisted motive, who maybe knew enough to get away with it.

What's the connection to Doc? I asked myself, and my brain came up empty as usual. No similarities in *modus operandi* except, of course, for the horrible methods of execution in both cases.

"Whatcha doing downtown this time of night, Annie?" Pepsi, the tall Sudanese man walking home, interrupted my thoughts. Pepsi didn't go to work until six p.m. and quit ten hours later, in the wee hours of the morning. It was about that time now, quitting time.

"Got a question for you, Pepsi," I said. "Do you know what happened here yesterday evening?"

"Yeah," he said and smacked his head. "I know—I work at City Hall, too, as well as Doc's building, but I didn't see or hear nothin' about the mayor before he got his balls blown off."

"What I'm wondering is the motive for killing Doc seems straightforward. Money and drugs. But what's the connection to Mayor Spacey?"

"Only the bad guys get handguns in Canada. Or maybe a law enforcement officer. What was it blew him away?"

I eyed the lanky Sudanese with more respect. "Maybe you could tell me, Pepsi."

"Yeah? Maybe not. You're barking up the wrong maple tree if you think it was me, Annie."

"You still clean, Pepsi?"

"Yeah. I haven't used dope for more than a year. Ask the boys at NA."

"Narcotics Anonymous, that's brilliant. Think I'll pay them a visit next open meeting they have. I might be able to get a lead there. Thanks."

Why hadn't I thought of that? That's what they paid me for. As for Lorne O'Halloran, my erstwhile boss? Lazy bar of soap hadn't solved a case in fourteen months without me, and needed either a safety net or a better job to pay his gambling bills. If he could pin Doc's murder on Pepsi or Samir and step into the mayor's chair, he'd be sitting like a pretty fat Republican president in a Republican Senate.

The bullet that blew away Spacey's balls? RCMP Ballistics wasn't that clever when the bullet went clear through the wall and they didn't find it.

Something niggled in the back of my mind. *They're not telling you the truth,* my voices squealed. *Listen to us. We're your friends.*

"Shut up," I said to the voices. "Let me think."

What if the killer wants you to think they're psycho? Just like you.

Tomorrow I'd go downtown to my first Narcotics Anonymous meeting. Everyone on the street knew they met in the back of the bookstore every Monday morning. Maybe I'd get some answers there.

You'll never solve this case. Do you want to see what's at the bottom of this filth? Do you really want to know?

Maybe they were right, and maybe I didn't want to know. I needed a job and the longer it took me to solve the case, the longer I'd be working on it, right?

Oh, you're a clever one, you are. Clever like Jack the Ripper but you'll get caught. What did they mean by that?

Sometimes the sun rose in the west not the east, and sometimes it didn't rise at all and it was night for twenty-four hours as I slept. Sometimes I was stupid and sometimes I wasn't.

I wasn't sure I wanted to meet the killer. Who would remove the brains of an old, overweight pill pusher, and who would be trusted enough by Security to sneak up in City Hall and blow off the balls of a crazy mayor, and leave him to bleed to death? Who would know enough to do that? Who would want to?

I made sure I took my pills the next morning, letting the antipsychotic wafer dissolve under my tongue. The voices whispered and mocked me but it kept them at bay for a couple of hours. I counted my fingers up to thirty under the breakfast table. Counting my fingers calmed me. *Oh, you're so friggin' serene, Annie.*

The Vespa bucked as it squealed down the street from my group home at the Powolskis. Everyone on the Island knew I drove a scooter. It was one of the hallmarks of Annie Hansen.

They didn't know much else about me. I liked it that way.

Chapter Eleven

The meeting of Narcotics Anonymous was an open meeting, as promised. That meant anyone could go, addict or not. Pepsi accompanied me to the back of the bookstore. I walked into the meeting, surprised at the joy in the room.

That's all. I promised I wouldn't tell any more, or the last names of who was there. I can tell you, though, that I talked to someone who knew the Doc very well. Someone on the street, a user, who dropped into NA occasionally as one would crash a tea party, Firewall Eddie, a big First Nations guy fresh out of jail, and a known hacker. He seemed too ready to talk.

"Meeting's starting," he said, though, and we left the huddle in the corner and joined the rest of the group.

I heard Eddie's story, for the gadzillianth time, sitting around that long table with the rest of them. How he used to use and now he didn't, and he had a good job as a Security Guard for the town. I heard all the stories and then the birthday speakers who were celebrating a year or more of being clean.

Afterward there was cake and coffee. Eddie said a couple years ago the baker had put booze in the cream filling. Eddie thought it was a true story. It sounded like another urban myth to me.

Many of the men and women in the room had multiple addictions—booze, narcotics, gambling, you name it. They laughed easily at themselves and others. I felt accepted.

Firewall Eddie took me to one side after the cake was cut and everyone started milling around the coffee urn.

"You want to know what I know, Annie?' He licked chocolate frosting off a plastic fork."Hizzhonnor…" Firewall's cheek twitched. "Hizzhonnor wasn't the good citizen he seemed to be. We all knew that here."

"He didn't go to any NA meetings? Not in this small town." I'd heard rumors about the cocaine parties at City Hall.

"'Course not. He was too smart for that."

Flames danced in a corner. I gnawed my nails and counted the candles on the cake. "Cocaine?"

"There was more to our Mayor than coke. Let's just say he knew Doc well."

A lean streak of misery came up behind Firewall and slapped him between the shoulder blades. "This guy telling you lies again, Annie?"

"Nice to see you, Pepsi," I said. "You're just in time to ruin a good convo. Let's go."

These were ordinary citizens that didn't mind coming clean. The five hard-core users didn't attend this meeting. They were all down at Hoyt Street being homeless.

But I'd got what I came for. I thanked Firewall and left. I had to go back and take a look at the memory stick the nurse had given me. I thought I'd get a lot of answers from that. Maybe enough so the cops could make an arrest.

That's what I got paid for. I smiled.

Chapter Twelve

The surf boomed deep in my ears as the Vespa squealed up the beach road to the Modge Bay lighthouse near the float house my mother owned before she died. Now it was mine, when I wanted it.

Over toward the right, the Indian nation slept. I would sleep that night on the float house, tucked under a white duvet on the second floor, rocked with the rain and the ocean, lulled by the sound of the old lighthouse like a Swiss alpenhorn.

The Powolskis had let me go home on a pass for good behavior, ha. My fingers gripped the handlebars. The Vespa's wheels flew over the gravelly road.

I felt little gratitude to the Powolskis or to Lorne. I had earned my keep.

I parked the Vespa and tossed stones at the giant cypresses in the rain forest at the top of the hill. I thought over the possible suspects. A red truck was parked on the road on the other side, a group of Haida First Nations arguing over a load of bales.

"Hey, man, half of that is for my ponies." A stocky dark skinned man in a white Stetson screwed up his face and spat.

"Hell, you say."

"Here, take the damn bales. Your ponies are half-starved."

"They're good horse flesh."

Where had I seen that truck before? My fingers flew, counting the raindrops.

More voices, one familiar. I threw a stone at the truck. Several hundred yards behind me, the lighthouse lamps flashed and flickered in the rain and dark. The surf boomed. The foghorn ululated through the inclement weather to the ships at sea. A Haida called, "Hey," and I grinned.

"Hi, Firewall."

"Annie, you funny bunny. What're you doing down here?"

"Looking for my mommy's float house in the dark. What are you doing?"

"Dealing drugs."

Another First Nations fellow guffawed. "Just like your boyfriend."

"Who?"

"The dude with the limp."

"He's kidding, Firewall."

"No, he's not. Ask his saner cousin."

Think, think, think. My head hurt. I lurched and slipped down the rocks on the trail to the dock, leaving Firewall and his phony friends behind. Samir had been home that night, I saw his freaky body in bed like a lump of dung, I'd got up a couple times that night to whiz and he hadn't moved. Had he?

I found the key where I'd left it under the window box so I wouldn't lose the damn thing (so trusting, stupid) and opened the door to the float house. Man, it was cold in there. I turned on the space heaters and lit the fire in the Franklin stove. I used the Porta-Potty in the bathroom, yawned, washed my face and climbed the steep ladder-like stairs to the bedroom on the second floor. The rain beat like my heart as I pulled the white crisp sheets over my naked body.

Something is missing here. I'm the perfect alibi for one of the suspects— Samir—but now I doubt my memory. Am I going crazy? I thought he was home that night, but what if I'm mistaken? My voices took over, drowning out my thoughts and my attempts at recollection.

We're everywhere, everywhere, you'll never get rid of us. Think, think, think.

The Screamer shouted. Sometimes I wished I were in jail. I might be safer there. The rain beat on the tin roof of the float house and outside something screamed in the night; probably a bird. I hoped so, anyways. Enough screams from my brain, enough screams in this town, and a bird would be so natural even though the pore thing might be missing its mate or attacked by a falcon. Nothing was sacred in this world where a God didn't care.

Chapter Thirteen

Next day, sure enough, I felt two hundred percent better when I got up, stirred the embers in the old Franklin stove and made myself something to eat. The coffee was pretty good, too, once I found the ground beans.

I counted to a hundred, which might have meant I averted something bad, or maybe something else I oughta do. Maybe I should be getting back to the Powolski house and see what's brewing there. I had a stronger feeling about it when I got a call from Samir's cousin Pepsi. I counted to ten.

"Better come quick," he whispered. "Your old man Samir's on his way out of town."

Sure enough, Pepsi's old Mercury was parked in front of our house and Mrs. Powolski was shouting at Samir, who had evidently packed his bags and was leaving. I knew the next ferry was due in about fifteen minutes, so I made a quick call to the only cops' office on Serendipity Island, turned the scooter around and headed for Burt's Landing.

When I got to the landing on my putt-putt, Pepsi and Samir were already standing on the pier watching the *Island Queen* pull in. He could go anywhere with what I suspected was quite a large wad of cash in his wallet and more than that, something to put up his nose to grease his brain as he traveled.

"Annie, what are you doing here?" Samir turned around and twisted his handsome face into a scowl. "I thought you was down at Modge Bay."

"I was. Last night. Today I'm here, hunny buddy, watching you leave town. Where you going?"

Pepsi started his old blue beater of a car. Black smoke belched from the exhaust and he backed it around just as the black and white van with the flashing red lights on top turned the corner and screeched to a stop in front of the ferry.

Pepsi left. Constable Tom, one of the only two cops on the island before the RCMP arrived, revved the van's motor, glanced at me, and I shook my head and pointed to Samir. The sergeant was sitting beside Tom.

"That's your guy," I shouted. Tom and his sidekick ran onto the ferry just as it was pulling out. Samir limped as fast as he could to the railing on the other side, his cane tock tocking on the wooden planks where the vehicles were parked on the lower deck.

"Hey, you!" The engineman saw what was going on, I guess, and the ferry stopped where it was, churning ocean water.

"You take his cane as evidence, Tom," I said. "You'll find blood on the tip, I betcha, and it'll be Doc Hubert's blood."

Samir had cleaned off his cane pretty well but there was still a blackish stain on the bottom. Plenty to indict him, I thought. *He's your friend,* my voices shrilled. *You friggin' traitor, Annie Hansen.* I tried to ignore them as my fingers flew beneath my coat, counting the gulls on the top of the poles near the landing.

The ferry started up again just as Samir fell, his cane clattering on the boards beneath him. Constable Tom and the sergeant plucked the evidence out from under the lanky Sudanese fellow who had shared my bed the week before. They hauled Samir to his feet; dragged and threw him off the ferry onto the landing.

The Moderator's voice cleared its throat. *Blood on Samir's cane? Where was he the night old Doc was murdered? Was he really sleeping in the bed next to you, or...who had that been? You did see him in the morning, pulling his jeans on, taking a shower, having a piss. How can that be? Boy, are you a piece of work, dumb like a doorknob.* I scratched my head and started up the Vespa again.

Samir was in the back of the van, the sergeant at the wheel. Constable Tom lumbered over to where I sat on my scooter, puzzling this out, sure something was rotten in Denmark somewhere, something fishy here, but what? It seemed so obvious, Samir had done it for drugs and cash.

"What about the mayor?" Tom asked. "By the way, thanks for the tip, Annie. Don't know what we'd do without you here."

"No worries," I said. "I know. What about the mayor? I've got some questions to ask around downtown." Drugs and money. Power. What about Lorne O'Halloran, and where had Pepsi veered off to in such a rush, leaving his cousin stranded in the back of a paddy wagon? Little prick.

"We'll scoop up his cousin in a few minutes." Tom pursed his lips and frowned. "We can't hold him though, just question him and send him on his way. No reason to arrest Pepsi. We'll send Samir's cane to the lab in Victoria right away."

"Next ferry's due in a couple of hours," I said.

"Does Samir have an alibi?"

"Yes," I sighed.

"What or who?"

"Me."

Tom's face got all lop-sided when he grinned. "We'll see you in court as a witness for the defense," he said. "Must be hard, you living together like that."

"No," I said. "I love it."

Something didn't fit. Betraying a friend (my *only* friend in all my twenty-four years) was the hard part, knowing in my gut that it was wrong but maybe right, and seeing his cousin Pepsi go free when something told me he knew more than he was telling.

My voices whispered. *You're so naïve and gullible. You'll believe anything.*

"No, I won't," I said out loud.

"What?" Constable Tom buttoned his blue serge jacket.

"Nothing. Just thinking out loud. Looks like we have the right guy."

"Yeah. I got to get back to the van, take him downtown and book him. Sure enough that cane has Doc's blood on it, just you wait and see."

"That's what I thought, too, first time I seen it," I said.

"When was that?"

"Hmmm," I said. "I don't remember."

I could hear the churn of the ferry starting up again and it sucked The Screamer right into its maw. When I looked over, I could see the warty green back of Drommit the Toad splashing toward the mainland. My eyes crinkled at the corners as I laughed at the sight straight from my Id. Plenty to laugh about there. Ol' Annie had some Irish in her and she enjoyed a good joke and a good glass of whiskey. 'Course I didn't drink anymore, I told myself soberly. I was a good girl.

Sure enough, Samir and Pepsi were free by noon.

Chapter Fourteen

One of the parrots was dead. Somebody had left the cage open and the cat got it.

"Who?" Mrs. Powolski cried. "Who would leave the door open so my Birdies got out? You all know Pussy was always sniffing around, waiting for them to get out."

"It's not Pussy's fault," Mr. Powolski said. "It's the nature of cats."

"I know."

I wasn't prepared to face this at this particular time in the morning, with Samir just out of jail and Pepsi—why had Pepsi called me to tell me Samir was on his way out of town? Was he not loyal to his cousin? *What's the matter, Annie?* My voices hissed. *Whose side are you on?*

The beautiful multicolored bird lay in a corner, feathers ruffled and strewn about the room, head neatly bitten off and missing.

Its mate huddled in a corner of the cage, now secured, pecking at itself and mourning.

"Do birds grieve?" I asked, mostly out of curiosity, but also I was buying time. Who had let the birds out? Was I guilty and didn't remember?

You remember, Annie. You did this before.

But not today.

You don't remember.

I can't.

You don't want to remember, Annie. You're as crazy as a rabbit with its ears caught in a sewing machine.

The cat was nowhere to be seen. Just as well. Mrs. Powolski cradled the dead bird with her stubby fingers, smoothing the ruffled feathers, blood on her hands. Mr. Powolski thumped his wife on the back, straining his suspenders as he leaned over to comfort her.

"There, there," he said. "There, there, Meredith. It's only a bird."

"Only a *bird?*" she wailed. "My baby!"

"He was beautiful, wasn't he?" Did I open the cage? Surely I hadn't done it. I wasn't home last night. Was I?

A flash of light as the sun rose through the west window, not the east. My visions again. The old yeller dog in the back yard howled and rattled his chain.

"Go feed that dawg, Meredith," Mr. Powolski said. "It ain't right he been chained up all night and now has nothin' to eat."

"How insensitive you are, Henry," Mrs. Powolski wailed. "I have to bury Birdie here. And where's our Pussy? Bad, bad Pussy."

"That cat has to go, Mrs. Powolski," I said. "Look what he's done now."

She turned on me with the fierceness of a mother lioness.

"You hate my Pussy, you dreadful girl," she shrieked. "You've always hated my Pussy. It's not her fault. It's the nature of cats. You know that, you bad, bad girl. You'll be happy to see my Birdies dead and the cat gone, won't you? Won't you?"

"Admit it," Mr. Powolski said. He sighed and scooped some Kennel Bits into a large bowl, filled another bowl with water and brought it out back to Old Yeller. There was silence again, just the tick-tock of the ornate clock and then the chimes to announce it was eleven.

It's true, I thought. You've always hated that cat and you didn't like the parrots much, either. Now there's one parrot left and the cat somewhere. Did you do it?

"I didn't do it," I said. "I'm sorry, Mrs. P, but I didn't open the cage."

"Okay," she said. "Who did?"

Chapter Fifteen

"The forensic lab replied with the results of the tests for occult blood on Samir's cane. They had Doc Hubert's blood type and DNA sample." Constable Tom frowned. "Nothing matched."

"Looks like we got the wrong guy."

"The sticky stuff was tar," Sergeant Ross continued, "I think probably from the newly-repaired sidewalk outside the Serendipity Hotel."

Yes, the Hotel where Samir and Pepsi often drank early in the morning and into the day, arguing over old battles fought and lost in the Sudan, or in the refugee camp where they were found by the missionaries and brought here. I could see the walks had been patched with burning asphalt last time I was there. It wasn't blood after all, let alone Doc's blood. It was regurgitated old tires or something.

"We had to let Samir go. There was no good reason to keep him, and we didn't find any coke or hash on him, either, or any big wad of cash in his wallet," Tom said.

"He was clean," the sergeant said. He fiddled with the big buckle on his belt.

"Looks like he's innocent," I said. My shoulders felt several pounds lighter.

"Yeah. Looks that way. We find his cousin a person of interest, though, and we haven't entirely looked the other way in regard to Samir."

"Could this be prejudice?" I'd run into it before, Samir and I downtown together, the looks we got, ebony and ivory so to speak, some folks didn't hold with mixing of the races here on Serendipity Island, not like the big cities where an interracial couple could go unnoticed.

"We don't exactly have a lot of suspects, Annie. Unless of course it's you." Constable Tom grinned his lopsided smile and chuckled.

There's truth in jest.

I flushed. "What about the Mayor?"

"Blown his balls clear through the wall, Doc's brains siphoned out of his head and stacked in a neat pile beside his body. Somebody's a psycho or just angry as hell. But why Mayor Rick?"

"Somebody's got a grudge," I suggested. "Or trying to shift blame."

"Keep on it, Annie. An election is coming up. We want to make sure the new mayor and next budget allows a police force to continue here on the Island like we been. We got to keep the electorate happy. And the administration."

"Just what I was thinking," I said.

"Seems like a cold thing to say about the people here, doesn't it?" The sergeant grunted and bit into his bacon burger. "What do you think they say about it on the street?"

"I don't know. But I'm going to find out."

"You better. Because it's looking more and more like an inside job. You're a sturdy young woman, aren't you?"

"I am." I began counting his chins under my breath. I stopped when I got to four and started with the buttons on his shirt. "What are you saying, Sergeant?"

"Just don't let us down, Annie."

"I won't, sir. I'm an obedient little bitch."

He laughed and Tom looked pleased with himself. I yawned in their faces, my mouth wide open, and I didn't bother to cover it with my hand.

Lorne O'Halloran, up for election…

A purple furry sun was rising from the trash bucket—and was that a pink snake in the corner? Could be; for all I knew, maybe I wasn't hallucinating. It was hard to tell sometimes what was real.

Chapter Sixteen

My mother, six years dead now, had dragged me from doctor to doctor when I was twelve years old, to find out what was wrong with me; the sunny, happy kid who turned sullen and withdrawn, so quickly then sunny again—"mercurial," my mother, Blossom, had commented.

My father tousled my dirty blonde hair and assured me I was a "normal teen."

It was "puberty," my pediatrician said, I'd "grow out of it."

Then when I started crying from bellyache, breaking up the furniture and setting fire to the drapes, Social Services got involved. I was diagnosed with amphetamine psychosis or mescaline intoxication. Perhaps schizophrenia.

The day my lawyer father left us for good, for a Dutch woman in Curaçao he'd met through the internet, I roamed through Woodworth's Department Store and stole at random, although I had money in my pocket. I was picked up and sent to Juvenile Court, then remanded for psychiatric examination.

They gave me a lot of tests. I assured them I didn't take drugs. Not back then. My mother began to pay attention to me. She came to see me in the locked psych ward every day. They weren't sure it was schizophrenia. I couldn't even spell it, let alone have it.

I got opiates for the bellyache; the pain was so bad, I would bend over with it and cry. They didn't know the pain wasn't real, ha. But there was the thing made me see the sun rising in the west not the east, and the furry colored animals running through the hallways, and that interested the psychs. When they gave me those paper tests, they frowned.

"It looks like acute intermittent porphyria," the doctor said. "It can mimic schizophrenia."

"What is that?" my mother asked. I sat there next to her, huddled in a plastic chair, and didn't care.

"There's a lack of heme leading to the lack of a key enzyme which metabolizes tryptophan. As a result of this, tryptophan accumulates in the brain and causes mental symptoms."

"What do we do about it?" asked my ever-practical mother. I remember the doctor smiled at me.

"This is a treatable disease. The patient is given heme and a high carbohydrate diet."

"What's heme?" I finally asked. Suddenly I cared. If they were going to inject me with something or give me pills, I wanted to know what. It might be fun.

"It's in hemoglobin, the red pigment in blood, but essentially is a group of molecules containing iron at the core."

"What are you gonna do to me?" My cigarette skittered onto the floor and I stepped on it. The doctor made a steeple with his fingers and frowned.

"Our labs aren't equipped to properly diagnose AIP," the doctor said. "We're not sure yet if that's what it is."

"She doesn't like needles," my mother said. She smoothed my hair.

"The vampire and werewolf legends may have come from cases of porphyria."

*Coo*l. I liked that, and I liked the oral opiates they gave me to stop the bellyaches.

Chapter Seventeen

Unfortunately, the tests showed I didn't have AIP or anything resembling amphetamine intoxication or drugs. I started seeing the sun in different colors rising in the west, not the east, by that time, and believed I was a special agent of God. I believed God was sending me signs. I saw the Devil in my room. I was fourteen at that time, three years before I hit the streets.

One morning, my mother came into my room and caught me sprinkling holy water (which I had blessed from the tap) onto a sunbeam, high up; it was the Devil's chest.

The bellyaches stopped when I was put on antipsychotics and Ativan. I did quite a bit of reading about paranoid schizophrenia. Cool. Ernest Hemingway had it, maybe Vincent Van Gogh, certainly John Nash of A Beautiful Mind.

All gifted and genius like me. *Cool.*

"What's this, Sunshine? What you been up to?" My father put his big, beefy hand on the top of my head and swirled his fingers through my frizzy hair. "Can't leave you alone for a few months, can we?"

His girlfriend smirked in a corner. My mother wasn't there this time.

"Her mother says she first noticed something wrong even before Annie was eleven and basically stopped eating," the psychiatrist said. "Setting fires and other acting out issues."

"Nothing's wrong that puberty won't cure," my father said. His girlfriend smiled. Her daughter glanced in a coy fashion at my father from across the room.

"I'm afraid it's more serious than that—may I call you Albin?"

"Albin's my name," my father said. "You may call me that."

"We're trying to get some history here," the doctor said. "Let's start with the family history, Albin. You can corroborate what Mrs. Hansen...er, Blossom, said. I understand that Annie has no siblings, is that correct?"

"Correct." My father crossed his legs in the bright orange chair at the side of the doctor's desk. "We didn't want any more after Annie." He laughed. The medical student's mouth twitched.

The doctor nodded. "Why is that?"

"Little Miss Sunshine here was always a handful," my father said. His girlfriend's daughter smiled smugly and his girlfriend patted her daughter's shoulder.

"Can you elaborate?" the doctor asked. "When did you first notice a problem?"

"The night we took her home from the nursery. She had colic as a baby, grew out of that then was diagnosed with ADHD when she was two or three. Grew out of that, too."

"Perhaps the diagnoses were wrong?"

"Maybe."

"Did you and your wife keep things running pretty smoothly emotionally at home?"

"Oh, I'd say we did."

"You're divorced, aren't you?"

"Are you trying to tell me it's *my* fault?"

"No, no, Albin, just trying to get a history so that we can understand your daughter better, and the genesis of her illness."

"Sounds like you're trying to blame the family?"

"No, we know now that schizophrenia has a large genetic factor."

"Oh, now it's schizophrenia?"

I started to rock back and forth, counting each movement forward.

"What are you doing, Sunshine?" my father asked. His girlfriend and her daughter gathered their Coach bags onto their laps and started to stand up. My father put his arm around the daughter and winked.

"Why don't the two of you go shopping?" he said. He pulled out a wallet and gave the girl five twenties. "Your mother has my charge card."

"Generous, aren't you?" I muttered, rocking. "Mag-na-ni-mous, I'd say, Father."

"She's soothing herself, sir," the doctor said. "With the rhythmical movements."

My father frowned. "Where'd you hear a word like that?" he said to me, as the door closed behind his girlfriend and her daughter. "Like your mother. Always her nose stuck in a book."

"Mom's a librarian, Dad."

"Hot damn."

"I think we might continue this by ourselves, Albin," the doctor said. He motioned to a nurse inside the doorway and she took me to the ward.

I was glad. My father drove me crazy.

Then he flew back to Curaçao with his girlfriend and her daughter. I haven't seen him since, though we sometimes Skype if I can borrow a computer.

Chapter Eighteen

Six years ago my mother died.

I'm twenty-four now. Which would make me eighteen then, the year I should have graduated from high school, only I didn't, 'count of all the days I'd missed. I was actually still seventeen when my mother died. We hadn't lived under the same roof for a couple of years, and I was on the streets. Mom sold our family home in North Vancouver and bought the float house on Serendipity Island, where she spent most of her final years until...

Mom.

The stomach cancer was very aggressive. It took her in less than six months, would have been a painful death without the Morphine they finally gave her toward the end. Her family doctor diagnosed a peptic ulcer and so, you see, she suffered until it became obvious, even to him, that he should send a scope down her esophagus and see what was happening.

My mother wasn't bitter at the end, but angry at first. We all were. My father didn't come back from Curaçao but he sent a long email. He sent a big wreath of yellow hibiscus and peach-colored roses, my mother's favorite, and that was the end of my family life right then. So when I was eighteen, I inherited the float house, my mother's Persian cat, and $150,000.

You didn't work for a living, then, did you, you good-for-nothing piece of liverwurst sausage? The voices ragged me from then on and I stopped being a Special Agent of God.

I'd been turned out to an adult group home but escaped onto the street, living underground mostly in Vancouver for the next few years. I had the keys and the deed to the float house but visited only a few times on Serendipity Island, long enough to know I liked it there. So that's where I ended up, using drugs, stealing, finally getting caught and sentenced to six months community service with the office of Lorne O'Halloran, Private Investigator. I stayed on with him later, after my probation was up, because he liked me and the Justice Department paid me to stay. Stayed on with the Powalskis, too. It was time to settle down. I was getting too old and too smart for the life I was living, wasn't right.

I hadn't seen my father since I was a kid, neither of us had cared to connect, but he would be glad to know I had a job now, and a friend. I'd spent all my inheritance.

I liked to read paperbacks, not the eBooks all the kids were reading. Sometimes I dreamed of our little family the way it was, in the beginning, my father teasing my mother and Mom laughing, laughing at one another, Mom blushing, and then me, setting fires and driving them crazy. Was I bad? Was the divorce my fault?

Chapter Nineteen

I talked to Pepsi at the Serendipity Hotel after his shift was done at City Hall. He stirred four brown sugar cubes into his black coffee. "I seen nothing here to match what I seen in the Sudan, Annie. Children with guns killing from the jungles, younger men abducted from Khartoum to forcibly serve in the Armies in the South and older men killed or ransomed, boys with machine guns mowing down Christians in the streets from the backs of open trucks, mostly Muslim there, some Christians, all hating each other like Allah commands it or as though God is on each side. How can God be with everyone, Annie? It doesn't make sense."

"No, Pepsi, it doesn't."

"My parents are still in the refugee camp in Yida, far as I know, my brothers and sisters dead or captured, that's worse. I used to be guerilla fighter in the jungles, would come back home to my family once every two weeks or more. That's no way to live."

"No, it's no way to live, Pepsi."

"We killed and raped the Muslims and they killed and raped us. Tortured, too, if we weren't lucky enough to be shot first. After they chose twenty Catholic men, forced them to dig a trench, lined them up in front of the trench and shot them all dead into the trench behind them. Then the women and children were forced to shovel the dirt over their blasted bodies. The two priests were tortured then released for ransom many weeks later."

"What happened after the men were buried?"

"Rape and pillage. Like in any war."

"Yeah, Pepsi, I'm sorry. And Samir? Where was he?"

"Samir was lucky. He was a paramedic, trained pretty good, came from rich family and was going to go to England someday for schooling. Then his father was taken away in the night, all their gold was taken away, the banks shut down, his mother and sisters were on the street. Samir don't talk much about it, does he?"

"No. I didn't know he was a paramedic."

"He took care of the dead and dying. Buried them sometimes, sometimes patched them up so they could be tortured again or killed."

"Sounds bad."

"Yeah." Pepsi fell silent, his black eyes unfocused. An ant crawled across the table through a small heap of sugar that had spilled from his coffee spoon. Without apparent thought, he put out a big black thumb and crushed the ant.

"Samir is trying to cast doubt on my sanity?" I asked.

"He give you the evil eye." Pepsi rubbed his hands through the cornrows on his head. His silky red and black jacket made a swishing sound as he rubbed his arms against his sides. He shivered. I reached out and felt his body trembling, the jacket smooth beneath my touch.

"He's my cousin. We're family, we traveled together from the refugee camp, thirsty, starving and exhausted. We knew each other in the villages. His mother is my father's sister. We're blood. We swore to be brothers always."

"You're not being disloyal, Pepsi. You're telling the truth."

"I've said too much already." His words fell on one another like dominoes collapsing onto themselves. "I told you, I knew him, there in our South Sudan village, he hid me in a truckload of rotting corpses and smuggled me out of the area at great personal risk to himself. We're blood brothers, I owe him my life. There was a ceremony, we cut our arms with stones and pledged to be friends forever. Enough said. I'm tired. Too much work at City Hall last night. Time for me to go home."

"Wait. What do you know about the mayor?" The mayor's death was a wild card in this game.

"Mayor Rick Spacey? He deserved to have his balls blown off."

"Why?"

"Check the expense accounts at City Hall these past two years, check the projects given to the mayor's buddies, check the corruption."

"City Hall has been corrupt before and nobody blew away the mayor."

"Maybe he knew too much."

"Do you think so?"

Pepsi finished his cold sweet black coffee and scraped to his feet. "Maybe he was dealing with the wrong guys."

"Dealing? Like in drugs?"

"It's no secret."

"Something's a secret, Pepsi."

"Yeah. Somebody's trying to protect him or herself. And that's all I'll say." He was gone out the door, hitching up his faded dropped waist jeans. I heard the old blue Mercury fire up.

Chapter Twenty

Why don't you suspect Pepsi? my voices mocked. *He's a likely suspect, too, now that Samir's been cleared and the plot is narrowing. He was there both nights, working.*

"Security cleared him that night," I said out loud. The barkeep looked me up and down then turned back to drying the Pilsner glasses.

"He has an alibi."

So does his cousin, and he said his cousin's trying to set you up, Annie. Be very, very careful. My voices began to chatter amongst themselves, some with nasty sniggering, some soothing me and encouraging me to take stress leave as soon as possible.

"Nothing's wrong with me," I said out loud.

Erna at the Justice Department hates you. She's trying to elbow you out of a job. She'll bring in somebody fresh, somebody good and just out of college.

"College?" My worst fear, being replaced by a college pro.

You'll never go to university or even college, dummy. Trust us, we'll tell you the truth. We're the only ones that will tell you the truth.

"I can't say you didn't warn me." The bartender glanced up at me and smiled.

"Who left the door to the parrots' cage open?" I asked no one in particular. The barkeep didn't answer.

Was it me? Who set up the birds to get eaten by the cat and plunge a dagger through Mrs. Powolski's all too emotional heart?

Why can't I remember?

How did Samir's shoes get muddy that first morning?

Then... *Annie. Did you kill the Doc then kill the Mayor to cover it up?*

"No!" I moaned. "I didn't do it."

47

Time to go down to Hoyt Street where the homeless lived. They may know something I didn't know.

I sure hoped so.

Chapter Twenty-one

I figured I'd see Firewall Eddie down on Hoyt Street, and his NA pals with him. Sure enough, there he was, sucking on a joint.

My voices whispered then screamed. *Go home before it's too late. We're the only ones will tell you the truth.*

"The guys who should know?" Eddie asked. "You know how to meet them as well as I do."

"I haven't been around. Things change quick on the street."

"You want a beer?"

"Sure. Okay." This is where I'd meet them, the streetwise who would know what's going down.

I bought him a beer and he sat hunched over his glass, hands cupping the coolness of it. He smoked and swore.

"No need to curse," I said. "It's me, Annie, remember? I don't like that kind of language around a lady."

"Yeah, Annie, I remember. Sorry."

"What do you know?" This would cost me, but I had to start from somewhere and might as well bite the golden bullet.

"How much you got?"

"Not much." I slid a ten across the table at him. He picked it up, turned it over, kissed the back of it and smiled.

"You'll have to do better than that."

"That'll buy you a bottle of cheap wine," I said. "Or even some pretty good stuff, if I remember right. You'll get another ten if you give me some answers."

Eddie looked sly. "About Doc Hubert?"

"Him. And others."

"Mayor Stacey? That's too deep for ol' Firewall. I don't know nothin' about City Hall."

"I understand. What do you know about the Doc?"

"Only that he was a high end pusher there on the street. When we run short of horse or coke we'd show up at Doc's clinic and get some methadone. Would tide us over until we had another shipment or another stash showed up from somewheres. No reason to kill the goose that lays the golden egg, right?"

"So you're saying it wasn't anybody on the street. No users?"

"I guess I could be saying that."

"Interesting. But what if somebody wanted some cash and drugs real bad? Wouldn't Doc's clinic be the logical place to go?"

"Yeah, and protected by a raft of Security and that little Sudanese pimp, and an alarm system, and Doc was a big guy. Also, he didn't carry a lot of drugs on the premises, just what he needed for the day."

"True. But why...?"

"Want to know what I think, Annie?" Eddie squinted and gulped his beer. He wiped the suds from his mouth and straightened. He looked sly again.

I pushed a twenty across the table at him. It was quite helpful.

"I'll tell you all I know. Because you're a friend, Annie."

He picked up the twenty, slid it under the ten and folded them both into his dirty suit pocket.

"I think the drugs and money was what they call a diversion. I think somebody had a grudge against ol' Doc and they didn't want the money or drugs at all, it was just a...a..."

"Red herring?" I asked. This was getting interesting.

"Yeah. They wanted Doc dead. Period. They had a key, you know, to the outside door and the safe. It was some kind of inside job. If you ask me, the nurse knows a lot more than she's telling you, Annie."

"How do you know about the nurse?"

Eddie looked uncomfortable.

A miniature lime green rhino hovered in a corner of the bar, over the spigots, and then floated with gentle precision to the top of a Bailey's. I stared. Too bad I didn't drink anymore. I never needed a twelve-step program, either. I was proud. I stopped by myself, two years ago.

But a drink would help right now.

Thinking about the nurse, I remembered something. Something about a memory stick and a hard drive. What was that Constable Tom had said? Doc's appointment book was missing. But who used an appointment book anymore?

His appointments would be on that memory stick. The nurse had said as much. I smacked my forehead with the heel of my hand. I pushed my chair back so sudden that Firewall's glass slanted off the edge of the table and shattered on the floor tiles.

"Sorry," I said, and put another ten on the counter. One, two, three... to ten. My fingers flew behind my back.

"That'll cover it," the barkeeper said. "But don't come back. I heard you talking to yourself. We don't want crazy people in here, sister. Take a hike."

"Another thing," Eddie mumbled. He put a hand on my shoulder. "That black lover-boy of yours is spreading rumors about you, Annie. You two had a fight?"

"I don't know about the rumors."

Eddie's fingers shook as he ordered another drink with my money. "That'll be another twenty if you want to hear it."

"Hardly," I said, and left.

I didn't want to know. It weren't true in any case. Samir was my main man.

Chapter Twenty-two

"You're trying to make me think I did it, dude." Fresh from Hoyt Street downtown and the implications there, I confronted Samir together in our little bedroom.

"I'm not," he protested. His teeth dazzled me.

"You're trying to make me think I'm crazy."

A slender pink palm caressed my cheek. "You are, doll. You are mighty crazy." His body, pressed against mine, smelled like vanilla.

"You know the Justice Department in Victoria tried to take me off the case." My breath caught in my throat. "They think I need a stress leave."

"You do, little baby-face, you do need a stress leave." His voice was gentle. His hand slid under my blouse at the front. I was stronger than Samir. I pushed him until one crooked leg buckled and he fell back, just catching his balance on the edge of the dresser.

He struggled to his feet, threw back his handsome head and laughed. "Oh, you are one wildcat, Miss Amazon."

His chest was bare to the midriff. A thick gold chain around his neck held a bronze Saint Benedict medal, an amulet to ward off Satan, he said. His shirt was white silk and his black trousers were pressed. He was some kind of germophobe, scrubbing with antibacterial soap, putting tissues down on the counter as a sterile field. How did his tennis shoes get so dirty the night Doc was drilled? No telling where the big ape had been tromping the past few days.

His lips hovered over my ear, then I felt his tongue exploring the lobe, his teeth nipping with tenderness here and there, the scent of vanilla strong in my nostrils. I shivered. His arms held me firmly but allowed me to lift my face to his mouth.

What are you doing, Annie Hansen? This is Samir, the guy who tried to ruin whatever reputation you have left with the Powolskis and their stupid birds. Everyone else too, from what I'm told.

Then he kissed me.

"I hate you," I said.

"I know," he answered.

I yawned in his face. Then I kissed him back. It was pretty good but I could do better, I was sure.

Chapter Twenty-three

I decided the best thing for me to do was leave Samir and the Powolskis and go back to the float house, live out my own life there, now that my probation was up and I didn't really have to work for Lorne. Who might have killed the Mayor and maybe Doc Hubert? My head hurt with all the thinking I'd been doing. Samir and my supervisors were probably right, I needed a break. A stress leave, and if I could do that and still get paid by the Justice Department, which I understood maybe would be the case, well, sweet.

After all, they hadn't drove me mad exactly, but they hadn't helped my sanity either. Giving me this case so much above my coconut head. It drove a wedge between my only friend and me, a break between him and his cousin, and suspicion on almost everyone I knew on Serendipity Island, including my boss.

You're a smart cookie, Anne. The Whisperer sounded pleased.

The landlords were the only ones I didn't suspect, and I suppose they could have done it, too, for all I knew. I didn't waste any loving feelings on the Powolskis, but I didn't wish them any harm, either. They'd been cleared by my employers to run an adult group home consisting of two people at the moment. There'd be more wanting to move in when Samir and I were gone.

The food wasn't bad and the rates were reasonable; we were always reminded how much and when. I never was too good with handling my own money. Look at the inheritance my mommy left me. All I had left was the float house and her cat's ashes in a jar. Something else too, in a jar behind the stereo, a few hundred dollars tucked away that nobody knew about except me.

The Justice Department was going to help me apply for the CPP Disability pension if I didn't get paid stress leave, which I probably wouldn't, being only part-time and all. My psychiatrist, Dr. Blanche in Campbell River, would have to sign the papers. I was sure he would. I was sure certifiable, a Special Agent of God like I was when I first strolled into his office, and now hearing voices and seeing lime green miniature rhinos floating on the Bailey's in the Serendipity Hotel. If needed, I could embellish the symptoms. I knew how.

Chapter Twenty-four

While I was deciding what to take with me to my float house home, I thought long and hard about a computer or a smartphone. A smartphone was a little beyond my experience. Half the time I forgot to charge the basic cell phone I owned. Lorne had given it to me first day I walked into his office so he could get a-hold of me, which he never did, being too busy down at the casino with his slot machines. I supposed I'd have to give it back if I quit.

It was just possible the Justice Department would spring for a laptop for me to use on the float house, if I explained to them that it might put me back in the workforce. Other than that, I'd have to use the few hundred dollars I had tucked away and bite the bullet, get a laptop or a tablet. I knew how to use the dang things from borrowing computers at the library or neighbors, or Lorne's, they let me use theirs when I was in their offices. I was pretty good at going online and chatting people up, or Googling, doing research online, that would be valuable to my future employers.

I liked to read and write, too. Maybe I'd write a novel if I got stress leave. A memoir. A regular soap. The more I thought about getting a new laptop, the more excited I got at the prospect.

Now that I couldn't use the Powolskis' phone at home, I'd have to use my cell phone. I plugged it into an outlet in the Powolskis' kitchen. Samir had gone out on his usual party with Pepsi and his Sudanese pals. I thought I'd give my supervisor in Victoria a call from my cell and ask her. Too bad for her she'd given me her cell number, too.

The Powolskis went to bed early, it was their custom, and I had the place to myself, until Samir got home, and that would be after midnight if I knew him and his drinking pals, and I did.

My supervisor, Erna, answered on the third ring.

"Hello?" Her voice sounded sleepy and wary.

"Hi. It's Annie Hansen, boss."

"Annie. How are you? Is everything all right?"

"Sort of. I decided to take you up on the offer of a stress leave, Erna."

"Good." Her voice sounded more alert. "But have you talked it over with Meredith and Henry Powolski? What does Samir think about it? I'm glad you've come to this decision, but I don't want it to be a hasty one that you'll regret."

"Oh, no. I won't regret it. They seem to support it, actually, and Samir has been trying to get me off this case for a couple of weeks now. I got some questions, though."

"Shoot."

An unfortunate choice of words, Erna. heh heh heh

"Does the Justice Department pay for stress leave? Say for six months?"

"Whatever your doctor recommends. I think it's for six months at a time, you're right, Annie. It would have to be through CPP, though. You'd have to apply with CPP first and then any disability pension of ours would be in addition to that, minus the CPP."

"Sounds like the Government, all right."

"Sounds like our insurance plan, Annie. That's what we'll do, but we'll make sure you're taken care of one way or the other."

"Okay with me. I don't need a whole lot. What will it be, do you know?"

"Should be similar to what you're making now, but no more, the insurance company will see to that. Anything extra you make will be deducted from your salary."

"I don't understand."

"Oh, I think you do."

Yes, you understand, Annie, I thought and smiled to myself. It's what you thought she'd say. *You greedy little witch.* "Another thing."

"Anything I can help you with. I just think this case is much too stressful for you right now, dear."

"I want to live on my mom's float house... *my* float house, you know, down at Modge Bay near the lighthouse there. No property taxes since it floats on the water, just maintenance fees, power and trash pick-up, that kind of thing, cheap accommodation. It's isolated except for tourists in summertime. Even then, very peaceful. I love it there. It would heal my soul."

Heal your soul? Oh, spare us, Annie. Shut up.

"It would mean leaving the Powolskis' house."

"What about Samir?"

"I don't know. He might stay there. He certainly wouldn't be coming with me."

"A divorce?"

"Something like that."

Liar, liar, pants on fire, tongue's as long as a . . .

Telephone wire.

"I think we could arrange that. I'd have to talk to my superiors about it, and of course, your psychiatrist. Can you arrange an appointment with him ASAP?"

"Yes. Sure. And Erna?"

"Yes?" I could hear her shift the phone to her other ear. I just *knew* when she did that. She sighed or something, there was a slight rustle… she was getting tired of the conversation. Time to zero in.

"You said any extra money I made would be deducted. That would be to the Department's advantage, I think?"

"Yes. Do you have anything in mind?"

"Yeah, actually. Writing and I'd have to do some research. Would need a laptop."

"A computer."

"Yes."

"Hmmm. Might be arranged if you could present a proposal to my superiors justifying it for any income you could make from its use."

Hotdog! "Thanks. I really need a laptop to network, too." I scratched my nose. "One more thing," I said. The pardon.

"What?"

Forget it. Not now. Don't be stupid and hasty. You've got what you wanted. Don't rattle the boat. You'll get your pardon later. Congratulations, you almost blew it. "Nothing, no, nothing else, sorry."

"Nothing else tonight?" Erna did sound tired.

Here's your chance, stupid. Blow it now. "A full moon tonight." I grinned. "All the crazies will be out."

"They already are." I could feel her grin back. We were pals now. I hung up. Don't count your chickens till the eggs hatch. Maybe I'd get that pardon yet; I could just feel how lucky I was going to be.

Chapter Twenty-five

Samir didn't come home that night. *Figures. He doesn't even like you, just shares a room with you because you're easy.*

In the morning, I could smell bacon frying and greasy eggs. I pulled on my best jeans and stomped downstairs. Mrs. Powolski turned and looked up at me, brandishing the egg flipper. Grease flew from the spatula into the air. I flopped into one of the fragile-looking vintage chairs.

"I'm leaving," I said. "Going to stay at the float house from now on."

"In the wintertime? Dang cold out there in December and January," Mr. Powolski said, then belched.

"You got permission to leave us, girl?" Mrs. Powolski asked. The lone parrot sang in its cage. His or her cage. The cat wasn't there.

"Yes. I'm taking a stress leave. The Department will get the signed emailed authorization here today. Head detective in Victoria took me off the case."

"That Detective Erna Sobey?"

"Yes. I'll never break this case. It's too much for me. And now Samir has turned against me, the little piece of cow excrement. Pepsi told me all about it, how Samir wants me to think it was me. I don't remember. I didn't do it. I couldn't. Could I, Mrs. P?"

"You wouldn't hurt a li'l ant, Annie," Mrs. Powolski said. "Don't you worry. It wasn't you. That cousin of Samir's is an evil man to tell you things like that, or else, if it's true, your Samir's an evil man to tell those stories about our Annie. He *is* your boyfriend, Annie, we know that you're not exactly legally hitched. Known that all along."

"But we liked you both," Mr. Powolski declared, picking his teeth with his thumbnail.

"I don't believe Samir would tell stories about me," I said. "Not Samir. He wouldn't do that to me. I'm too strong, I know what's true."

"Yep, he's trying to throw suspicion on our Annie. Don't you believe it, honey," Mrs. P patted my frizzy blonde head.

"That boyfriend of yours is trying to make you think you're crazy. You're not any more crazy than Meredith's black cat out there," Mr. Powalski snorted. "And I'm not so sure about it."

"Thanks, Mr. Powolski. I think."

"Where is my Pussy?" Mrs. Powolski asked. "Pussy came back just the other day, didn't she, Henry? She knew she'd done wrong. Bad, bad Pussy."

"Bad Pussy," Mr. Powolski agreed.

"But we'll forgive her. Because she's our little Sweetums, Pussy Puss-Puss, isn't she? Isn't she?"

Meoo-rrr-ow-w-w.

Oh, no. Dang it, the bird sang and preened, then started to screech.

Pussy leaped at the cage and swung by her front claws to the bars as feathers flew. The agitated bird flapped its red and green wings as its cage spun in ever-increasing circles, goaded on by the cat.

You picked a good time to leave, Annie Oakley, the voices whispered. I detected a note of glee.

"Bad Pussy, bad Pussy!" Mrs. Powolski swung at the cat with her Swiffer. The head of the Swiffer flew off and struck Pussy on the back of her neck. She fell like a stone to the ground with a last mighty *Meeooorrrwwwwww.*

Mr. Powolski lit a cigarette, striking the match on the bottom of his steel-toed boot. "I think you've killed her, Meredith." His voice was mild.

Sure enough, the cat on the floor was motionless as a salt cod in Mom's freezer. The last remaining bird lay feet upward in its cage, surrounded by bright feathers. Soft red-green down floated in the air. I began to count the feathers.

There was silence. Mrs. Powolski stood as though carved out of a salt block, arms raised with the Swiffer pole hovering in the air like a Samurai's sword. Mr. Powolski paused with the cigarette partway to his mouth. The bird lay apparently dead. The cat lay apparently dead.

I froze in horror at the scene in front of me. How will she clean up the mess? was my first thought. Then, let me outa here. I didn't do it, I know that, this time I'm innocent. Bad Pussy.

Suddenly the tableau came to life. The bird flew to its perch and began to groom its ruffled feathers. The cat lurched to her feet with another screech and flew out of the open door. Mr. Powolski choked a great wad of grey smoke into his lungs and let it out with a "Whooosh." Smoke rings spiraled above his head and encircled the red-green down that floated in the air by the Swiffer pole. Mrs. Powolski jerked her arms about and flung herself down the hallway to their bedroom, wailing.

I thought of red herrings and the Mayor's death. I thought how I'd so much enjoy the trip down to the float house and how I'd find the key under the window box, where I always kept it, I'd try not to fall in the narrow drink of salt-water in front of the outside door and I'd make the leap from the dock to the porch. I'd light the fire in the Franklin stove with the box of long matches my mother had stashed there in a drawer. I'd put my feet up on the windowsill and watch the ocean.

The voices were with me. *That's your plan? Boy, is that smart. You got it right this time.* I grinned as the wailing continued from the bedroom. Mr. P grinned back at me.

Yes, my voices agreed. *Maybe you'll read. You'll write a bestseller and be written up in the New York Times. You'll be on Oprah. Eventually you'll be pardoned and spend the rest of your life on a CPP disability pension, living in your mother's old float house with us voices until you're old, at least forty-five.*

Then it wouldn't matter anymore.

Chapter Twenty-six

A month later, some exciting mail came to the marina office where I lived in my float house. I was afraid to open the envelope from the Justice Department. It looked like a check. It smelled like a check. It felt like a check. But was it a denial of benefits? I put the letter on the counter for five minutes. Then I tore it open.

It was a check for two months' salary, retroactive to December. I kissed the ink. I kissed the stamped impression on the envelope, and I would have kissed Samir if he had been here. That's how desperately happy I was to see that check.

I got my laptop at Best Future Store down on Port Street, a new phone, a WiFi, and a black and white laser printer, then set them up in the float house. I paid for them with cash, including the Acer notebook. I set it up at home on the float house. Easy peezy. It asked me for a password and I typed "Bite Me" then chuckled. The notebook came with the latest software. The Justice Department was generous. I installed a freeware antivirus program, two fire-walls, a new browser and email program, then Netflix, which I paid for with my secured Visa. I hadn't been careful with money but still had a bit left from my inheritance. I spent it carefully, like now. Mom would have been pleased.

I started to download a bunch of games, sat cross-legged in front of the kitchen table in my cozy room and grinned. I could even use my eReader now I'd got a wireless router, though I preferred to read my books the old-fashioned way. The eReader had been a gift from Lorne, and I was not one to look an O'Halloran horse in the mouth, ha ha.

I inserted Doc Hubert's memory stick. I know I wasn't supposed to be work-ing but I had the thing, so why not take a look? Nobody else knew I had it, far as I knew, except of course for the nurse.

Pages of pharmaceutical directories and subdirectories came up. Files with lists of drug reps and addresses. Apparently personal phone numbers. I flipped through the files and directories, and the subdirectories. A few letters came up in the files. Nothing incriminating or interesting.

Then—a patient list. In descending alphabetical order. Clients, with code numbers beside their names. Some with phone numbers.

Eureka! I found the Doc's appointments for the past two years, apparently from when he bought the computer. Went right up to the night Doc died. Let's see. Someone with MS at two o'clock in the afternoon. A code number beside the initials. No help there. John Doe with an H beside his name at three o'clock. A drug rep came in at three-fifteen, blocked off an hour of his time. I squinted but couldn't make out the code name. Looked like Pfizer. Six o'clock dinner break for half an hour, he had typed in 'Molly', the nurse, and a phone number for a local fast food restaurant.

Neatly on the right side of the list there was a dollar amount and health care numbers.

I scrolled down. Nothing for another hour. Then seven-thirty and another John Doe with 'AA' beside his name. Alcoholic? Did he go to meetings? Seven forty-five just 'Irvine and Dorothy'. Eight o'clock Teresa Coons Littlebear… Nine p.m. a line drawn through the rest of the Excel sheet.

Nothing more until eleven forty-five. Bingo! A name. I squinted, fingers trembling, color high. Then the disappointment. I didn't recognize it, unless it was a code name. MASER, followed again by 'MS'.

Two of his patients had multiple sclerosis. So what? Did Doc have a drug for that? I scrolled back to his two o'clock appointment. Another 'MS', no name given that time.

Stuck, I sat with my hand on the mouse and stared over the screen to the islands beyond my window. The Discovery Islands decorated the ocean as far as I could see, swelling like mountains to the northeast of Modge Bay. The lighthouse swung its automated lamps. Darkness shadowed Serendipity Island — suddenly, the foghorn blared. My neighbor in the boat tied up to the dock next to my float house swung his curtains shut. I could see slivers of light in the dark.

In my float house, only the blue light of the laptop illuminated the top of the table and bounced off the near wall. I got up and turned on some lights. Disappointed, I flicked through the rest of Doc's files. He had been a secretive man. I found his health care billings. I puzzled over John Does and who had 'MS', and the injection indicated as Dolophine. After some research, the formula was revealed as $C_{21}H_{27}NO$, or methadone. Nothing new here.

'MS' again at midnight. I googled a dictionary of abbreviations. It came up with multiple sclerosis, Mississippi, the female salutation Ms., Master of Science, Manuscript, Microsoft..., dozens of words which 'MS' stood for, and how could I know what he meant? He was a doctor, therefore perhaps Multiple Sclerosis was my best guess.

Next I noticed the asterisk next to the initials and followed it down. Urgent, it said. *Bingo*, I had something or someone, near or at the time of Doc's death, and he / she / it was marked Urgent.

The lights flickered in the kitchen and went out. Dang. I'd overloaded the generator again. I opened the front door, high-stepped over the expanse of salt water onto the dock and flicked the circuit breaker in the shed halfway up the hill.

The Franklin stove was cold with ashes. I hugged myself to keep warm. I switched on the space heater and built a fire in the stove. In the drawer where the matches nestled, I saw the book again, tatty and unloved, Agatha Christie's first novel: *The Murder at the Vicarage*. What had made me think there was a clue here?

Chapter Twenty-seven

Farther back on my mother's shelves in the main room of my float house, there were a couple other books: *The Purloined Letter*, a short story by Edgar Allen Poe, and *The Scarlet Pimpernel* by Baroness Emmuska Orczy, all in equally desolate condition. Once these books had been loved. I figured my mother must have read through them on many a day, many years ago, perhaps before I was born, and she brought them with her here, old friends like books often are.

Purloined. An obsolete word, no doubt. What did it mean? *Google and find out, Annie Fanny. Let me count the ways... you're a modern woman with a laptop. Why don't we look on-line? Can count on-line, too. Five, six, pick up sticks.*

Shut up.

The Purloined Letter. The Stolen Letter. Oh. By Edgar Allen Poe. Oh, yes, I took that in school for my GED, the last year of the program we had to read one great work of literature and a famous short story, and this was one of them. I didn't remember anything about it besides the unusual name.

The Scarlet Pimpernel, the story of a British nobleman who rescues French aristocrats sentenced to the guillotine. He leaves behind a small red flower (a pimpernel). It was about his love for his wife, from whom he must keep his activities secret. I spent the rest of the evening reading, with the pontoons creaking against the floorboards of the float house, the wind moaning across Modge Bay, and the lighthouse strobing the night from the rocky cliff two hundred yards away. Every so often I'd hear the foghorn like a Swiss alpenhorn playing a brief concert just for me.

I read two of my mother's old books until dawn extinguished the lamps from Modge Bay, until the foghorn no longer sounded in an automated sweep, until my eyes closed as I shut the final page of the last book. I stroked the old sepia cover of *Murder at the Vicarage*, and vowed to read that one next. I felt there was something in that book that would help me solve this case.

As I dragged myself up the ladder-like stairs to the bedrooms on the second floor, my mind whirled with formulae, lists and code numbers and abbreviated names. I couldn't focus on any one of them. My recollections were like confetti whirling around in my brain.

When I got to the top of the stairs, I emptied my pockets. My body slid between the crisp white sheets and my head sank onto a stack of soft but firm pillows, so that I was half sitting. A glass of water was cool between my fingers. Meds are over-rated, I thought as I swallowed my morning pills.

My BlueBell iCell phone on the night table played 'Dixie', and I peered at the display. It was the Serendipity Island Police Station. That wasn't any of my business. I was on stress leave.

I didn't answer the call.

Chapter Twenty-eight

I met Firewall Eddie at an NA meeting the next morning in the back of the old bookstore on Main Street. I was curious to see who'd be there. It was the end of the month so an open meeting, a birthday meeting again, and I knew Eddie would be there to eat the cake and drink the coffee. He was.

After the meeting, we got started talking about Doc Hubert, rest his soul.

"I never even met the guy," I said. "Just lucky, I guess."

"The cross-eyed old coot is dead and I don't care," Eddie said. He wiped his mouth with a dirty hand.

"What did you say?"

"He's dead and I don't care."

"No, the first part. Cross-eyed?"

"Yeah. Doc Hubert was cross-eyed from birth. His ma didn't take him to no doctors and by the age of seven or eight it was permanent. Used to wear an eye patch most days when he was working at his clinic."

"Strabismus," I said. "The nurse didn't mention that."

"She wouldn't. She thought Doc was a Greek god."

"So he had no depth perception."

"What do you mean?"

"Strabismus sometimes affects depth perception. If he wore an eye patch it most definitely would. Maybe affected his work as a surgeon?"

"Maybe that's why he pushed pills instead of cutting people open. I don't know. He wouldn't be much good at surgery, I suppose, with both eyes wonky and one covered with a patch."

"His nurse used to be in OR."

"She tell you that?" The room was half full of recovering addicts gathered around the coffee urn. A long table was pushed against one wall. The meeting was over and now it was time to socialize. Eddie edged me away from the group to a less crowded corner of the room.

"Yes," I said as I sipped on a cup of lemon chamomile tea.

"You never met Doc Hubert?" he asked.

"No. Interesting," I said again, and left it at that.

"Molly Dewitt is one patient woman."

"The nurse? Why do you say that?"

"Doc had quite an eye for the ladies."

"Never reciprocated?"

"No willing women that I know of. He had to pay for it."

"Was he a good looking man? Molly seems to think so."

"No, not particularly, though Molly always looks pretty pulled together. Nice looking woman."

"I didn't know that about Doc. About the ladies."

"Oh, yeah. Used to keep his clinic open late so's the ladies could get in, after hours. Certain ladies work those hours, you know, Annie, my naïve little friend."

"No." I laughed.

"Yes."

"Interesting." Was that all I could say? I began to feel uncomfortable, like I was out of my depth. Wouldn't be the first time with this case that I was out of my depth. Officially, I was off the case. Eddie didn't know that. Yet.

"Lots of ho's went through that office late at night. Some of them from the reserve off Modge Bay."

"The town paid for that office space. Somebody should have put a stop to it."

"Looks like somebody did."

"Hmmmm."

What Doc did with his free time was up to him. But it did put a new twist on the case, one I hadn't thought of when I talked to Eddie last week. A twist that Firewall Eddie didn't mention at first, the little bastoid.

Chapter Twenty-nine

At home in the float house the next morning, I thought I'd visit Molly Dewitt again right away. I wanted to surprise her but I had to be careful I didn't offend anyone, or I'd be in trouble for still working this case. But there were more unanswered questions after talking to Eddie.

I was quite relaxed now that I was off the case and on stress leave, it was true, but I just couldn't leave it alone. I told you before how I'm OCD. That means I'm like a terrier when I get a-hold of some idea or other. They should know that at the Cop Station downtown. I gave them plenty of reason to be glad I never let go of a case.

Then I remembered they'd called me, and I hadn't called back. I bet there was a message on my cell if I could figure out how to retrieve it.

While I was trying to get my messages, I decided to let Molly know I was coming over. Her card was in my pocket. I hoped she hadn't told Tom or the sergeant that I had the memory stick and hard drive from Doc's computer. They'd be on me like fleas on a dog if they knew.

I never did get my messages until later that day, which made it possible for me to do what I did next.

There was a "For Sale" sign on Molly's little house when I drove up on my scooter. Made sense. Why would she stay here when her employment was in the sink, down the drain, her employer six feet under and pushing up roses? Nothing left for good ol' faithful Molly here now.

I pushed open the gate and knocked on the door. The hinges creaked when she opened it. I noticed again that she had a tan. Hmmmm. Had she been on vacation? Nobody had said anything about that.

"I opened up Doc's appointments for that night," I said. "May I come in?"

"Of course." The door swung a little wider. Inside, the furniture was mostly covered with sheets, and boxes were stacked in the middle of the floor.

"Moving?" I asked. She nodded.

"I've got a new job down in Surrey," she said. "The OR there needs an experienced nurse."

"Don't leave town just yet. I might need you."

"Soon as I sell the little place I'm leaving. Have to be in Surrey by the middle of next month for the new job. I might have to leave it to Hot Air Real Estate here in Serendipity."

"You could rent it?"

"I could, until it sells. This is the start of tourist season. I put a big sign out front, someone might like some vacation property."

"They might." It was time to cut the chit-chat and get down to business. "Molly, did Doc treat anybody with MS? Multiple sclerosis? That shows up quite a bit in his appointments for the day. Just 'MS'. I thought it might have something to do with his last appointment of the evening."

"I wasn't aware he had an appointment so late." Molly sat down on a modern sofa that was half hidden in boxes. "He tended to keep his appointments in code to maintain confidentiality. I looked after the bookings for him and the billings, if he was able to bill for a service. He was a very kind man and if someone wasn't able to pay he would treat them anyway."

"Does the name 'Maser' mean anything to you?"

"How do you spell it?"

"M-A-S-E-R." Five letters, I thought. I gulped air into my lungs, feeling like I was suffocating in front of this woman, who was a murder suspect, and sane.

"No. But Doc didn't work with MS patients other than if someone was in pain, he would help them out."

"I see."

"I was there until nine o'clock then I went home. I thought Doctor Hubert would be right behind me." I scratched my nose and smiled…I'm sure, I thought.

"MS could be this Mr. or Ms. Maser, couldn't it?"

"Could be anyone with initials like that."

"Or anything."

"Yes, anything. He would often remind himself of little idiosyncrasies of a patient, made it easier to work with them, especially with his clientele."

"I'm sure."

"You must understand the doctor was a humanitarian."

"Yes. I understand that. A good man." *Oooo he was a womanizer, little Molly, and now let's hear what we can hear.* "Molly, this is very important. Is there anybody you suspect the doctor would meet at such an odd time of the night? Midnight? The appointment was written in for that time. He must have been alone from nine o'clock to midnight, that's three hours, unless there was something else he was doing to fill in the time. Do you remember or know anything about that night?"

"I don't know," she said. "He had a lot of paperwork and I wasn't always able to complete it in a day, if it was a busy day, as they usually were. He was working on a medical paper for a journal, I think, about the effects of oral methadone versus injectable. He did research on his own. He had friends, he might have been on the phone, or emailing his many contacts over the world. He could have been on Facebook. I don't know what he did in his spare time." Her voice was firm.

Facebook! Why didn't I think of that? Names, faces, places might be on his Facebook page. They almost certainly would be.

I pushed back my chair and got up. It was mid-morning. Both Molly and I were apparently early risers. "Thanks," I said. "I think I have enough to keep me busy for a while. And Molly?"

"Yes?" I noticed she was wearing yoga pants and a blue tee-shirt. Her tennis shoes were by the door and a gym bag seemed packed. Molly works out? A new gym had opened on Serendipity Island last summer including a tanning bed and a class in Martial Arts. Would explain the tan.

"Keep this visit to yourself, will you, Molly? Do me that kindness. I'm sort of out of favor with Lorne and my boss in Victoria, they wouldn't want me knowing too much about the case." The best defense is a good offense.

"Oh, I see," she said. "Yes, of course. It's time I got going. I have a class in twenty minutes."

"The new gym?"

"Yes, karate," she said. "I'm working on my second-degree black belt."

"I'll be danged. How long have you been doing that?" I asked.

"Since I lived in Abbottsford," she said. "It's a hobby of mine."

"Since Abbottsford. That's a few years. You must be able to take down a roomful of men by now."

She smiled.

Chapter Thirty

I never thought living on the float house would be permanent, but after the fight I'd had with Samir, it seemed like a good idea. Confronting him with Doc's death didn't seem like a good idea in hindsight. Of course, he'd got defensive. Of course, he'd denied it. I shouldn't have confronted him at the Powolskis' home, in retrospect.

"You and those flatfoot cops tried to pin this on me once before!" he'd shouted. He banged his fist on the table. "Took me right off the ferry and I hurt my leg again."

"I'm tired of hearing about your dang leg!" I shouted back. Mrs. P peered up the stairwell at us. She'd likely report this outburst to our social worker.

Samir's cane leaned against the wall. The tip of it was stained black. He pointed to it. Veins stood out on his forehead. His face turned a funny shade of eggplant purple. I had to grin, but that was a mistake.

"That's not funny, you *miwat*. My parents *pisth*. Raised me to be *guop la wic*. You *puou ayur*, *miwat*." He lapsed into a Dinka SW Rek dialect and I almost died laughing.

Good thing I didn't know what he was saying, but I could get the gist of it. What he called me was not nice, I'm sure.

"What I said was, how come there was mud on the floor that morning and where were you at midnight?"

"I right here in bed next you." He lapsed into pigeon English. I grinned again.

"You're enjoying this, aren't you, you little *miwat*?"

"Children, stop it," Mrs. P called up. "Can't have you fighting like this. It ain't seemly for a couple."

I doubled over laughing again. Samir hobbled over to his cane and shook it in my face.

"You were testing me."

"Of course."

"You know I didn't do it."

"Why would you?"

He grinned. "I know how to use a surgical drill."

"I'm sure you do."

"I could pile Doc's brains in such a neat heap by his empty skull."

"I know you could."

"But did I? No!" He slammed the cane on the floorboards, which caused Mrs. P to yell again. We looked at each other and burst out laughing.

"Don't follow me to the float house," I said. "I want to be alone."

"You vant to be alone," he mocked. "I leave you alone, then, Miss Greta Garbo."

"How you know about our old movie stars?" I asked.

"We watch American TV all the time. Old movies. Old jokes." He slapped my back. I coughed real hard and sort of phony-like.

"Children, make up," Mrs. P called. I heard her stomp back to the kitchen. The remaining parrot squawked.

"Go to your float house, Annie." His body was very close, his pink palms entreating. I could smell his musky but clean smell, like vanilla over honest sweat. An arrow went through my guts.

"It won't be forever," I said. "I just got to think things out."

"Take your time." He pinned the Canadian flag back from the dirty little window. The old yeller dog whined on his chain in the backyard. "Dog needs feeding, Mrs. P."

"Close the door on your way out," he called as I turned my back and stomped down the stairs. "I hope you're tested real good."

It was the last thing I heard him say to me for two more lonely weeks.

Chapter Thirty-one

I managed to retrieve the phone message later that day when I was back home in the float house. My dinner was cooking on the propane stove in a corner of the kitchen, all cheery and everything. I was getting quite domestic.

Annie, you little witch, get off the case. Yes, that was Constable Tom on the voicemail.

You get down to the station right away. You've got something that belonged to Doc Hubert. His thumb drive is missing from his laptop and I think I know where it is. I hope you have it.

I do.

If you don't have it, maybe you can tell us where it is. We know he kept his patient list on it.

I phoned Tom right away but he'd left already. That's the trouble with a small town, it rolls up its sidewalks at six o'clock. I had his cell number, though. I considered. Suddenly my phone gave a little squeal and shut off. Oh, dang, I'd have to plug it in and recharge it. I kept forgetting to do that. I dug around in one of the drawers by the Franklin stove and found the charger, plugged it in, and the lights went out.

It wasn't crucial, there was still light outside. After all, it was only March. The big window reflected the ocean outside. The dock was pretty empty except for the float house and a few boats wintering until spring was really here.

I stepped out over the gap between the front door and the dock, where the Bay was pretty shallow but still, I didn't want to fall in. I climbed across the rocks to the little shed where the circuit breakers were and popped it back on, then returned.

My dinner was delicious. I wasn't finished eating when the noise began in this very quietest of sanctuaries. The door almost buckled with serious thumping from a beefy pair of hands.

"Annie? Constable Tom here. Open up."

I sighed and opened the door. Tom almost fell into the drink.

"Okay, Tom. I got what you wanted. Sorry. Molly gave it to me the other night and I kept it."

"Oh, for Pete's sake. Did you look at the info?"

"I opened the thumb drive. That's memory stick to you."

"I know that."

"Here, you can have it back." I popped the USB out of the laptop.

"Thanks. You know, I could arrest you for this, Annie."

"You wouldn't." I sucked my thumb.

"No, I won't, but you're on stress leave and Erna took you off the case. So stay off it, Annie, stay out of these murders. I can see why you're on stress leave. It's too much for you. Molly Dewitt says you've been over there snooping around." *The bitch.*

"Send me to Lorne for instructions," I said. "I'll listen to him. He's my boss, or was."

"You don't need any instructions other than what I'm telling you, girl. Stay out of this. Now stay home and let's not hear from you again or you'll find yourself under arrest again, and this time you won't be getting away with community service and a pardon."

"You know about a pardon?" *Sounds good.* I felt the color rise in my face and I smiled. My fingers flew behind my back, soothing me.

"Erna said something about it."

"That's exciting."

"No promises, I think, girl. Just stay off this case. We'll handle it."

"How's it going so far?" *Cheeky little devil you are, Annie Hansen.* I grinned.

"A fellow's coming from Victoria to help out. Name's Detective Snow. Mark Snow, friend of Erna Sobey. You won't meet him if you keep your nose clean."

"Good, someone capable, I hope," I said. After a few more pleasantries along that line, Constable Tom stepped over to the dock and left.

Darn. I'd have to be more careful.

Chapter Thirty-two

I patted *The Scarlet Pimpernel* and Poe's very clever short story, *The Purloined Letter.* I think the eighteenth and nineteenth centuries would suit me. Yes, a gentleman of breeding who rescues aristocrats who are about to be guillotined by the French Revolution, leaves a blood red flower (a scarlet pimpernel) behind in their place, and gallops off to his home, where his wife eventually joins forces against him, but he finally rescues her, as well, and her brother. A hero after my own heart.

The Purloined Letter, a mystery and love story, dramatic and tragic, by the mad Poe. Both books made me yearn for an age when I could flaunt learning and cut to the quick of the action, but think my way out of a mystery and into a solution, be brave and *be a man.*

The fire in the Franklin stove crackled amongst the charred and blackened logs. My eyes began to close and my head kept dropping to my chest then would jerk up again as I briefly awakened.

Finally, legs stretched out on the orange and gold-blanketed settee by the bay windows, now dark with night, I allowed myself to doze. The room was warm and the last I remembered of the room was the sound of embers hissing in the belly of the stove.

I was the baron Sir Percy, my calling card a small red flower that I left in place of nurse Molly, who wore a flowing red and white gown, then suddenly we were on my scooter escaping the King of Clubs who wanted to cut off our heads. No, it wasn't the King, it was the French Revolution and the year was 1792, the start of the Reign of Terror. The King was dead or dismembered, he lay on the chopping block behind us, and the flowers which covered him had begun to bleed. The blood overflowed onto the street, onto walls and floors and followed us in a flood of scarlet. The scooter disappeared and I was swimming in flowers. Molly followed, arms flailing, wearing a black karate belt and little else. I was embarrassed, in my dream, and averted my eyes.

Pepsi was at the side of the road with his blue Mercury. We got in and he drove us to a ruined castle. When we got there, Samir appeared and Molly swirled down a drain in a cascade of scarlet flowers. I embraced Samir and he slipped from my arms. Flowers sprang up all around us, covering the blue Mercury. My Vespa was suddenly there. I tried to ride away, but flowers choked the wheels and overran me, my mouth, my eyes, my nose. Then I looked down and saw the flowers were blood and my hands and arms were covered with it.

I moaned in my sleep and was aware it was a bad dream. I tried to control it, tried to scream and wake myself up. Molly was there in a white nurse's uniform with a scalpel in her hands. I struggled to awaken, saw myself sleeping as though from above. I realized it was a dream within a dream, a sleeping dream, I enjoyed the softness of the settee, the warmth of the blanket, and looked at myself with fondness.

"Watch out!" someone shouted, and I woke up.

Gollywogs only knew where the letter was, I thought, still drowsy. I turned on a light and looked at one of the many alarm clocks scattered around the float house, a legacy from my OCD mother. It was eight o'clock. At night or in the morning?

It was eight o'clock at night and the phone was ringing. It must be recharged, I thought, and lurched off the settee.

The call was from Lorne. He sounded upset. I couldn't imagine why. I was the one should be upset. I should be troubled, not the jerk Private Eye on the phone. I'd just had a terrible dream and I couldn't shake it.

The light flickered. Red flowers floated in the middle of the room, swirled into the shape of a funnel cloud and tried to devour me. It wasn't pleasant, unlike some of my visions.

A therapist had once tried to tell me they were pseudo-hallucinations because I knew they weren't real. I wore my schizophrenia like a badge in the beginning and he was trying to knock me down, the son of a bitch, make me less proud of my differences. Okay, I had nothing in particular then to distinguish myself other than the visions and voices. I'd learned to fight for myself since, but at that time I believed in the doctors and eventually the lawyers who told me I wasn't anybody unique. That idea had been knocked out of me a long time ago.

Though I saw the sun rising in the west in glory, not in the east, and sometimes a lot of noise, and I thought I must be a Special Agent of God, how else could this be explained? We're all special agents of God in our way. Me, too.

Chapter Thirty-three

Now Lorne sounded upset and the phone was so small. I tried to listen and then talk, but the phone was too small to put to my ear and my mouth at the same time. I had an awful time with it until I figured out the mike was sensitive and all I had to do was hold one end of the phone to my ear. Somebody had tried to tell me that once. I think it was Samir. Lorne was saying something important on the other end and I couldn't quite grasp it.

"Stay away from the evidence and stay away from the case, Annie. You been pulled for a reason. I got a call from Sergeant Ross at the station downtown. He's got a new gumshoe there, a Detective by the name of Mark Snow."

"I know."

"How'd you know that, you brat?"

"I talked to Tom earlier today. Or maybe yesterday, I don't know when it was."

"Have you been drinking, Annie?"

"You know better than that, Lorne. It was one of the stips of my contract, no drinking, and I know what that would do to me, let alone put me back in jail."

"You're darn right, young lady, but you sound awful fuzzy."

"I had a bad dream."

"This detective has the hard drive and the memory stick. They said you were hiding evidence. That right?"

"Sort of, I guess so. But I didn't mean any wrong, Lorne."

"I believe you. But it wasn't the right thing to do."

"I know. But I found out who might be the killer."

"Who?"

"The last appointment of the evening, at midnight, somebody called 'Maser.' Molly says it must be a code name. As well as somebody with initials 'MS'. Or something like that, somebody or something. I could have cracked the case, Lorne."

"You could crack up, too. Stay away from all that thinking and take it easy there at the float house. You think too much. Let the experts figure it out. They've got the mayor's murder to think about, too."

"I *am* the expert. Life on the street is my thing. I've talked to Crazy Leroy and Firewall Eddie, Pepsi and Samir, I'm *this* close."

"You are not."

"Okay, I'm not."

"You're on stress leave and you keep it that way."

"Have you thought the mayor's murder might not be connected?"

"They're both too damn creepy. Must be the same guy."

"This detective Snow. He any good?"

"I think so. Seems to have more brains than the sergeant and Tom put together, just between the two of us."

"You know better than to say that, Lorne."

"Ha, ha, don't threaten me, girl. I can put you behind bars yet."

"No, you can't. Nobody can anymore. I'm getting a pardon and I've been straight for two years."

"You can't get a pardon."

"Yes, I can. Erna promised me."

"You're turning over a new leaf these past two years, I gotta hand it to you, kid."

"I'm a new woman." The red funnel would devour me. It swirled in the middle of the room then just as suddenly sucked itself into a hole in the floor, which opened up and I knew it went down to Hell.

"Just be careful," he said.

"This Detective Snow, his first name is Mark."

"Yeah. I know, 'MS'."

"Yeah, that's what I was thinking. He's new to town, you're sure?"

"That's a stretch, what you're thinking."

"Everything's a stretch," I said. I put a hand to my forehead. The room was clear again, no red flowers, no funnel, no hole leading to Hell. I felt relief and then started to squint into the corners, afraid I'd see something, but willing it to appear.

The visions made me very special.

Lorne was talking but my voices were getting louder, drowning out his rambling. Eventually he hung up.

"Little Molly's a martial arts brown belt," I said to no one in particular. That sort of scared me. I was tough but a brown belt could beat the heck out of me and probably anyone else we all knew.

I flung myself onto the settee again, then thought of something really brilliant and hit the floor in another 'Hulk stomp'. There was a YouTube Nollywood movie I had to watch again about a Nigerian woman who'd killed her husband and was in an asylum. I saw it on the web the previous night. It was like I had to watch this movie because it was by OKIN Partners from Yoruba in Nigeria. Haha, that came from watching too many mystery movies, but it was about this schizophrenic woman treated by a doctor who sleeps with her to cure her.

The movie had very bad reviews. It was pretty bad, but it mentioned the 'evil eye' and I remembered Pepsi talking about the evil eye. A lot of Africans believed in it. Greeks, northern Europeans, Asians, and Arabs, and immigrants brought the idea of the curse to North America. It could be done unintentionally, or with envy, especially blue-eyed people were suspect. I'd like to have been one of these dudes who dig up graves and stuff, scrape off old bones with a toothbrush. I really loved movies about other cultures and I liked reading about old stuff, too, different ideas. This movie interested me because I thought Samir probably believed in that stuff, too.

But anyways, I thought of something brilliant and it had to do with the movie. I had to do some research first. *Stay away from the case, you'll never figure it out and you'll go crazy trying to do it.* That was actually good advice from my voices. Way to go, voices, you're finally making sense.

I missed the Powolskis, and I missed Samir and Pepsi. I'd isolated myself long enough. I knew what the problem was.

I was lonely. I almost never got lonely because I had my voices and my visions to keep me company, but now I was lonely. Maybe I was finally becoming human. I looked at my hands. A red flower floated on my right hand. It faded and died away, but I was happy, because I loved myself for being beautiful with a scarlet pimpernel on my hand. I didn't even have to count the petals, I was that happy.

Chapter Thirty-four

Seemed to me I spent too much time in the float house but it was so relaxing and such a peaceful time to watch the ocean storms without getting ratcheted about, the pontoons are that secure, and the place reminded me of Mom without Dad, a good thing actually. But I was feeling a bit grey in my mind, a low mood.

I was stirring a pot of chowder, when a knock came on the door. It was the time of day that photographers don't much like, sun high in a cloudless sky, not the golden hour at all, but a time of day I really loved. I was sure tired of the rain and sleet.

The sun is my friend and it was March, almost spring, when I opened the door and a stranger stood there.

He flashed a badge and asked if he could come in. *Don't let him in. He'll kill you, dummy. Look at that, he's got the evil eye.*

Oh, shut up, voices. Yes, he had bright blue eyes and an engaging smile, rather like a brother, I thought. I never had a brother.

"Mind if I come in?" he repeated. "Detective Snow. I've been talking to your friends Constable Tom and Sergeant Ross, and they sent me here."

"I guess so." I gestured toward the small room. The Franklin stove had gone out and it was a bit cool, even for March at the coast, in spite of the sun outside.

"You can help me, if you're Annie Hansen. Guess I should have made that clear. I'm from headquarters in Victoria, I work with Erna Sobey."

"I know. I heard."

"News travels fast in Serendipity."

"News travels fast on any island."

"Nice here." He looked around.

"Sit down," I invited. *Stupid, he'll snoop through everything, he'll find the stash.*

84

What stash? You ain't got no stash.

"What?"

"Nothing." I ran my fingers through my frizzled hair. "The voices," I explained. He nodded professionally, looking like an owl, then frowned. He took a step back and leaned against the counter in the kitchen, by the stove.

"Oh, yes, Tom told me."

"Nothing to worry about. I'm harmless. I don't have no brown belt." He laughed.

"That's actually why I came. It's about the nurse, Margaret Dewitt."

"Oh, you saw Molly?"

"Yes, Molly, and she didn't tell me much, was on her way to a class, really wouldn't talk a lot, but she did mention she'd talked to you and told me to check it out with you. Tom and Ross said the same." Darn Molly, she promised not to tell I'd spoken to her.

"Did you talk to Lorne O'Halloran?" I wondered how much he knew about me being off the case and now—talking to Molly Dewitt.

"Yeah, of course. He knows you pretty well, had some good things to say about you. Said you'd taken a leave."

"Yeah, stress leave."

"He didn't say. But apparently you're off the case? Officially? You work sort of under the table anyhow, I understand."

"Sort of. They hire me to do the dirty work on the street. And yes, I saw Molly. She's about to leave town, Detective."

"Call me Mark." He leaned against the counter and folded his arms across his chest. His blue eyes swept the room. He was tall, I'd guess six feet two. A bit of a paunch. Handsome.

"You live here full-time?"

"I do now. Have you talked to Meredith and Henry Powolski?"

"No, not yet."

"Might be a good idea. Samir lives there, or did." *You little snitch. Leave him out of this. We don't like Detective Mark Fark, the Snark.*

"Who's Samir?" He put a hand in his pocket and brought out his iPhone, started typing something there, I don't know what. Never could figure that out, I don't even text. *Stupid, you'll never figure this out, either. They're coming to get you.*

"My phone doesn't even take pictures," I said.

"Oh, I'm sure it does," Mark said. His thumb patted the tiny keyboard. "Mind if I take a photo of you and this place?"

"Sure." I posed with a hand on my hip and smiled for the Detective. He took a couple more shots of the room and the view. I glanced at my photo and didn't like the sloppy, overweight young woman with the wild peroxide hair. I wondered what Mark thought of me. Samir never seemed to mind despite his teasing.

"You didn't answer. Who's Samir?"

"My boyfriend and former roommate at the Powolskis. You're not a very good cop or you'd know that."

"I just got here two days ago. Have pity."

"You look kind of young."

"Thanks, but wisdom doesn't always come with age." He grinned. "I'm thirty-five and do have credentials. Graduate of UBC in Criminal Studies, ten years' experience on the force in Victoria and Campbell River, got promoted last year."

"Congratulations."

"You know anything about this Samir or Molly Dewitt you haven't said?"

"Nope."

"What do you know, Annie? This will help a lot with the case."

"Don't know nothin'. But have you talked to Samir's cousin, Pepsi?"

"The janitor at City Hall and the medical building where Doc worked? Yes. He's got an alibi."

"Sure, I know, Eddie the security guard. Have you talked to Firewall?"

"I can't find him yet." The voices snorted with glee. I glared in their general direction.

"You're covering all bases. Good luck. You do know Molly was in love with Doc Hubert?"

"No, I didn't know that. They have an affair?"

"I don't think so. From what I hear he was pretty busy in the sex department, though. Or the sex trade, I should say."

"Who told you that?"

"Eddie. He saw a lot of comings and goings. I bet Molly knew all about that, too, and it must have put her knickers in a knot to know the Doc was–"

"That's gossip. But keep it up, Annie. What more do you know? Do you think Molly blew him away? Would she have the strength?" His thumb flew over the keyboard. I noticed a little light blinking.

"You recording this, Mark?"

"Yes."

"Off the record, Mark." He thumbed a small button and the light went out.

"What?"

"No, I don't think it was Molly. Just a feeling, I don't think she could have done it."

"I agree," he said. "Just a gut feeling. I don't think she hated him enough."

"I think we're looking for somebody with the initials 'MS' and somebody whose name, or code name, is Maser. I saw the doctor's appointment list for that Saturday. The cops on the beat downtown have the thumb drive, and the hard drive, and they probably know more than I do."

"My initials are 'MS.' " He winked.

"You're pretty casual for a strange cop."

"It's my modus operandi."

"Get a lot more people opening up if you're friendly?"

"Works better if my partner is surly."

"Good cop, bad cop. Are you ever the bad cop?"

"Oh, yeah. We take turns."

"You don't have a partner here?"

"We can't spare anybody else. A couple of RCMP are over to City Hall investigating the mayor's murder. We're splitting the two cases, we don't even know if they're connected."

"You're sharing what you learn, I presume?"

"You know a lot for somebody who's off the case. I wouldn't ask too many more questions," he said. "You're on stress leave, remember that. Erna speaks highly of you. Don't want to disappoint her and get yourself in trouble with the powers that be here in Serendipity."

"I know that, I've been warned. I just can't keep out of trouble, Mark." I sat down in the old armchair that was in the kitchen near the stove. "Say, you ever hear of Nollywood?"

"Yeah, Nigerian movies."

"Bingo, you clever fellow. They're big on the evil eye, aren't they? Especially blue-eyed dudes like you. Be careful around Pepsi and Samir. They won't trust you. I don't think they trust me all that well. And look out for Mr. or Ms. Maser, and whoever 'MS' is. I don't think it's you."

"Could be Mayor Spacey," he mused.

"Mayor's first name was Rick."

"I know, it's a long shot. We're trying to cover all the bases."

"Good luck, gumshoe." A purple giraffe glided across the room, across his toes, and out the closed door with a puff.

I couldn't help but stare.

"We've told Molly not to leave town. I'm telling you the same thing, Annie." He snapped his phone case shut and pushed himself away from the counter. The chowder bubbled on the stove behind him. Man, it smelled good. I hope he appreciated what a good cook I am, what a domestic goddess and everything. *Oh, you're completely harmless, aren't you, little murderer? He doesn't like you. Nobody likes you. You might as well drop right into the drink and be done with it.*

"I might as well," I said.

"What?"

"Drop into the drink and be done with it."

I restrained myself from counting.

"Oh. Of course. You can help out, and this is off the record."

"Sure. Anything I can do. I love mysteries."

"You got one here," he said. "For sure. The boys at City Hall aren't any closer to solving the mayor's death than we are to solving the doctor's murder. Looks a lot like it might be the same psycho."

"Right here in ocean city," I said. "There might be two psychos on Serendipity Island."

"Say, the lighthouse there. Who runs it?"

"It's automated."

"What time does the light come on?"

"Dusk, I suppose. I never noticed. Stupid foghorn keeps me awake some nights."

"I suppose."

I opened the front door and leaned against it. "Did you think we still had keepers?"

"I don't know. Wondered who lives in that broken down shack next to it."

"That's boarded up in winter. Derelicts and homeless sometimes shack up there."

"Yeah, I know you checked them out downtown."

"If you mean Crazy Leroy and Firewall Eddie, yeah, I did."

"Good for you. Mind if I come back sometime?"

"Be my guest," I said and leaned against the door as he stepped out onto the dock. Just before he left, he called back.

"By the way, Annie. Mollie was married before."

"Really? What was her last name?"

"Guess."

"I don't know."

"Schneider."

"Doc know that?"

"Changed her name back to Dewitt two weeks ago."

I heard an engine start up about five minutes later, when he would have got to the top of the hill where the parking lot was. I thought about the visit. My voices were quiet, for a change.

They must have been thinking it over, too.

Chapter Thirty-five

The moon was a crescent hanging over the island, the ocean a silver wash upside down in a grey sky. We'd taken down my mother's sheets from the window and a single candle flared in a corner of the float house. Samir's silhouette was a cut-out against the moonlight.

"We never have a date night, Sugar," I whispered. My voices were still and only the moon was bright like a copper earring, my visions still too.

His lips moved. I thought he was sobbing.

"What's wrong? Did I hurt you?"

He didn't answer. I felt his arm tighten across my shoulders.

"What you see in me?" he asked finally. "I'm a no good for you, Annie."

"What do you mean?"

"I should have died in the refugee camp, like Moses. Samir took his passport, maybe Moses Nijam Suliman wasn't really dead."

"Life is for the living."

"I did bad things in my life, Annie. Maybe I got HIV."

"No, you were tested when you came to Toronto. You all were." *Were they?*

"Don't want to touch you, Annie, I'm unclean. All we do is kiss. I feel your boobs. They feel good. I missed you so much."

"I want you to touch me," I said.

"You're right. We never have a date night. I go out with Pepsi and my buddies like Eddie and Crazy Leroy, sometimes African friends from the big Island, sometimes girls."

"Yes. I know."

"You know, Babes? You still like Samir?"

"Yes."

"You want a date night? I know you don't want to stay at the Powolskis anymore. We shared a room, it was nice, we could both pay for it. I could afford that. Now I can't afford to stay there no more," he said.

"That's not true, Samir. They'll adjust the rent."

"What does that mean?"

"You won't have to pay so much as the two of us did."

"I only paid half."

"Yes, you're right." I sighed and stroked his dark face in the shadow of the windowsill. The crescent earring had sailed overhead and was covered with cloud.

"I'll talk to my worker," he said. "She'll... what did you say? Adjust it."

"Let's have a date night," I said.

"When, Sugar?"

"Right now."

"What should we do?"

"Let's go out on my mother's motorboat, in the moonlight, or what's left of it."

"Your mother only had a little boat. Not safe in the ocean."

"We won't go far. It has a radio. My neighbor can look out for us."

"Your neighbor in the big boat? He keeps his curtains shut. He don't care what happens to us."

"I've talked to him. He's a nice guy. His wife, too. They keep to themselves. People around here don't trust the people who live in boats or float houses. We don't pay property taxes, they resent it. Him and me got a lot in common," I said.

"But he don't *always* keep his curtains shut," Samir said.

I whipped my head around. What did he mean by that? Before I could ask, he crushed me to his manly chest. Oh, my gosh.

Slowly I put both arms around his neck. My cheeks were wet with his tears. He was crying. We never did go out in the motorboat that night. There wasn't time.

I almost told him that night that I trusted him. I almost told him I loved him. But what do I know of love?

I know a lot about loneliness, though. Those Christian people in the church downtown never visited little Annie. Not good enough for them and their pious stick-it-in-your-face religion. My gut ached sometimes, I was so lonely. Especially after I moved out to the float house where my mommy used to stay.

I wondered if she had been lonely, too, with my father gone and me on the streets? I never thought of that at the time.

Samir and me never had a fight. We just drifted apart like the ships around the spit that come too close to the lighthouse and were warned away. I could hear the foghorn most nights.

That dang foghorn played a concert for big, tall Annie in the night. It kept me awake, it did. I loved to lie and listen to the foghorn, see the sweep of the lamps if I looked in the right direction. Sometimes I counted the sweeps.

That lighthouse kept me company, though it was automated, as they say, still, somebody might live in the broken down shack beside it. If they did, it was a secret to me. I never saw nobody come and go from that shack.

Until much later, on the night I found out who killed Doc Hubert and why somebody would want to kill Mayor Richard Spacey, the high flyin' friend of the doctor, or who was 'MS', though I guess we'll never really know that for sure, that's what Mark said, my blue-eyed gumshoe. He should know. He helped me solve the case. Some things you never really know for sure, he said.

But that didn't satisfy Annie Hansen, the OCD private eye, you know. I wanted to *know*, and by gum, *I did.* It didn't make me happy, but at the end, I knew it all.

Samir went home early that morning. That's the last time I seen him before I moved out to the float house permanent. Lordy, he was one handsome, screwed-up fellow.

First, him and me would tumble beneath the big white duvet in the bedroom upstairs, fall acrost the embroidered pillows and the crisp linen sheets, his lips soft and hungry. I told you Samir was my first boyfriend.

He was like an arrow piercing my soul.

Chapter Thirty-six

I'd like to become more attractive, I thought. I had looked at myself in the photo the Detective took the day he came knockin' at my door, didn't like what I saw. I'd put on a lot of weight since starting the psych meds I was on and thought maybe Dr. Blanche could give me something different. I might do something with my hair. I pulled it back. It was bleached white and the brown was growing out. Hmmm, violet eyes, not bad looking face, rather round, but my face tended to be oval shaped when I didn't weigh so dang much. Twelve years ago my hair was blonde. It had darkened and I did something about it, maybe the bleached white wasn't a good idea at my age. I was only twenty-four and looked like a hag.

Something could be done, I thought.

I could hear the rain drumming on the tin roof of the float house. When I looked outside, the ocean was speckled with rain. I put on a yellow slicker and opened the door, ran up the wet dock, laughing, fell up the hill to my Vespa parked at the top. My hair was wet and my sneakers were soaked. It was fun to putt-putt through the rain and sleet along the little road to town.

I stopped at the Powolskis' house but Samir wasn't there.

"Well, well, it's our lovely Miss Hansen." Mrs. P greeted me warmly. "We miss you around here. It's pretty dull without you, dear."

"I miss you, too, Mrs. P," I lied. Mr. P grunted and turned up the television.

They were watching the news. The investigation was on the local news from Campbell River. They hadn't had a break in the case yet. I knew that.

"Yer old man's with his cousin at the Serendipity Hotel, if you're looking for him," Mrs. P said.

"I suppose drinking beer and playing Chinese checkers." She pinched my cheek and I leaned over her and stole a gingersnap straight from the oven. Mmmm.

So I drove through the pouring rain to the hotel. Sure enough, Pepsi's old blue Mercury was parked out front. I strolled through the door. Samir was sitting at the bar drinking coffee. Good for him. He looked up when I came in and his face lit up like candles on a Christmas tree.

"You look good," was the first thing he said. "Where you been?"

"You know I've been at the float house," I said. "Where you been? You never come see me, you piece of turtle dung." He laughed.

"My leg's been hurting bad."

"We'll have to get that fixed. They've been wonky ever since the soldiers broke your legs and you didn't get them set. We've got healthcare here in Canada, you maroon. We can fix them maybe."

"Maybe. Doc wanted me to go for treatments."

"Doc?" He didn't answer.

Pepsi was sitting in the corner drinking coffee too, staring at a game of Chinese checkers that was unfinished, presumably his cousin had grown tired of the game. Guess they'd had their quota of beer for the morning. Neither one is an alcoholic, I thought, but they sure start drinking early when they get together.

"Bad magic spells on my legs," Samir said. "Soldiers put a spell on them back in Juba."

"Voodoo," Pepsi called from his place at the window in the corner. The barkeep wiped down the tables. There were no other customers in the place. Guess he'd have to be glad about the Sudanese, they gave him something to do mornings like this until the other regulars came in.

Speaking of which, Firewall Eddie and Leroy came through the door. They must have heard what Pepsi said just as they entered the room.

"Whatcha mean, voodoo?" Firewall said. He sat at the bar next to Samir.

"They don't want to talk about it," I said. "Bad luck."

"Yeah, me, too," Firewall said.

"That's bad magic with us, too." Leroy nodded. "That what happened to your leg?" Samir nodded and played with the Saint Benedict medal he wore around his neck to ward off evil.

"They took his father first, then his mother," Pepsi said. "He was working on a first aid truck, hid them in the back of the truck and brought them to the refugee camp at Yida."

"Saved a lot of people that way," Samir said.

Pepsi nodded. "Soldiers found out about it, broke his legs."

"It was bad magic." Samir put an arm around me. "Missed you, Anne the Can."

"You did a good thing," I said. "I didn't know that about you, Samir." I looked at him with new respect. There was more to him than met the eye. "We'll have to get in touch with your worker. She'll arrange for some medical care. How long you been in Canada?"

"About five years. I'm a citizen now." He was proud of his Canadian citizenship and didn't make a secret of it to his Sudanese buddies, either. He encouraged them to do the same, because... "Now nobody can send Samir back to Sudan."

"That's right, and we'll get you some medical care. I'm going to Campbell River next week to see my psych, try to get some new meds. I phoned him and set up an appointment. His nurse got me in on a cancellation. Why don't you come with me and we'll see the clinic about getting your legs fixed? I bet they can do something for you, Samir."

"They sure hurt," he said. "Never got them fixed. Bad, bad magic."

"No, it's not magic, silly."

Crazy Leroy and Firewall weren't so sure.

"Big magic there in Africa," Firewall Eddie said, and ordered a Canadian Club.

"I thought you'd quit," I said to him.

"He sure quit his job some nights," Leroy said.

"I'm there every night," Firewall said. He winked and tipped his glass. "Here's to you, Annie."

I didn't drink.

"So you were a paramedic in the Sudan," I said to Samir. He nodded. "Couldn't you do something like that here?"

"He's not really trained," Pepsi said, and belched.

"I'm not trained by no white doctors," Samir said.

Eddie laughed and ordered another whiskey. "Witch doctors."

"No, they got a good hospital there in Darfur," Samir said. "I was there for ten months learning how to patch people up, but I didn't finish. The rebels took over part of that area and I joined them for a while, then was recruited by the government soldiers. I worked for them."

"He helped the people if he could," Pepsi said. "That's how we both escaped and ended up in the refugee camp in Yida with Samir's parents. He drove his truck straight in there and left it, somebody else drove it back, they escaped, too. Samir's a good guy."

"How'd you get here?" Firewall asked. I sipped on my coffee, black.

"Missionaries helped us escape with somebody else's passport," Pepsi said. "Plane full of refugees and they flew us to Toronto. We were there for about two years, then we came here. First Vancouver, then Serendipity Island for Samir and me. Samir got citizenship in Vancouver, now uses his real name. Came here as Moses Nijam Suliman under someone else's name."

"I know," I said. I put down my coffee cup. My hair was beginning to dry. I took off my yellow slicker. Samir's hand slipped from my shoulders and I shivered. His arm had felt real good, warm and strong.

"You think the white doctors could fix my leg?" Samir asked. I looked down at the crooked limb.

"I think so," I said. "We could try."

"They didn't say anything in the clinic in Toronto," Pepsi said. "But we got our teeth fixed right away with dentists."

"Soldiers broke my teeth." Samir grinned, exposing perfectly-capped incisors.

"I know. You're a hero, loverboy. I didn't know that before, I never thought about it, but you know, we don't live like that here in Canada. Explains a lot about you guys. For example, when I lived in Vancouver, there was a Sudanese community there, they went to a Christian church and some of the men worked for a packing plant in Burnaby, some violence would erupt every now and then, but I think I understand."

"Yeah, it's part of our culture," Pepsi said. "All we know for years now is soldiers raping and murdering, can't trust our neighbors, many children left orphans, saw their families shot and killed right in front of their eyes. I did. I'm only twenty-one, like my cousin here, and saw lots I don't like to think about. Children used rifles, learned to fight and swear real young. Had to survive, sometimes didn't, lots of people die, tortured, murdered. Fact of life."

"Ages you fast," Samir said.

That was more than I'd heard the two men say about it since I'd met them. They explained a lot I didn't realize about my two friends.

Firewall Eddie and Leroy were talking between themselves, arguing about some load of hay or horses or something. People were starting to come into the bar and the coffee shop was filling up with senior citizens getting together with their buddies. I thought maybe it was time for me to go, but not until I'd made some arrangements.

"What about it?" I asked. "You coming with me next Monday to Campbell River, see the doctors at the clinic, while I see Dr. Blanche?"

"Guess so," Samir said. "Not the first time I thought about it."

"It's time to take some action," I said. "I'm tired of hearing you whine about your danged leg."

"It hurts," he said.

"It didn't hurt so much two weeks ago when you and Pepsi went fishing out on the ocean in Henry's boat."

"That was good of Henry."

"Yeah, he doesn't get out much himself."

"But what happened to make it so sore?"

"Guess I hurt it."

"Let's get that leg looked at."

"Okay, Annie, you win, I'll get my leg looked at. They maybe fix that evil voodoo spell."

"Bad magic like a soldier hit him with the butt of a gun," Firewall Eddie said.

"That's real bad magic." Pepsi laughed. He pointed to a scar on his face. "Me too, got hit with machete when I was hiding out in truck."

"Voodoo," Samir said. "Bad luck to talk about it." He made the sign of the cross.

"Superstitious bunch of rabble," I said.

Leroy and Firewall Eddie turned around. Samir squeezed my shoulder and raised his eyebrows. "Not to us," he said. "Voodoo is real. It very Christian, too. Really, Annie. Lots of Christian crosses in voodoo religion. Death and resurrection, too. Ask Haitian brothers."

"Say," I asked, to change the subject. "Do you think I'm fat?"

"Meds put on weight," Samir said, and I knew he was trying not to be rude. Sometimes the guy could be quite tactful like.

"I've been thinking of joining that new gym," I said.

"You got more money?"

"I could afford a drop-in once a week. Maybe karate, what do you think?"

"Good idea. Protect yourself."

"I always thought you was pretty strong, Annie," Firewall said. "Always could pull your own weight in a fight." *He thinks you're fat, you ugly cow*, my voices whispered.

"Isn't that what nurse Molly does? You want to be like the nurse?"

"Yeah," I said. "I want to be like Molly."

"Could do something with your hair." Samir pulled my hair back into a ponytail. The barkeep pushed an elastic band across the bar to me. "Here, try this."

I looked in the mirror. Hmmm. Not bad with my hair pulled back, made me look younger.

"You look like you're nineteen," The barkeep affirmed, lifting his eyebrows.

Samir pulled a bit of lint off my blue shirt. "Just maybe get some clothes not so baggy, sis."

My fingers flew under the counter, to nineteen, then I started over again for luck. I felt guilty for being so obviously OCD, and stopped. "Sis? Yes, brother Samir."

He grinned and I thought hard about where to get some new clothes. I couldn't afford Nancy's Dress Shop downtown. Then I thought about Thrift Village where Samir got his shoes. He always looked pretty spiffy.

"Yeah," I said. "I could do that." The voices jeered but they sounded a bit worried.

The hotel was beginning to fill up. I didn't like a lot of crowds. When I went out the door, into the drizzle outside, I wasn't sure where I was going, to the thrift shop or home again. It seemed to me I'd been stuck inside long enough and I started the scooter. We chugged down Main Street to Thrift Village, the Vespa and I, and my voices were silent.

When I got there, I saw a mannequin in the window all dressed up in khaki cargo pants and a chocolate brown striped shirt that looked to me like it would fit. Maybe I'd get some capris and maybe one of those long skirts the hippies wear.

There was a burger place next door and it was getting on for noon, but I didn't stop in. I'd make a salad at home.

It was just like New Year's Eve when everyone makes new resolutions. What a lot of fun.

A clerk glided toward me when I opened the door to Thrift Village. She was followed by a zoo of colored monkeys hopping and skipping, and then they all got sucked through a hole in the floor down to Hell. At least I expected it would be Hell, that's usually what was down one of those holes I saw in my visions.

I remembered the dream about the Scarlet Pimpernel, and the red flowers that turned to blood, and thought all these visions and dreams must mean something, but it didn't matter much if they did, because the important thing was that I was going to get well again. They were pseudo-hallucinations and I knew that.

"Annie, I like your hair," the clerk said. I preened a bit, one hand on my bleached white hair that was pulled back into a ponytail, and said, "You got anything that would make me look ten pounds lighter, Sugar?"

"Just the thing," she said.

I got a lot of help that morning picking out some new outfits. When I finally plunked down my thirty-five bucks, I felt like a new monkey woman. That's a joke. I made a stop at the drug store next and bought a box of hair coloring, light brown like my frizz really should be.

My voices sounded desperate. I was getting too good for them. *What is this all of a sudden, Annie Tin Pan Alley Cool Girl Sally? You too good for us? Stay with us, you know you need us. We're your best friends. You won't find nothing make you look any better than you do. You know that. Annie? Annie?*

I found I could laugh them away. What had brought on this change in our Annie?

That Detective sure had piercing blue eyes, like he could look right through me. That picture he took, would he take another one now? I'd changed so much since then. I glanced in the mirror. This new chocolate brown shirt with the vertical stripes didn't make me look chunky at all. The cargo pants fit my big hips pretty well, too.

Annie, you look damn sexy.

Chapter Thirty-seven

I figured that Miss Marple was just about the smartest character there is. Agatha Christie was a genius when she created the elderly sleuth. That's what I wanted to be when I got old. Just like Miss Marple.

For example, *A Murder is Announced*. I watched about all the Agatha Christie tee vee series on Netflix and that one was my favorite, except for the weird gardener in it. It made me think, though, that not all is as it appears, which wasn't too obvious to me in previous cases here on the Island, where they were pretty well all wrapped up for me. No, this time I was in over my head and so much so that my boss lady had even put me on stress leave.

There was so much going on in *A Murder is Announced*, as there was in all the Miss Marple mysteries. Agatha Christie excelled at red herrings, and it made me think, here I am with all sorts of red herrings right here in ocean city, so to speak, Samir being only one of them. In the movie, the two sisters were interchangeable. I thought, something is significant there, who would know in a small town that the sister was really Charlotte, and the hotel clerk had met the sisters in Switzerland and would know them by sight, hence she had to knock him off? All the clues were in place, as they probably were in this case of the doctor and the mayor and the nurse who was a brown belt karate expert. Maybe I made too much of that, though.

I would have to let it go or I'd be in big trouble with the folks in Victoria.

I was wearing a blue and white broom skirt down to my thick ankles with a little sash around the middle and a white tank shirt. My stomach was making hungry noises but I quieted it with an apple. There was only one mirror in the whole place and that was in the bathroom. That's where I headed next, to do something with my hair.

I wasn't used to wearing make-up but a powder compact that I had picked up at the same time as I bought the hair coloring, sort of smoothed out my somewhat-mottled complexion. I needed a lipstick but all I could find was a jar of blush, so I stuck my finger in it and smoothed it on my mouth. Hmmmm...

Looked in the mirror. I looked like a damn tart.

The door creaked open. It was Samir.

Chapter Thirty-eight

"Annie?" was all he said.

I rubbed my face hard with a wet washcloth. The color on my face came off. Angry with myself, I threw the cloth into the sink and pulled the combs out of my hair. *One, two buckle my shoe.*

"Annie, don't."

"I look like a clown."

"No, you don't. You look real good. I never saw you lookin' like a... a *girl*."

I hesitated. The change was too abrupt. People would laugh at me. If they recognized me at all. I pulled off the blue ribbon in my ponytail, leaving an elastic band to hold the sudden waves of golden brown hair.

"Why you getting all dressed up, angel pie?"

I didn't answer. I hardly knew why myself. I untied the sash around my waist and let the broom skirt fall to the ground. My lips still held a hint of ruby blush, a souvenir from my mother. Mom always looked good. She had tired of showing her only daughter how to apply makeup, how to dress. I never listened. Now, too late...

Mom.

Why was I getting all dressed up? Because someone might look at me and smile and like what he saw, someone might take a fancy to my thick ankles and round fat face, my sleek arms...

Nobody would look at you twice, you look like a freak, get back in those jeans and tee shirts, Annie Phony Baloney. Pride, that's what it is. We know who you are.

Who?

You're nobody. That's who. Nobody and less than nobody. You're a sideshow in your underpants and dirty makeup.

I answered back. No, I'm not a freak and you can all go to blazes where you came from. You can't make me feel bad about myself anymore. You can't.

The voices were silent then they started again, all at once, in a welter of noise. I couldn't even make out what they were saying. They sounded angry and scared at the same time. I had to smile. I'd bested them for now.

The sun rose behind Samir and he was all in a glory. He was one who made a difference in my life.

"Angel?"

"Yes?"

"You look real good. I never saw you in a dress before."

"It's a skirt."

"Here, wear those jeans you left on the kitchen chair. They'll look real good on you. I don't think a dress looks so good on you. I'm not used to you wearing a... a skirt. It's real pretty, though."

"I got it at Thrift Village."

"Oh, you clever witch woman. You put a spell on ol' Samir."

"Does my cell phone take pictures?"

"Sure it does. They all do."

"I can't figure it out."

"Here, Angel." His thumbs flew over the keyboard. He held up the phone. "Here. A picture of something pretty."

My face was smudged. I scrubbed again at the makeup and blush until my face was clear again. Then I applied just a bit of color to my lips and cheeks. "Take another one," I urged him.

He snapped me leaning against the door jamb, pulling on my red jeans. He pulled wisps of hair over my forehead to create bangs. "You cut your hair," he accused. Then..."Looks good."

I patted a bit of powder on my shiny nose and chin.

"Where you going?" Samir asked. He frowned and a small muscle next to his mouth twitched. His hands trembled. He danced from one foot to the next.

"You have to go to the bathroom?" I teased. He shook his head. "Where should we go?" I held out an arm for him to take it. Instead, he wrapped both long black arms around me and squeezed. Breathless, I broke away. My fingers flew behind my back as I counted to seven for luck, twice, just to make sure. "We're going to catch a red herring," I said. I remembered Detective Snow and his warning, "Don't leave town." *Yes, we are going to catch a red herring. You're it, Annie.*

Was I? Suddenly my shiny new hair and red jeans didn't seem so hip anymore. The voices had won and I wanted to stay home, but Samir already was escorting me out the door. The blue Mercury was parked at the top of the hill. You couldn't separate Pepsi and Samir. On our way out, I noticed my neighbor watching us from the boat.

Chapter Thirty-nine

That Saturday was a night to remember. The three of us went for a drive and that's all I wanted to do, go for a drive with Samir and Pepsi, in my new red jeans and shiny gold brown hair. But they wanted to show me off, so we went down to the Lebanese diner and had dinner there. That's where the folks went who didn't drink, and also some of the higher society who went for ethnic food on a Saturday evening before going out for drinks at the Red Ox Inn.

La Shish was crowded. Samir got to show me off to the interim mayor and her family. She didn't know who I was but I was pretty sure she was one of the alderwomen/men who had opposed Hizhonnor when Hizhonnor was alive. So she was all right in my books. Already City Hall had started to be cleaned up and Rick Spacey was just a bad memory.

Somebody had done Serendipity Island a favor when they blew away the mayor, but it was a messy and probably painful way to go. Some said he'd bled to death. I'd heard the murder took place at six o'clock on a Monday evening but others whispered the mayor had been fixing the books late at night when he shouldn't have been there, and the cops had tried to cover for him. That made more sense to me, that it wouldn't have happened in sun bright daylight, and also made certain people more suspect than they had been before.

It was my opinion that the two murders might not be connected, but the modus operandi seemed equally bizarre in both cases. Maybe we were dealing with some sort of witchcraft here that specialized in spilling brains and balls. That made me think of the tribe I'd read about in a south American jungle who ate brains and got a rare brain disease that was pretty epidemic in that particular tribe, because they got it from brains, something like meningitis I thought, but I couldn't remember. *Oh, Annie, you can't remember nothing, can you? What would your mother have thought? Your very intelligent mother and father, with a moron for a daughter.*

Shut up, I thought.

Maybe somebody had tried to eat the doctor's brains and somebody thought the way to justice was blowing off the mayor's testicles. Maybe they ate the testicles. Now who would do that?

Annie, you are one crazy woman. Sick, sick, sick. I'm ashamed to know you. Who said that? It sounded like Dad. He's still in Curaçao far as I know, doesn't know anything about all this, and wouldn't be any help if he did, him and his big bosomed Dutch girlfriend and her daughter. I don't miss him.

Don't you? We're ashamed to know you.

After we left the Lebanese diner we went out to… guess where? The Red Ox Inn. Yes!! The stuff of legends on Serendipity Island.

We got turned away because I was wearing jeans. Samir and Pepsi argued but they were wearing nice black pleated dress pants and I was wearing red jeans and a white tank top. I looked pretty good, though, but not good enough. Samir was very embarrassed, I could tell, but I wasn't embarrassed at all. I expected to be turned away from a posh place like The Red Ox Inn. I'd never been welcome in a place like that before. Why that night, when all that was different was a bit of blush on my lips and a new hairdo?

Pepsi was very impressed when he saw me, and Samir had been steppin' high and grinning when he'd escorted me to La Shish. I put my hand in my jeans and counted the letters on the big billboard that turned in front of the Red Ox Inn. Including the adverts there were thirty-one letters.

Just before we got turned away from The Red Ox Inn, I saw somebody familiar coming out the door. He passed by us without apparently recognizing me but I knew him. Those ice blue eyes couldn't belong to anyone other than Detective Snow. Should have called him Mr. Frost. I did a double take when I saw who he was with. It was Molly Dewitt, the nurse, and she was walking two steps in front of him. When I turned around, they'd gone, but not before I felt a surge of satisfaction. She looked angry and I heard him laugh. Maybe there was justice in this world.

I clung to Samir's arm and pretended to be annoyed with the doorman who had turned us away, but really, I could hardly wait to get home. I had another call to make tomorrow, and it wouldn't be to church.

Chapter Forty

The float house on Sunday was like a church to me, all bright and honey smelling from the candles I lit, almost holy. I'd never been to a Catholic church but I thought the sweet-smelling incense and the gold and silver pouring through the stained glass windows there must be like a glimpse of heaven. There *was* a stained glass window in the float house. Reds and purples sparkled on the white boards of the walls. The ocean splashed against the sturdy pontoons under the creaking old structure, and a sort of joy welled up in my breasts to think of spending the summer here.

I wore my new khaki pants and the striped brown shirt, and a pink lipstick I'd bought at the twenty-four hour drugstore yesterday after we'd left the Red Ox Inn. *You should have bought the coral lipstick, it would have gone better with your chocolate brown shirt.*

Shut up. I counted the tiles on the kitchen backboard.

At least you're wearing lipstick, you murderer, you'll look fine when they arrest you for leaving town tomorrow.

That's right, Samir and I were going to Campbell River tomorrow so I could get my meds changed and he could get his leg looked after. Reminded me I should phone and confirm my appointment with Dr. Blanche. His office was a bit too laid back when it come to keeping to a schedule. Dr. Blanche seemed anal enough though, something like me, maybe that's why we got along. I should call his secretary. She called herself an administrative assistant, oo la la, how times have changed. I remember when she was called a receptionist and glad of the job. Now without any promotion or pay raise at all probably, she was suddenly Miss Important.

I'd figured out how to take pictures after Samir showed me, but right now I was more interested in dialing the psych clinic in Campbell River. I squinted at the tiny keyboard. Lordy, they made these phones so dang small. I missed being able to use Mrs. P's landline, I did. But I took a couple of pictures of the ocean swelling outside the big bay windows, dolphins or otters or something leaping near the shore, a silver-grey wash across the abandoned logs adrift on the silver waves.

"This is Annie Hansen, Liz." I had to leave a message, of course, the voices were right, I was stupid. It was Sunday and the clinic wasn't open on weekends.

"Confirming my appointment at one o'clock on Monday. It's just for a med change, if the doctor will agree."

The Orthopedics clinic was drop-in twice a week so Samir would have to wait there until a doctor was available, but somebody would see him for sure. That meant I'd have to wait for him after I'd seen the psych. Dr. Blanche seldom kept me waiting. He was a stickler for being on time and keeping his appointments to the fifty-minute hour. Liz hadn't figured that out yet and sometimes double booked or worse. I wondered how she'd kept her job so long, but then one look at her and I figured it was her big boobs or maybe her butt that interested her employers.

That was pretty mean and I immediately had to punish myself. I counted to a hundred backward before the voices started in. If I got a proper med change I might not have to put up with the voices and the visions much longer. *You'll miss us, Annie.* They sounded worried.

I snapped some more photos of the place, the Franklin stove crackling with flame shooting out the partly-opened door (it wouldn't close proper), the cheery flowerpots in the alcove in front of the bay windows, the settee with the orange and gold afghan on it, so cozy at night when the glass seeped moisture and a draft from the ocean outside.

I loved this little place.

I peered at the cell phone. The latest picture was on there and with a little manipulation, I was able to see the other pictures, too. Now if I could just find the cable that connected it to my laptop and printer I'd be able to put the photos on my computer, even print them off. I'd like to show the photos to Firewall Eddie, who would know exactly what to do if I couldn't transfer them. I turned the camera around and snapped myself, grinning like a fool or the clown that I looked like, all dolled up. Then I started to leap around the living room and kitchen, making faces, snapping pictures. I whirled and staggered in circles until, laughing and exhausted, I fell against the settee and collapsed on the cushions.

That's when the call I'd planned last night to make sort of gelled in my coconut brain. Imagine my surprise when the phone rang. *Dixie* and it was him.

Chapter Forty-one

"Sorry to call you so late on a Sunday night," Mark began.

I picked myself up off the settee and arranged my beautiful hair.

"I thought we could have a talk about this case," he continued. "You have some good ideas, and you know the people here on this island better than I do."

"I thought you told me to stay off the case," I said. I made circles with my finger on the front of my cell phone.

"This will be off the record."

"Off the record? Maybe I could crack up off the record."

He chuckled.

That isn't funny. That is a possibility, you groovy chick, I thought and grinned into the phone.

"Molly said you were asking questions."

"Molly? Oh, the nurse. I didn't know you knew her. Of course, she's a suspect, isn't she?" I pretended innocence. *Of course, you saw them together on Saturday night. She didn't look happy, did she? Congratulations, ho.*

"I saw you and your Sudanese friends the other night. I was with Molly then, on business, I had some questions to ask her and felt the best way I could get some answers was over a meal and drinks."

"You sly fox."

He chuckled again. "Annie, how about it? Should we get together and exchange notes? Off the record. I don't think you'll crack up, by the way, I think you're the most sensible person I've met here on the Island."

"Then why did you all take me off the case?"

"I had my orders, too."

"Maybe I was getting too close to the truth?"

"Maybe you were overstepping somebody's boundaries."

"Could be, M.S."

"Doc Hubert's Facebook page is interesting."

"Really? Oh, yeah, nurse Molly mentioned that. I'll have a go at it, Mark, thanks."

The sun started to rise in a corner of the float house, the opposite corner from where I sat with the phone. The stereo was gilded in golden light and there were faces flicking much too fast through the ether to be real, even I knew that, right in the middle of a pseudo-hallucination. Dang, I didn't want this to happen right now, when I was talking with somebody like a special Detective from Victoria, and this could be important. I could be learning something new or made part of something really important, or maybe he just liked me.

There was some more small talk, which I'm not good at. We agreed to meet on Tuesday afternoon, tomorrow being Monday and my appointment with Dr. Blanche, the psych, and Samir's appointment at the Orthopedics clinic, which was more important than mine, IMHO.

After the conversation with the blue-eyed Detective Snow, I grinned like a banshee in heat. His call seemed a pretext to talk to me. Mark had only wanted to say hello, I thought. *Is that right, Annie? He likes you! Surprise, surprise, wait, he'll be just like all the others... maybe...*

The voices sounded faint and tapered off at the end. Their threat was pretty vague, like usual lately, I thought they were losing their power on me. Monday I'd get a med change and maybe the *voices* would be history. I smiled some more, but for a different reason now. I'd never thought Annie Hansen could live a normal life. Maybe I was wrong.

I reviewed my conversation with Mark. Silly me, I'd forgotten all about Doc's Facebook page. I fired up my laptop and signed onto Facebook. The clever little site remembered me. I was always pleased when I could log on somewhere without trying to remember my password. I had a different password for everything, and it got tricky trying to remember them all, that's why I had them all listed on a sheet of paper. If I could only remember where. But most of the time clever little Acer remembered for me. I could kiss those guys who made it so easy for hackers, what the heck, I had nothing to hide. Identity theft was overrated, in my books. Could always be fixed, and it didn't hold a match to convenience.

Doc's Facebook page was a surprise. It wasn't filled with pictures of pretty girls, like I expected, and there was only one picture of the Doc himself. It was a handsome picture, obviously touched up by Photoshop, and he wouldn't have had the expertise to do that, so somebody helped him, I thought. It was taken three-quarters face to the camera so his wonky eyes didn't show up all that obvious, and somebody had airbrushed out a double chin, if he had a double chin, which I suspected. His one eye showing was a bright robin's egg blue and he had a sort of secret smile on his kisser. The man looked a bit dashing.

His page was all about drugs and doctor stuff. It wasn't what I would have thought at all. It looked quite professional actually, and there were pictures on there of Nurse Molly, too, bending over patients in what I supposed was his methadone clinic. He had a lot of notes about helping patients with their addictions and also some ads for Alcoholics Anonymous and Narcotics Anonymous sprinkled at the side of his page. It looked like he had quite a network of online doctor friends and drug reps featured there. I thought his page looked more like a professional or business set-up and wondered if the Doc had thought of all that himself or if somebody younger and more hip had helped him with his Facebook page. Who?

There might be a clue there, and I bookmarked it. Then I called Detective Snow back. It was late, and Samir and I had a big day tomorrow in Campbell River, but I wondered if maybe Mark would like to meet us there. The lights from the boat next door glimmered through the bay window. Shadows chased themselves around the Franklin stove and the snakes of flame that gleamed orange and red and white, blue at the center, faces morphing in and out amongst the ashes.

"Hello, Mark?"

"Annie." I could hear him gulping a liquid, maybe a glass of cold water, I thought. *It's probably Scotch, be careful, Annie,* my voices warned.

"Shoot. I misdialed," I said and hung up. He would think I was a crazy woman, or brazen, to call him this late and invite him to Campbell River with us on some sort of thin excuse to see him again. So I lied and hung up. *Darn, darn, little girl, you are one cowardly woman. No wonder the only man you got is a murder suspect.*

No, not Samir. He was cleared two months ago.

Wasn't he?

The phone rang again. I looked at the call display and saw Mark's number. I picked it up.

Chapter Forty-two

Water crinkled away from the great engines, so that the ferry's wake washed like plastic wrap behind us. We pulled out from the Serendipity dock with ten cars and my scooter on board, going to Vancouver Island by way of Campbell River.

Samir and I stood on the observation deck and held hands. With his other hand he gripped a black coffee. The Regional Hospital had given him a referral to the adult orthopedics clinic in Campbell River. I clutched my bottle of antipsychotics and prayed to Athena or whatever goddesses there were, that Dr. Blanche would be understanding and change my meds. I'd do anything to cooperate, though I mustn't make it too easy for him. *My voices chuckled in agreement.*

My new golden brown hair streamed behind us and my fake designer shades, picked up for a song at the thrift store, made me feel like Greta Garbo. "You going to be all right, man?" I asked the tall dark man beside me. I could smell his aftershave, a hint of vanilla and spice.

"Yeah. I never thought I'd get a script for a new leg."

"Maybe two."

"Only one really bugs me."

"Go for two."

"How about you?" He shivered. The engines labored through the shiny swath of ocean, picking our way through the dozens of islands dotted there.

I looked up at a screeching gull. "Jonathan Livingston," I said.

Samir didn't understand my reference to a book I'd read in summer school between GED Grade Twelve classes.

"What?" He withdrew his hand. My own was cold and pale.

"A bird who found freedom in a short book riddled with clichés," I said. "The hallmark of a 1970s lost generation, my mother's generation."

"Hippies," he grunted.

"Yes, and they were right."

"What about?"

"Freedom, for one thing. We gave it all away, slow as molasses in January, but it's gone."

"You bag, you don't remember that." Samir smiled at me, his sideways smirk. The touch of his leather sleeve was like rhino skin. Then his hand closed on mine again.

"Scared?" I asked.

"No, not me." He sipped on the coffee.

"It's okay to be scared."

"I'm not."

"Oh," I said, snuggling closer.

"When do you see Dr. Blanche?" he asked. "I have to be at the bone clinic by one."

"Twelve-thirty," I said.

"That's your appointment?"

"Yeah. What did they tell you over the phone when you called, Samir?"

"The bone clinic covers casts," he said. "Other stuff is billed to the patient."

"That would be you."

"I'm on CPP. I got benefits."

"That's right. You're copacetic. I think we're there," I said to him. "Yes."

He threw his coffee cup over the railing into the ocean. I frowned and sighed at his lack of environmental concern. That was Samir, though. Everything focused around him and his own needs. Even me. Maybe constant pain did that to a person.

Dr. Blanche was stocky and white-haired, some would say silver. A beautiful head of hair. I'd heard it was a wig. He peered at me over his professor glasses and placed his hands into a steeple. His big mahogany desk was between us. I gazed at the diplomas on the wall, at his glass and wood bookcases, at the spines of his learned books. I sighed. "Samir's getting his legs fixed," was all I could think of to say.

Dr. Blanche's face appeared starched, like his coat. Like his silver mustache. His mouth twitched a bit. Far off, I heard a gull screech. "Is he? What do you think of that?"

"I think it's about time. He walks like a drunk goat. He's in pain like all the time."

"What made him decide to do something about it at this time?"

"I don't know." I fiddled with the bottle of pills in my pocket and counted the tiles on the wall.

"Did it have anything to do with you? You've changed quite a lot since I last saw you, Anne."

He insisted on calling me Anne. I snorted and pulled a face. "Not really. A few cosmetic changes."

"Your hair is very becoming. I like it."

"Thank you."

"Does Samir like it, too?"

"I don't know. I didn't come here to talk about Samir."

"What then, Anne?" He seemed pleasant enough, like a Schnauzer before it pounces.

"My meds. They make me sleepy and they make me fat."

"I did tell you they may lead to some weight gain. I told you to be careful. Remember?"

"Some?" I snorted again. "I look like John Candy."

He smiled. "What would you like me to do about it?"

Then he started to explain the pharmacology of drugs, what the meds did, how they worked, yap, yap, yap, ad nauseous. I listened until I couldn't listen anymore, then I interrupted. "Wait. Is there something else I can take?"

"Do you promise to take it?"

"Sure."

"You're sure?" He fiddled with his prescription pad. "I'm going to try you on a depot injection."

"A what?"

"We'll give you a long-acting medication with a needle every three weeks. It's called Flupenthixol." He tore off a sheet of the prescription pad and passed it across the desk to me. "Take this to the pharmacy, Anne."

"Thank you." *You're not gonna take any injections, Anne, from the man.*

"Do you understand you'll have to come back here every three weeks for the injection?"

"Do I have to come here?"

"Anne, we've discussed your noncompliance issues before. You do want to be rid of the voices and the hallucinations, don't you?"

"Yeah. Okay."

He hadn't convinced me a lot, but I wasn't afraid of needles. I wouldn't have to swallow pills anymore. Might not be so bad. A blue snake slithered from Dr. Blanche's open mouth to the desk then dropped into the chair beside me. I studied it. It looked back with glowing eyes, then slowly morphed into a pile of books.

"That's better," I said.

"What do you see?"

"A pile of books."

"Is that all?"

"Yes."

"You're sure you're all right now? We can chat again in three weeks. Go to the pharmacy, get this filled, bring the vial back here to the nurses. They'll give you the injection."

"In my arm?"

"Probably in your hip."

"Hip. That's a laugh." Euphemism. He wasn't laughing and neither was I. "Buttocks, you mean." He smiled.

When I came back to his office from the pharmacy, the nurse made me wait. By the time I got out of there and charged over to the orthopedics clinic, Samir was gone from the main room. Later I found him huddled in the waiting area, holding a sheaf of papers, a large envelope that said, 'X-ray film', and a couple bottles of what I made out to be Flexeril and OxyContin. He was giggling. His funny black kisser was relaxed for the first time I'd ever seen it like that. His legs were bandaged and he wore a brace on his poor left leg. When he saw me, he stood up and brandished his African cane with the ivory head. He knocked twice with it on the hardwood floor.

"I'm so glad to see you, Annie. Docs said they could fix my legs."

"Really? When and how?"

"They have to break da bones again, reset it in proper alignment like, bones will knit together, they said. Top bone doctor in Victoria comes here every Monday."

"Did you see him today?"

"Sure did. He gonna fix up ol' Samir good as new brass monkey."

A dust mote was caught in a sunbeam spilling through an open window. My voices were silent. I looked at the brace, at the tensor bandages, at the pain meds. The doctors had made Samir happy. Happy for the first time since I'd known him. "That's wonderful," I said. "But I don't believe it."

"Believe it, sister," he intoned, then laughed and hobbled out the exit behind me.

What would I do if Samir were made perfect? The only reason he liked me was because we were two broken people that came together in the middle of their growing up years, before the 1970s drug guru Timothy O'Leary's cut-off date of thirty. What if there was life after thirty? My new black gladiator sandals made a click-clack sound as I sashayed down that hall with my guy. Samir's cane echoed the click-clack of my heels as we lurched through the exit door and then dove out into the day. The sky was grey with a steady drizzle.

I'd never seen him so happy. He glowed. I thought it must be the drugs.

We got home without any visions. My voices were still. My hands trembled and I felt flushed and excited about what the future held for Samir and me. He lurched on ahead with the new brace on his poor left leg, and his old cane in his right hand. He was singing *Scream and Shout*.

Yes, it must be the drugs.

The shot in my butt seemed to be wonderful magic, I thought, that Dr. Blanche sure knew what he was doing. I'd have to make sure I showed up at the clinic in three weeks to get some more of this stuff that fought with my visions and voices and *won*.

Chapter Forty-three

You may have figured out by now that Detective Mark Snow didn't come with us to Campbell River like I sort of planned. The phone rang again the night before, in the float house, and it was Mark, but he was all professional and apologetic for ringing so late, not to mention that I'd been the one who phoned him and then chickened out. At the time my voices were still nagging me and I was seeing little colored animals in every corner of the room.

The improvement was pretty dramatic after our visit to Campbell River on Monday, when my voices were quiet and the visions didn't appear very often. When they did, it was more of a muted sort of shadowlike movement on the sidelines, not the active little purple monkeys and blue snakes that I'd been used to since I was sixteen. I did love animals and sort of missed them. Sometimes I'd try real hard to squint and make my vision sort of go off a bit, but they didn't come back unless I was tired or stressed. Then, like I said, they were more of a flickering and morphing of real images into movements that weren't real, but not as dramatic as my colored animals. The new illusions were scarier, though, because I didn't know at those times if something in the room was going to move and attack me from sideways, a ghostlike assault rather than funny, happy pictures.

The night before Samir and I went to Campbell River, Mark phoned and told me he didn't think he'd go with us. "I trust you," he said. "I know we all told you not to leave town, Annie, but this is something to do with medical appointments and your psych is important. He practices in Campbell River, and it's not far, you'll be there and back in a few hours, I expect. You can accompany Samir and make sure he doesn't go anywhere. He's been cleared, but anyone to do with this case should stay on the Island, you know. You're off the case officially but you can be a great help to me personally as you know the people involved and you know the Island. I don't see that you're unstable at all, though I know your diagnosis. Go ahead and visit your psych in Campbell River tomorrow."

He said personally, my voices exulted. I hadn't received my new depot injection yet, this was the night before Samir and I went to Campbell River. So that little phone call from Mark made that last night brighter and more magical. I had a good night's sleep before the trip on the ferry to the big Island (Vancouver Island), where Campbell River sprawled on the shoreline and the ferry left every hour for a ten-minute trip to Serendipity. I loved Campbell River, the sleepy little city at the edge of the crashing waves, and I loved the big Island. I loved Serendipity Island, and I loved Samir.

Oops.

I did. He was mostly kind to me where nobody had been kind before, at least not a lot of menfolk had been kind to Annie Hansen. His cousin Pepsi tried to make me think that Samir was putting me down, that he was using me for his own purposes, and that he tried to make me think I was crazier than I already was. I knew that, big-boned and tall, I wasn't graceful or delicate like a lady, in my mind, should be, but I more than made up for it with my character, I thought. At least, Mom had always told me that I needed to attract friends with my personality, not my looks. Dear old Mom hadn't done much to make me think I was movie star material.

I wiped a little leak in my eye and thought about Mark. He seemed to think I was worth talking to like a normal person. That made me think about Lorne and how he had helped me when I was down and arrested for shoplifting from Woodworth's, doing community service with his office. Maybe I deserved better than what I'd always got from life. Maybe I ought to put back more than I did.

I slid some Spanish combs into my lovely locks and smiled into the mirror over the bathroom sink. Someone had shoved an Avon cosmetics booklet under my door while we were gone to Campbell River. It was a sign, I thought. I'd never bought lipsticks and makeup from a catalogue before but it was less embarrassing and less trouble than going to the drugstore late at night. Yes, I was embarrassed that I was trying to change my appearance. People might notice the difference and mock me. I squinted into the mirror. Where were my voices, mocking me? Still two weeks until my next injection. Was it possible the voices had been my own mind, something I'd picked up from childhood, maybe, my parents, my teachers, my companions?

I sighed. I often found myself short of breath, a psychological thing, I thought, or maybe my heart. I put my hand on my heart and grinned. 'I love you,' I mouthed to the image in the mirror, the pink lipstick, the foundation that evened out an uneven complexion. I did look a bit like a clown.

Mark didn't think so. Mark had said *personally* and he had called me back.

I scrubbed my face with the white washcloth hanging on the towel bar. The washcloth turned amber and pink. I studied the face that was left. I still didn't look half bad. The kimono I was wearing was covered with delicate orchids. Purple orchids. When I am old I shall wear purple.

I was twenty-four years old and Samir was twenty-two. I would have a birthday in April and I would be exactly a quarter of a century old. I thought we would go to the Red Ox Inn the night of my birthday, and I would wear my long broom skirt and the coral lipstick that was in the Avon catalogue for four ninety-nine. Coral kind of went with my complexion better than pink.

Then I sashayed into the kitchen and sank on the wicker chair. I had a grin higher than the old barn and the little calf, too. What, was Annie getting vain? You little poop, I thought. You vain little shithead. I laughed and laughed, threw my kimono off and bounced my breasts up and down with the flat of a hand.

That was when the phone rang again. I looked at the call display and it said, Mark. Snow.

My breasts were still bouncing when I answered.

Chapter Forty-four

I settled down in the tawny cushions of the wicker chair in the kitchen to talk on my cell to Mark. I was a bit worried I hadn't charged the phone lately.

A wash of sunlight fell through the window above the counter and splashed on the hardwood floor in front of me. I tried to count the dust motes. That hadn't changed, still counting, I thought. My fingers flew, tapping out a rhythm of motes.

"Hi. Mark?"

"How are you?"

"Better than you think."

"How do you know what I think?" He chuckled. I yawned.

"Am I boring you?" He's teasing me. Cute. "I always yawn when I'm excited," I said.

I knew he was grinning from his tone of voice. "I have that effect on pretty women," he said. "They get breathless."

"You got it right. Pardner. Now why'd you call?" I was all business, just before the phone died. Dang. My BlueBell iCell phone never did give me a signal that it was dying, but I thought the little battery indicator should do that. It seemed to be full all the time, unless I was misreading it. I peered at the icon. A little light had gone on. So I found the cord and charger and plugged it in. I'd missed the important part of Mark's call.

I wasn't too surprised when fifteen minutes later there was a knock on the front door. Well, it was the only door. Mark stood there, poised between the dock and the threshold, staring down into the watery space at his feet.

"Come in, stranger," I said, and opened the door wide. Maybe too wide. 'Don't be overanxious, Annie,' I cautioned myself, hearing an echo of my mother's voice in my coconut brain. She had always thought I was a bit too optimistic in the romance department, being somewhat homely like I am and everything, kinky hair and buck teeth. I sucked on my lower lip and smiled. Mark didn't seem to notice the overbite. Good on him. He was a prize worth keeping.

Typical of us delusional alcoholic thinkers, Firewall Eddie had told me about the movies he ran in his head when he met a new girlfriend, the wedding and settling down in a petunia-covered trailer and everything. Right after he met someone. I was like that with a new guy, not that I'd ever had one except for Samir. Of course, it never worked out for ol' Eddie, or me, either. I went right back to hallucinating and he went right back to using drugs and drinking, a lot of the time as far as I know, girlfriend or not.

That worried me a bit. Something niggled in my brain about Eddie and the night Doc Hubert was downed and drilled.

"I want to talk to you about the case," Mark said. He ducked when he came in the door. The door jamb was pretty low and Mark was more than six feet tall. He had a bit of a paunch, too, I noticed, and was a bit thin on top, with greying hair around his temples. He was at least ten years older than me. There you have it, thanks, Mom, ruin this for me, too.

His blue eyes redeemed him in my books. "You have some of the pieces I'm missing. You know Firewall Eddie and the guys on the street. The boys in the office at City Hall are beginning to think there's a connection between Doc's clients and the murder, that we're on the wrong footing here. It was nothing more or less than a killing for drugs and the cash he kept in his wallet. A street killing, or maybe revenge."

"And Mayor Spacey?" I asked. Mark settled in the settee near the bay windows with me on the other end. Nice.

"Could be not connected at all. Or could be the mayor was there the night of Doc's murder and saw something he shouldn't have. Could be he was killed to shut him up. Word is on the streets and in the offices of the Aldermen that Mayor Rick Spacey knew Doc very well."

"I heard that, too," I said.

"What about Firewall Eddie? You said you knew something."

"Word is, Eddie's been drinking and using drugs, missing work," I said.

"He was Pepsi's alibi."

"Exactly." I sucked my thumb.

"And Pepsi was working that night."

"Yes."

"Pepsi said he didn't see anybody come in around midnight."

"He was Samir's alibi, too. Actually, *I'm* Samir's alibi. He was in the next bed to me that night."

"We've ruled out Samir. I think. Are you sure?"

"Unless his bed was packed with straw. There was a long ugly heap of black Sudanese in that bed all night."

"Hmmmm." Mark's hand massaged his chin, which was struck through with the beginning of a reddish blond beard. He hadn't shaved that morning. I looked at my cell. The green light wasn't on yet. I was glad it had died and brought Mark to my house. Looked like almost noon coming up. Maybe he would expect lunch? I was a pretty good cook when I had to be, liked to experiment with my mother's recipes. What could I make that would be quick, delicious, and impress him with my homemaking skills?

Nothing, that's what. I sat up straight.

"Want to go out for lunch?" I asked. He looked surprised.

"Sure. My treat."

"I'll pay my own way," I declared. "The Golden Arches is fine for me."

"We'll go someplace like that," he agreed and stroked the reddish blond stubble on his chin. "I'm not dressed for going out. When we were disconnected..."

"I didn't hang up."

"No, I didn't think so. When your phone died, then..."

"Yes."

He looked into my eyes. I don't know if I've mentioned it, but my eyes are my best feature, a pretty violet blue just like my daddy's, probably what attracted the Dutch woman from Curaçao at first, and then her daughter... little witch that she was, mesmerizing my daddy. Now Father was in the Caribbean, thousands of miles from my mother's home and me, and he didn't even come back for my mother's funeral. Only came back later to see me, with his new family—I bet, because he figured there was money here.

Double damn, I thought. He won't come back for you again, Annie, no matter how much you want him in your life. The SOB, the Slimy Old Boy isn't your father anymore, he left you and your mother way back when you were twelve and he hasn't been in your life since. Much. Quit dreaming and face reality, Annie. You don't have a family at all.

My thoughts were depressing, so I looked back at Mark, batting my lashes like I'd seen Madonna do in *Dick Tracy* or even *Dangerous Game.* No, Dick Tracy it was, my favorite show of all time. Warren Beatty was so much like a dark-haired Mark. Mark was so much like a blond young Warren Beatty. Cute, all he needed was a yellow raincoat and I'd be Pussy Galore.

Chapter Forty-five

Mark and I leaned over the square white table in McDonald's with our legs wrapped around the red plastic chairs, enjoying each other's company and sharing information about the Case of the Purloined Brains. I liked the way his mind worked, typical detective, trust no one, clickety-click, very observing, cut and dried, but caring just the same.

"How'd a gentleman like you get interested in the force?"

"I wanted to make a difference," he said.

"That's a tad old-fashioned."

"I'm an old-fashioned gumshoe. Lots of footwork. Cops used to wear rubber-soled shoes so as to move quietly, like a thief. That's why they called us gumshoes." He was looking at his cell phone and his thumb was busy on the keypad. "Post-modern technology makes things a lot easier, though. A lot faster to get an ID on someone, for example, or get in touch with my colleagues."

"Like now."

"I'm never out of touch," he said, and put down the phone. I looked at the screen but it was blank.

I raised my nice full eyebrows at him and crinkled my nose, half smiling.

"I turned my phone off," Mark explained.

Oh.

He played with his box of chicken nuggets and fries. I dived into my cashew teriyaki salad and looked with envy at the teens at the next table gorging themselves on Big Macs and cheeseburgers. I didn't own a bathroom scale but figured from the way my clothes fit that I must have lost a few pounds in the past two weeks. I licked my fingers and watched Mark's eyes.

"Who do you think did it?" he asked. The question was abrupt, his food was untouched, his gaze direct and searching. My fingers fluttered to my cheeks and I felt myself flush. Who did I think did it? So I told him.

"There are difficulties with that," he said. "For one, you're his alibi. You and Pepsi."

"Pepsi had an alibi," I said. "It was Firewall Eddie, who was the security guard on duty that night, and he said he saw Pepsi working in the basement at midnight, when the murder apparently took place."

"Our forensic guys are very exact now. No more guessing about times anymore, like when I first started with the force."

"I know the labs are real important," I said. "They can pinpoint DNA from a shaft of hair, for example, I knowed that. Why couldn't they do that with ol' Doc Hubert and the Mayor? Pinpoint who done it that way. We have lots of suspects could supply samples."

"Been wiped clean," Mark said. "Of course, samples like Samir's cane were sent to Victoria for testing, nothing came up on that cane except oil slicks and tar. And Samir's fingerprints. We were surprised as you. Thought we really had something there, Annie. Guess you did, too. But aren't you relieved? Samir's a good friend, after all."

"Yeah, I heard what he's capable of though. Life was brutal back in the Sudan. Both Samir and Pepsi learned to kill and lie. Samir was a paramedic there, too. Came from a family who wanted to send him to London for more training."

"All shot to hell, probably, I heard his parents are still in a refugee camp. They could be dead by now."

"Yeah, Samir's lost touch with all his friends, but he thinks his parents are still alive. Word gets out somehow, leaks out with the missionaries, people send messages to their friends and family in Canada."

"Does he talk about it?"

"No."

"Typical. Also doesn't talk about how he got out, I suppose?"

"On somebody else's passport," I said.

"Typical again. They learn how to manipulate, how to fight, how to murder. How to lie."

"Mostly he says he wants to kill himself. Don't be too hard on them. They're the victims."

"Yeah, they're the victims, that's right. Little children, women, old people, they're all the victims, and the men of the villages were often lined up and shot. Samir and Pepsi took the smart way out when they signed up with the government soldiers."

"All they could do. They don't talk about so much of it."

"What do you see in him, Annie?" Mark pursed his lips. "Do you really think he did it? Instead of killing himself, he killed others mindlessly like they did at home in the Sudan."

"I think he's capable of it."

"Why was he cleared?"

"Have you ever watched *Murder at the Vicarage*? It's an Agatha Christie, Miss Marple, story."

"I think I've read it. Yes, the obvious suspect is cleared at the beginning of the mystery, then turns out they arranged an alibi right away so they wouldn't be suspected again. Clever."

"Yes, I think maybe Samir made his cane a red herring and when Pepsi phoned me from the ferry to tell me Samir was making a break for the mainland. I think Samir had put his cousin up to letting me know, so that I'd go there with the constable and arrest him, put him through interrogation. He knew he'd be cleared because he had an alibi and his cane, which was the object of our suspicion, turned out to be clean. Thus Samir was cleared, too. Doesn't really add up, does it?"

"Not when you put it that way, Missy Anne."

"He was taking advantage of human psychology."

"You must know a lot about psychology, with all your experience with doctors and therapists, I expect."

"Yes, I have a bit of that."

"Have you ever thought that Pepsi and Samir are a little too close? Maybe Samir's covering for Pepsi. You've already said that Pepsi's alibi doesn't hold up because Eddie might have been off work that night. Eddie's drinking and using drugs again, you said."

"That's what my man on the street says."

"We can easily check and see if Eddie was there that night. Odd they didn't check earlier. Must have trusted Security."

"Let's do that. If he wasn't, then Pepsi could have done it because that would blow his alibi."

Mark started munching on his chicken nuggets and put ketchup on the fries. I gazed at his meal, mouth watering, and forked salad into my face. "Why would he?"

"Pepsi's been drug-free for a year now. Could start again at any time. Or maybe to cover for Samir? Blood's thicker than water. Don't forget the nurse, too," I said. "Molly Dewitt also known as Molly Schneider. She loved the Doc maybe too much, couldn't stand his dalliances with the ho's after hours. That night was just too much for her, made it look like theft?"

"She could have but I just don't get that feeling from Molly Dewitt. She wasn't as upset as maybe she made out to be after Doc's murder, but I don't think she's a killer."

"Still, she could have done it," I said, pushing back my Styrofoam box. I patted my glossed lips with a napkin.

"She had the karate training to use her strength against a bigger opponent like Doc. She also had the opportunity to take him by surprise."

"What would she have hit him with? We never found the blunt object."

"That's crucial because it would have the fingerprints or DNA on it that we want."

"Did I tell you the prosecutor wanted me to leave a sample of my DNA with his office when they arrested me for shoplifting? No weapons, either, for four years."

"You don't have a weapon."

"I know. My lawyer laughed about the DNA sample. The judge struck it down. Prosecutor recognized me from the street, wanted to hang me."

"That's his job."

"I know. That's our job, too, if we do it right."

"To hang somebody? No death penalty in Canada."

"You know you're being too logical, Mark."

I was surprised when I saw Samir walk in. Mark looked up just as Samir glowered like a piece of burned Winnipeg Goldeye. Mark leaned quickly toward me. His lips brushed the napkin and he stood up. Not before I heard him say, "I'm not logical when it comes to your lovely violet eyes, lady Anne."

Wow. That was the nicest thing anybody ever said to me. Then Samir strode over to the table and Mark was gone, just asking me once if I needed a ride home, that's the gentleman he was. He might not be as handsome as I gave him credit for, but I thought he was distinguished. The detective was a very nice gentleman who made Annie Hansen shiver and die a little inside when she thought of the way he moved.

Die a little to look at those ice blue eyes, and then Samir sat down and I started to cry.

Chapter Forty-six

The Avon rep lived on the Upper Heights of the island. It didn't take her long to take my order over the phone, now the BlueBell was charged. I offered to come pick up my order when it was ready in two weeks, just to get away from home and meet somebody new. Her name was Tess Russell. She sounded attention deficit to me, couldn't focus on the conversation, but real friendly. We were pals by the time she finally got my order right. A coral lipstick, a blush, and some shower gel. There was only a shower in the float house. Gosh, how I missed the big ol' soaky tub at the Powolskis. I thought a bit, leafed through the pages of the catalogue, and added a pedicure set and some clear nail polish.

"Coral nail polish?" Tess asked. "Or what about blue? It's on page nine of Campaign eight. Crazy."

"No," I said. "Clear."

"Coral it is. Anything else?"

"Clear nail polish." I spelled it out. "C-L-E-A-R."

"Blue really gets attention. Or too cool Go-Go Green with nail hardeners."

"No, I don't think so. Not blue or green. I want clear nail polish, please, and a pedicure set. Number 147-632. The small one, with the green toe separators."

"Green?"

"The one with the green toe separators, please." I sighed.

"Sure thing." I could hear Tess scribbling. I was afraid to ask her to read it back to me. She told me the order would be ready a week from next Monday and I hung up after a few more pleasantries like that.

I stood on the dock, looking at the big boat and the open curtains, now that it was daylight. I could see my neighbors moving around inside the galley kitchen in their boat, where space was really limited. They saw me watching them and came on deck. I felt kind of sorry for them, living on a boat, but they took their craft out a lot in the summertime and would be getting it ready now for their next trip. Had to scrape the barnacles off, fit the engines, give it a coat of paint, I expect.

He was about five feet eight and squat, in his mid-fifties. His wife was a similar size, with something like my build. Both of them wore gosh-awful Hawaiian shirts and sand digger jeans with rubber clogs, tromping around on the deck. His wife waved and they both came down the ramp to the slippery dock, about fifty feet from where I stood.

"Ahoy there," he called. "My name's Brent Hoffman. This here is my wife Catherine. Welcome to the marina. You've been here a while now, haven't you? Like the float house?"

"Yes," I yelled. "I'm Annie Hansen. Do you remember my mother? She owned it. She died about six years ago."

"Oh, I'm sorry, dear," Catherine Hoffman said. "No, we didn't know your mother. We've only been here for the last three."

"Take it out a lot?" I asked.

"Oh, yes, for months at a time come May or June. We cruise up the Alaska coastline, down south to the Big Sur, in and out of the islands dotted all along near Prince Rupert, have a small dinghy to go to shore in, weather permitting."

"We do a lot of salmon fishing," Brent offered. He was drinking a glass of something dark, maybe port or burgundy. I smiled. To the left, I thought. Any port in a storm. One of Samir's little jokes.

"You've been staying pretty close to the float house this past month," Brent observed. "We keep a sharp eye on our neighbors, neighborhood watch kind of thing, don't want anything bad happening on this marina."

"No, for sure," I said. "Me too."

"You had a visitor last fall by himself, almost fell in the drink in front of your doorway there, Annie. Slipped something out the door and into the water, appeared to get rid of a poker, wouldn't you say, mommy?"

"Yes, dear," Catherine said. "It was definitely a fireplace poker. Now why would he do that, dear?"

My ears perked up like a Schnauzer on the chase. That explained why I couldn't find the poker last fall. I still used a stick to stir the fire, dang it. Now why would he do that? I felt cold and shivered, although the sun was orange and hot—a big ol' flaming basketball in a blue west coast sky.

"What did he look like?" I asked. "Just curious."

"Yes, we thought it was a curious thing to do. Seen him around here since then, too. A tall, thin black fellow, wore a baseball cap and dropped waist jeans."

"Did he limp?"

"He could have. Don't rightly know if the fellow had a limp. I didn't think to look for that, I didn't want to stare, you know, he looked like he could get ugly and for a while he had that dang poker in his left hand."

"Port side," I said. "Any port in a storm."

The Hoffmans looked at me real strange. "What do you mean?" Catherine asked. The sun blazed from a cloudless sky. It was a quarter off three in the afternoon and I was still cold.

"I mean," I said, "he could have been left-handed."

"Oh."

"Maybe not. That's stretching speculation a bit far, young lady," Brent said.

"I'm just hoping it's not who I think it is," I said.

"A good friend?"

"Yes. Actually, a very good friend, and one who needs a friend."

"He could have dropped the poker accidentally, you know."

"He could have. Easy to do with this watery space here in front of the door."

"Yeah, could have been stirring the fire, heard a noise, maybe us, came out of the door with the poker in his hand, dropped it into the drink."

"Yes. That's what happened, I'm sure."

"Anyone else got a key to your place, Annie?" Catherine asked. "This guy got in somehow, and you weren't there. We were a bit worried, almost called Constable Tom and the sergeant."

"Why didn't you?" I was curious. "And yes, Samir has a key to the place." *Everyone knows where the key is, you trusting little ho.* I was surprised to hear one of my voices. A breakthrough with my Flupenthixol, I thought, time for another injection soon. I counted the yellow Hibiscus flowers on Brent's shirt.

"Samir?"

"Could have been my good friend."

Catherine sniffed. "Be careful who you call friend, young lady. Certain groups are sure to be trouble."

"Like African-Canadians?"

"We call them blacks." *Oh, oh. Red neck troublemakers next door in the boat.*

"Why didn't you call the police?"

"He didn't seem to be doing any harm. He knew his way around your place, and we seen him before around here, with you. We hadn't been introduced to you yet, dear."

"Thanks for not snitching on my good friend."

"It just seemed odd, dropping the poker in the water."

"Yes. Odd." I tried not to think of it, what he would have been doing with the poker, and why he had to get rid of it.

Maybe Mark would dredge the bay under the float house. Shouldn't be hard to do. I stopped yelling at the Hoffmans as though they wore ear trumpets.

"Come over for a drink sometime," Brent said. "We'd love to show you around the *Catherine*."

"Thanks," I said. "What about now?"

I was lonely. That was after my talk with Mark at the Golden Arches and I had a lot of thinking to do that I didn't want to do right now.

"Sure. Come right over. We'll give you the super special tour of our floating home."

"Just a minute," I said. "I'll put on some lipstick."

It didn't take me long. But I noticed in the mirror when I brushed on some blush that my dark roots were showing. I sighed.

Mark had said *personally.* I tried not to think what else he had said, just before Samir got there. Who'd have known that big Annie would have two guys after her plump body?

Maybe it wasn't my body, I corrected. Maybe Mark really liked me.

Chapter Forty-seven

The tour of the *Catherine* was interesting and it was great to get out with other people for a change, other than my little circle of acquaintances. That decided me that it was time to get away for a while. This was supposed to be stress leave. I was sure Erna didn't expect me to walk away from the case and then do all the work from home. I sort of resented the pull on my time and brain power that the cops demanded because they weren't competent to put things together themselves. Of course, I hadn't put it all together yet, either, but Mark and I had a fine beginning to it. We'd figured out the possible suspects, or some of them, and what we'd do about it. I had more ideas, too.

I smacked the side of my head with the flat of my hand, making my curls bounce. Cut that out, Annie, I yelled to myself where nobody else could hear. You've got to take a day off.

I did take a day off, the next morning, after a late snowfall and a dip in temperature. I decided to go to the bookstore up on the Upper Heights and get a guide to hiking trails, take my scooter up as far as the start of one of them trails and head off into the rain forest that brooded green and wet over Serendipity at this time of year.

There was melting snow on the trail but I wore thick rubber hiking boots and broke off a willow branch for a walking stick. After the up and down sunny warm days this past week, I thought this kind of weather would maybe spin me down into a bad cold or be the start of a flu season. I never got a flu shot at my age and didn't need one, seldom got sick. Annie Hansen was strong as the cable on the Capilano Bridge, but I didn't want to take any chances.

So before I left the Vespa behind, I asked at the counter if they had any Vitamin C or zinc tablets, and they didn't but they did have some Cold-FX. I bought a bottle of that and took it with me along with a couple bottles of water. That about cleaned out the cash I had in my pocket. If I was more ladylike I'd have carried a pink backpack with me or a handbag, but I didn't ever see the need for anything like that when a girl had pockets.

"We enjoy our Island," Alma burbled at the counter. "I hope you have a real good time on your hike today, hun. That's a good guide book you got there."

"Yes," I said. "I see the trail ends near the Modge Bay Lighthouse, close to my place."

"It does," she said. "You'll be almost home."

"I'll have to come back here and pick up my scooter," I said. "Or walk all the way back."

"You can leave it here overnight if you choose," Alma said. "It'll be safe here. We'll put it under the carport and keep it dry. Funny weather this, yesterday was above zero and today it's colder than the inside of an icebox. Did you hear the wind last night? Reminded me of winters on the prairies when I was a kid. Wind whistling and roaring around the shakes on the roof, practically tearing them off."

"Then the snow," I murmured. "I'm all for global warming."

She laughed.

The trail struck right up between the cedars in the rain forest on top of the hill behind the little bookstore. I shoved my scooter under a canvas carport and proceeded on my way like a pilgrim. I stumbled on some roots at first but got used to picking up my big feet. I tried to clear my mind of any deep thinking and just focused on the ground in front of my boots and the tap, tap, tap of my walking stick on the hard earth. I looked for spongy olive-colored moss on the sides of the trees to see if it was true that moss grew on the north side, but then I lost track of directions and instead enjoyed the slow slogging of my trek through the woods. Occasionally a squirrel would chatter at me and scold from a low branch, then would run backwards up a tree trunk and into the upper reaches of the cedars, where it rained cones and seeds on my head. Birds called and I saw a few I almost recognized but I wasn't very good at names or songs. There were gulls, of course, even this far inland, as the Island wasn't that big and where there are oceans there are gulls. I saw a cormorant wheeling high overhead, or maybe it was a vulture preparing to pick my cold bones…

The steady tromp, tromp of my feet was almost hypnotic. It lulled me into a sort of a trance. The forest was dark and sloppy green, water snaking down the sides of ferns and into puddles on the trail. The snow was almost melted but I was glad for my waterproof boots and jacket. I had started on the downward curve of the path.

Within an hour, I realized that I was nearing the shore and the beginning of the spit where the Modge Bay Lighthouse warned ships at sea from the rocky coast. I slid down the rest of the trail to the back of the lighthouse, stood there and looked up at the huge lamps that so far were unlit. It was automated, so why did the shack next door look occupied? I'd never noticed smoke curling from the crooked little chimney before, but someone had lit a fire in there today.

The windows were small and dirty. I could see movement inside. I peered through the grey panes, wiping them clean as I could with my mittens so I could get a better view. Sure enough, there was two Haida Indians in there, a couple of First Nations fellows I knew all too well. They huddled around the potbellied stove in the middle of the room, and were smoking dope, I could see it, and drinking something clear straight from a narrow necked bottle.

It was Firewall Eddie and Crazy Leroy sharing a joint and a bottle of vodka.

Son of a ghost rider. I poked my head down real quick in case they seen me, but the glass pane was so filthy with smoke and dirt, and they were so high, that I don't suppose they'd have known me even if they'd looked that way. They wouldn't have figured out somebody would come out on a day like that and look inside the old shack. I wondered how many times they'd been out here and if this was the first time they'd lit a fire.

'Course I could have been real unobservant. I took a swig off one of the water bottles I'd bought at the bookstore, and wiped my mouth with the back of a hand. It sure didn't take me long to go native, I thought, grinning at the pun or double entendre, as they say. It was almost noon and my Vespa was miles away, back up the hill then down again. It would be closer to go home and then hike up to the bookstore from there when I'd rested a tad.

Mind you, we were not far from the First Nations reserve on the Island and the Xa'ida Lodge was just next door, where some of our tourists would be gathering from the States or Eastern Canada or the Prairies, come to see the culture and history of the Haida, including some of their rituals and their crafts, totems, pottery, jewelry and so on. Something to be proud of here, the Haida Indians we boasted of, their trading and skill as artisans, living mostly on what used to be called the Queen Charlotte Islands, and many of them had come from overseas, Alma said once, quoting a book. From Europe and Hungary and so on. Haida Gwaii they called the Charlottes now, about forty-five percent of the population on the islands were First Nations.

So I was kinda proud of my part Haida blood. When I slopped over to the Xa'ida Lodge, I wasn't sure who would be there, but sure enough, there were some natives and some tourists and at least one stranger. Yes, I was on the case again!

I shook my sorry head and cornered the stranger, an anthropologist from the Western Michigan University at Kalamazoo. After a bit of chit chat, he told me something about the Haida I didn't know before. The young post doc graduate student with the beard indeed had information about Leroy's and Eddie's culture. That made me think that Mark and I had been too hasty in pinning this on Samir and his cousin.

How you hate that, Annie dear. You don't think well, do you? No, you dummy girl, you should go back to your bottle and your shoplifting and stop trying to be more of an educated ass than you are.

My voices were back. My fingers flew behind my back, counting the acne on the young anthropologist's face.

Chapter Forty-eight

The anthropologist, Peter Humming, was staying on the reserve for the summer, working on his post-doc thesis. He seemed eager to share his knowledge of the Haida, indeed, he struck me as lonely as I was. Far from home, he talked too about Kalamazoo, Michigan and his family there.

He showed me pictures from a leather wallet with a monogram 'PH'. The wallet looked brand new.

"A gift," he said, "from Dawn, my girlfriend. Here she is." Young, childlike, fair-haired, with a broad brow and hair pulled back in a ponytail.

Why didn't I think of doing something with hair that day? I stroked my lovely gold-brown locks and wished I'd finished touching up the roots that morning instead of taking off on my half-cocked hike up the trail and down to the Lodge. "Is that your mother?" I asked, as he proffered a snap of a middle-aged, brown-haired, rather plump woman in front of a veranda.

"No, that's Auntie Em," he said. "She's the unmarried aunt of the family, a sort of surrogate mom to us all. She's a librarian. Plans to retire in Kalamazoo in about eight years' time and raise chickens and plants. My favorite aunt."

"And those? They're your parents?"

"Yes." A rather plain-looking elderly couple clasped hands and smiled for the camera. He must have been a late child.

"Are you the youngest?" I asked.

"The only child," he said, understanding my question. "They couldn't have children and weren't able to adopt, too poor, and then I came along in their fortieth year. Surprise." He smiled. "I'm very spoiled."

"I don't think so," I said. "But put your photos away, Peter. I want your professional advice."

He raised his brows and made an "O" with his mouth. He stuck the photos back into his wallet and slid the wallet into his back pocket, buttoning the flap over the sleek leather surface.

"There," he said, and took my arm. We were standing near the front door of the Xa'ida Lodge. A few tourists milled around. A First Nations woman sat in a chair made out of moose antlers while a small girl shyly danced. One of the men played the drums on a synthesizer in a corner.

"Shall we go somewhere quiet to talk?"

"This will do," I said. I didn't want to be alone with a man anymore, not after recent developments. My head had begun to spin with the attention.

"Let's sit," he said. I followed him to a sort of couch made out of moose antlers and hides. He sank onto one end and stretched his long legs out in front of him. I curled up on the other end, muddy feet tucked under the couch. Reaching down, I undid the laces and took my boots off with a sigh. Then I pulled my knees up to my chin and studied him. Could I trust him?

"Can I trust you?" I said. He looked surprised.

"Of course."

"We've just met."

"What is it?"

"We've had a double murder in the town."

"Yes, I'd heard. A doctor and a councilman."

"The mayor, actually."

"Oh, too bad."

"Not really," I said. "He wasn't well liked, but nobody had that much against him that they'd want to kill him like that."

"Yes, I heard it was nasty. It was on the local news every night for a while. It seems to have gotten buried now that the police can't find a suspect."

"We're working on it," I said.

"We?" He raised a thick brown eyebrow.

"Yes, I'm sort of involved in the investigation. That's why I need your help."

"Do you have any ID?" he asked.

"Yes." I peeled back my credit card holder and showed him my private investigator certificate from last year. They hadn't taken that away, thank gollywogs.

"It's not current," he said.

"They took me off the case. I'm supposed to be on stress leave."

"You're honest."

"I'm what they call emotionally fragile."

"Oh, I see." He didn't see at all, I could tell. *He hates you. He's just pretending to be your friend. Don't trust him,* the voices shrilled.

From behind the door, a miniature purple rhino ran under the couch. I'd missed my colored animals and was happy to see him. Then a snake ate him and the couch morphed into a hot air balloon. I shrieked and threw my arms into the air. Peter twisted his hands in front of his body and sat like a stone. He acted like he knew what to do.

"You're like a shaman," he said at last. A shaman? Me?

"Don't they do what they do because of drugs?" I asked.

"Often. Not always. Sometimes they're schizophrenic or have epilepsy and so on."

"You know a lot." My face reflected my awe at his knowledge of shamans and mental disorders.

"I'm here to investigate the role of shaman in the post-modern Haida society. That's been the focus of my work so far. I do know a fair bit about it." He was so modest, this Peter Humming, PhD. "I think if any witchcraft is involved in your murders the Haida shaman could very well be involved."

"Who's that?"

"Why, they're both not here right now. You know him as Crazy Leroy, and his friend Firewall Eddie is an initiate."

"They're both drug users," I objected. "They aren't holy men."

"That's a matter of opinion. The shaman use medicinal plants, or drugs, for spiritual purposes. Often, in post-modern society, of course, the drugs get mis-used. The Haida were all but destroyed by disease introduced by Europeans a few generations ago. They're just beginning to rebuild their culture. The shaman and artisans play an important role in passing along ancient knowl-edge through word of mouth and knowledge of the rituals involved in binding together the two major clans, the Raven and the Eagle."

"Leroy," I said. "He's important?"

"Yes. I tried to find him yesterday but he'd slipped away. I want to learn what he knows, as far as he'll tell me. I'm living now with his grandparents and small brothers. I'm part of the family, as far as they're concerned."

"How long have you been here, Peter?"

"Most of a full year. I'm due to go back to Michigan at the end of this summer. My research grant will be up then. No moola, no study."

"This doctor who was murdered, he gave drugs to the Haida and the street people. Others, too. Some people think he was killed for the drugs."

"I think they could have got the drugs free, from what I hear."

"Probably. He had money in his wallet, that went missing."

"Enough from the day. Not enough to make it worthwhile to kill him."

"You have the mind of a cop," I laughed. "You're better than me."

He slid his hands into his pockets and crossed one long leg over the other. "The natives talk a lot about this case. They're scared."

"Scared?"

"Scared they'll be implicated. The doctor had a nasty little vice… women."

"Yes. And some of them were First Nations women."

"A few young women are just like anybody else; young, foolish, poor, looking for drugs or money, selling their bodies."

"What would the elders think of that?"

"Very bad. They'd be sent to the sweat lodges to make atonement, get spiritual again. But it wouldn't work if they didn't go willingly, and someone like the doctor, I heard, had drugs and money plenty to lure them away."

"Would that be a reason to kill him?"

"Maybe."

Hmmmm. I thanked Peter and pulled my boots back on over my damp socks. I asked him if he'd give me a ride up the hill to get my scooter back and he said he would. Turned out he drove an old green Jeep Wrangler with "ultimate 4x4 capability". Nice.

Chapter Forty-nine

My depot injection was starting to wear off and I was hallucinating again and hearing voices. It had been more than three weeks since Samir and I went to Campbell River to the clinics. I thought Dr. Blanche had said every three weeks but I forgot and stretched it to almost four. An old story with me. His office would be calling soon, I expected.

I was feeling at sixes and sevens, like my mom used to say, late in the afternoon on a warm but rainy Sunday in late March. The Powolskis had invited me over for Easter dinner with Samir and Pepsi. I thought that was real nice of them. Probably Meredith's idea but Henry wasn't a bad fellow either, as my science teacher had commented about a fellow student in grade ten, "Under that shoulder holster beats a heart of pure gold."

I thought how my Avon order should have been in the previous Monday but I hadn't heard from Tess, and I was getting tired of only one lipstick color and using my mother's old blush. I had a shower in the cramped and cold little space reserved for bathing in my float house, toweled myself off as best I could, and applied make-up, trying not to look like a clown fish. Mrs. P had never seen me wearing make-up or with my hair fixed up. I'd touched up the roots with a wand that came with the hair coloring I'd already used. It didn't look half bad and I pulled it back into a ponytail like Samir had done that first day in the Serendipity Hotel. Like Peter Humming's girlfriend wore her hair. I found a couple hairclips and tamed the waves a little that made me look like Shirley Temple gone wrong.

"Lemondrops, child, you look so thin and peaked," Mrs. P exclaimed when she saw me. "Poor girl. We miss you something awful, but Samir is still here and his cousin moved into your bed when you left. We make do with the rent, but it's not the same without our Annie."

"Yeah, well, I got my own place now, Mrs. P," I mumbled.

"I know that, and it's only right a young lady like yourself should have her own place. I never did think it was right you pretending you and Samir was married when we knew very well you weren't."

"It helped save on rent," I said. "That's the only reason we moved in together."

Mrs. P didn't reply. She looked a lot like an owl when she gazed at me from over the rims of her eyeglasses and pursed her lips together like that. I let the silence go on and then noticed the parrot in his or her cage, and the big ol' mean black cat curled up in his dog bed in the corner. He hadn't made a meal out of the remaining bird, too bad.

"Pepsi and Samir aren't home yet for dinner," Mrs. P said. "Henry's lying down for a grandpa nap downstairs. The ham's in the oven, the potatoes are peeled and soaking in the pot, the green bean casserole and the yams are ready to be popped in the oven next to the ham when we're ready to eat. I guess I've thought of everything, but it's too early now to cook anything until I know when the boys are going to be here."

"Pepsi and Samir? They'll be down at the Hotel drinking beer," I said.

She sniffed. "Not today, not on Easter Sunday. Hotel's closed today."

"Oh," I said. "Where are they then?" As though there was no alternative. I grinned. They could be anywhere. They could be… let's see… they could be smoking dope with Eddie and Leroy at the shack near the Modge Bay Lighthouse. If we put all the suspects into one small building together at the same time, we could just blow it up and have done with it. I must tell Mark I'd found a solution to our problem.

"What you grinning about?" Mrs. P asked. She was suspicious of any good humor on my part. My fault for being so surly all those months I lived here.

"You know I see visions," I said. "Just something amusing I saw."

"Oh. That again?"

"Yeah, a blue frog just ate the cat."

"Oh, it did not. I don't believe that, Annie, you wicked girl. You're just making that up to upset me."

"I *am* tired, Mrs. P. A wave of fatigue just washed over me. Maybe I could lie down in my old bed for an hour while we wait for the guys to come home and

Henry to wake up from his grandpa nap? Why don't you just take it easy. I'll help with the rest of dinner when I get up."

"Sure, hun, I'll give you Pepsi's bed to lie on. You'll find a clean sleeping bag in the next room and you can put that on top of his bed. Here's a nice clean pillow, and Samir has more pillows in that room, you might remember. He likes to sleep with lots of support."

I knew that. I trudged upstairs with the sleeping bag and the pillow, leaving Mrs. P behind in the kitchen to talk to the cat and feed the bird, who squawked a heck of a lot more than I remembered. Maybe it missed its mate. I'm sure it did, poor thing. How did they get out of the cage that day? I didn't think I did it but you never know, I sure am crazy as a coyote with its tail caught in a sewing machine some days. Can't trust myself.

I tossed the sleeping bag and pillow on Pepsi's bed, my old bed, and threw myself down. The bed conformed to my shape perfectly as it always had, I remembered the springs and the sagging mattress and everything about it, comfortable and soft and yielding. The sleeping bag and pillow smelled clean and fresh, must have just come out of the dryer with those dryer balls Mrs. P used to fluff them.

I remembered to take off my shoes, and when I did, I remembered the night of the Doc's murder and how the next morning Samir's shoes were muddy and mine weren't. The Powolskis' front yard was always muddy when it rained, no grass there to speak of, because they didn't take proper care of their property. Was it raining that night in November, the night of Doc's murder? I couldn't remember. It probably was, it rained almost every day and night here in November. Would explain the muddy shoes if Samir had gone out that night.

The old yeller dog was still chained in the back and still howling. I tried to sleep in spite of the cur's gosh-awful wailing. I heard the radio snap on downstairs and the voice of CBC soothed me to sleep. I dreamed of the Scarlet Pimpernel.

When I woke up, a little red flower fluttered on Samir's bed, a vision left over from my not-altogether-unpleasant dreams. Then I thought of the reason for the flower, someone saved from execution in the French Revolution, an aristocrat like Mark. Samir's family had been wealthy, too. Could the Scarlet Pimpernel save him? I smiled and stretched beneath the comforting bulk of the sleeping bag.

I heard a door slam downstairs, and men's voices.

They were home.

Chapter Fifty

The meal was really, really good, and I mean Mrs. P is a dang good old-fashioned cook. That ham was a Virginia ham, pink and white and perfectly marbled, and the garlic mashed potatoes were to die for, the casseroles and the dinner rolls fresh out of the oven, the wine with the meal (which I couldn't drink, of course, being a former wino myself as everyone knew), the pumpkin pie and brandy whipped cream (which I ate) for dessert, the pickles and relish and salads, oh my, we were stuffed like turkeys when that meal was over. Only thing is, we had to say grace before the meal, being as how it was special and all, Easter and everything, but besides that, it was a very good day.

Pepsi kind of sly brought up the subject of the one remaining bird and how someone had left the cage open and the cat got its mate. How I got blamed.

"I'm not sure if I didn't do it," I admitted. "I might have. I can't remember."

I didn't like the look in Mrs. P's eyes when I said that, and Pepsi must have caught it, too, because he said right away, "Meredith..." He called her 'Meredith' because he was less respectful than the rest of us. "Meredith..." he said, "I know it wasn't Annie did that heinous deed."

"Where'd you all hear a word like that?" Mr. Powolski asked. "I don't even know what that means and I'm not sure you do, either. 'Heinous.' And have some respect for my wife, young pup. She's *Mrs.* Powolski to you."

"Sorry, sir," Pepsi said. He leaned back in his chair and stretched, popping a couple of buttons on his too-tight Italian shirt. "I learned that in ESL. They said that a 'heinous deed' meant you did something pretty bad. I know who did it, don't you, cuz?"

Samir glared at him.

"Yeah, he tried to put the blame on Annie," Pepsi said.

"What are you saying? You set my pussy on the birdie on *purpose*, you dreadful boy?"

"I admit it, Mrs. P," Samir said. "I let the birds out. So the cat could catch them. I wanted Annie to think she did it."

"Why on earth would you do that?" I asked. It seemed implausible that someone would want to just hurt me like that without any reason, and someone I thought was my friend, too. *We told you so,* my voices whispered, almost below my level of hearing. Mrs. P was mumbling, too, and I wasn't sure she said what she did or my voices did, but then I realized she was speaking louder now, her voice growing to a roar, then she raised her mighty bulk up from the vintage chair at the end of the dinner table and *splat,* she grabbed a broom, hit Samir over the head with it, and chased him out of the house.

"Son of a bitch. Don't you ever come back," she screamed at the tall, thin Sudanese. Pepsi was laughing. Samir laughed too, ducked the broom and ran out the front door into the rain.

"We're going, Mum," Pepsi called, and followed Samir out the door. "We'll get a beer and play checkers at the Red Ox Inn, the only restaurant open today, we sure don't need a good meal anymore, thank you very much, Mrs. P."

Pepsi grabbed his rain slicker with his left hand on the way out the door. I noticed then that was the hand he favored. *Hmmmm and what of that?*

Something I must think about, but in the meantime a funnel full of red flowers opened up and tried to swallow the bird. The cat morphed into a snake and slithered under the door.

You haven't heard from Mark for two days, Annie Fanny. Shouldn't you have a lot to say to Mark? After all, he's your main man, isn't he? Oh no, sorry, your main man is Samir.

Mrs. P sat down, red-faced and puffing. Henry was patting her between the shoulder blades.

Interesting. I'd forgotten that Pepsi was left-handed. I must tell Mark. This party was getting rough. Time we all put our pants on and went home.

Chapter Fifty-one

Guess it was my fault that Samir became a guest in my float house the night after Mrs. P sent him packing with a broom to his head. He was still laughing when I got home and found him camped there on my settee with the blanket pulled over his lean black body. Pepsi was there too, drinking white grape juice from my little apartment-type fridge and eating Frito-Lay chips.

"It's only for tonight," I said, and turned on some lights.

"Yes, sis," Samir said. "You know it's *his* fault, the snitch."

"I'm a whistle-blower," Pepsi agreed.

Samir sat up straight and slid his jeans to his knees. "She'll be over it in the morning. Let's get a good night's sleep first, cuz."

"Where am I gonna sleep?" Pepsi asked. He brushed crumbs onto the area rug and ground them in with his boots.

"There are two bedrooms upstairs," I said. "One of you or both of you can sleep in the biggest room. I take the smaller room in the back. A yoga room my mom fixed up is just off the main bedroom, if you don't mind the cold."

"Yeah, it gets cold here still," Pepsi agreed. "I'm glad for the space heaters. Can you light the fire, Annie?"

"I could," I said, but didn't move from where I stood in the alcove. "I don't think I will, though. It's time you two went to bed, and I want to stay up a bit and read."

"Read then," Samir said. "I'll go upstairs and sleep."

"Yeah, we can share the fart bag," Pepsi said. They both skittered up the ladder to the upstairs bedrooms, like two monkeys, Samir with his shirt tails hanging out and his boxer shorts showing. I tried not to look at his black behind. He was agile in spite of the brace on his leg.

I knew Pepsi had a half bottle of rum in his back pocket and expected they'd finish it before the night was over. I half thought better of my plan to leave them alone upstairs, but figured I'd be better off without them to worry about right now. Before I settled down I might do some reading, as I'd said. Now that they weren't going to get too comfortable down here, I lit the Franklin stove with kindling and papers, then settled down with *The Purloined Letter* to mull again over its truths.

I liked Dickens and Poe and all the old masters, got that from my mom. Her taste was all over the shelves here in the float house, evident in all the books she'd loved and left behind, although the pages were yellowed and some of them were water stained. I felt closer to her now, knowing that her fingers had touched the same pages. It was her coffee that had spilled and left the stains on the pages. Her love of Poe and the old masters had been passed along to me, her only child.

I thought about how 'purloined' meant 'stolen.' The stolen letter was put in the solicitor's keeping and no one knew it was there. It wasn't stolen after all. Poe was a genius, I thought. Is it the same with the blunt instrument that felled Doc Hubert? The poker was the most likely suspect, and it was under the bay beneath the float house. According to my neighbors. The purloined poker. I smiled. *You're so funny, Annie. They all hate you, you know.*

"Shut up," I said. It was time for my injection. The voices were getting too familiar again.

The bay under the float house should be dredged. Or a scuba diver should go down and try to find it. I almost called upstairs to the two hoodlums in the spare bedroom, drinking rum and telling funnies, to ask them which of them had taken the poker and dropped it in the drink. I thought that confrontation might be the best option after all, but couldn't make myself do it. *Annie, you coward.*

I didn't really want to know, I guess that was it. I had too much invested in my relationship with Samir, and I didn't really believe that Pepsi did it.

The cell rang *Dixie* and I answered it first ring.

Chapter Fifty-two

The fire in the Franklin Stove burned hot. It felt warm on my face even from a distance. With Samir and Pepsi in bed upstairs, I felt safe down here in the armchair by the stereo. Mark thought Samir did it, I knew that, and I thought he didn't. It was a matter of trust in my gut instincts, which didn't belong to a Private Eye at all, Lorne would say. I disagreed with that, too. I thought gut instincts were my most valuable possession. That and the coral lipstick. *Hee, hee.*

I answered the phone. It was Tess, the ADD Avon rep, and she had my order. I hoped she had it right.

I checked my wallet. I didn't have a checking account, used cash and my preloaded credit card. I thought it was time I opened up an account like everyone else but too many bounced checks made me an undesirable client at the Big Six banks. Maybe I'd mosey on down to the Credit Union near the docks tomorrow and give them my valuable business.

No more bounced checks, Annie.

"I promise." Sure went through a lot of money this month already. The end of my money was going to be here before the end of the month. I sighed and tried to fill my lungs with air. As I mentioned before, it was sometimes difficult to get a breath, especially when stressed. Psychological, I'm sure. Which was more necessary, hitting Lorne up for a loan or visiting the clinic in Campbell River tomorrow for another injection?

Maybe I could do both.

Chapter Fifty-three

Before the ferry left to take me across the bay to Campbell River the next morning, I stopped by the Credit Union at the docks and opened up an account. I gave them twenty-five dollars. They gave me a set of blank checks, a couple of brochures the same color as a twenty-dollar bill, and a smile from the manager. I took one of their pens as a souvenir and spurred the Vespa onto the ferry just before the gates went down.

Dr. Blanche saw me for ten minutes and said I looked good. I told him about the voices and he increased the dose to 60 cc. I moseyed on over to the Orthopedics clinic and asked about Samir's surgery. They said he was still on the wait list. Figures.

On the ferry on the way home, I bought a salmon filet sandwich, ditched the fries, and drank a bottle of Diet un-cola pop. Mark met me at the other side. "I'm on my way to Lorne's," I said. "Are you coming with me?"

"Just the place," he said. "Why haven't I heard from you lately, Annie? Are you giving me the cold shoulder now that Samir's no longer the gimpy guy he was?"

"He's still gimpy," I said. "That was never the issue."

"Of course not. That doesn't give you a lot of credit. He's pretty excited about the surgery, though. Will make a new man out of him."

"The pain killers already made a new man out of him."

"Yes, chronic pain can wear a body down." Mark scratched his smooth chin. "What's this about Lorne O'Halloran? You still work for him or for yourself?"

"Annie works for herself now," I said. "But I keep in touch with the authorities. Don't want to lose their goodwill. I know how close I can be to court again, or jail."

"Erna's well on her way to getting you that pardon, guess you have that in mind all the time, do you?"

"Sure do. That would be the break I need to start a new life."

"You got your break when you worked for Lorne."

"That's true. I'm gonna boogie right now, Mark, he's expecting me. I gave him a call from the ferry and he said to come right over. Guess the slot machines where Lorne hangs out will have to wait."

Mark slid into his car. "Do you want me along, Annie?"

"Don't you have nuffin' else to do?"

"No. Just trail along with you."

"Okay, then, but you'll have to stay out in the waiting room."

"Lunch after?"

"Sure, I'll dress for it this time, and I see you've shaved."

"The Red Ox Inn it is, then, Annie."

I didn't tell him I'd already eaten.

Lorne smacked his big coffee cup down on the oak desk. "I knew I could trust you to ferret out the truth, Annie," he said. "So now you want us to dredge the bay under your float house? Do Mark, Tom, and the sergeant know about this?"

"Not yet. Just you and me," I said. "My neighbors on the big boat to the north saw a tall, thin black man drop the poker in the drink last fall. Sounds a lot like Samir, could be Pepsi, though. I asked them if the fellow limped and they couldn't remember."

"Seem to me, they would have remembered a limp like Samir's."

"Yeah, that's what I thought. Pepsi has an alibi, though."

"Firewall Eddie."

"Yeah."

"Who could have been using and drinking again."

"Right, which blows Pepsi's alibi."

"We've got too many suspects, Annie."

"Including you, Lorne. You could have reason to blow away the mayor."

"But not the Doc?"

"The two murders may not have been connected."

"That's a stretch. In this little town, two murders a couple nights away from each other, first murder in forty years, then two of them? Not connected?"

"I'll tell you how it looks. You needed the money, Lorne, you're tired of a low-end gumshoe job here in the dregs of downtown. You got the gun that blew him away. You got the motive. In the meantime, after Spacey's murder, you lost to the interim mayor, an alderwoman. That's ironic or what? You bitter about that, Lorne? The mayor gets blown away, maybe you did it, and then you didn't win the chair anyhow."

"Yeah. Yeah, I'm bitter. Life's not fair." He took a huge slurp of the cold coffee and slammed his fist on the desk. "I should be sitting pretty now, not that old hen in City Hall who slept her way up the ladder."

"That's not a nice thing to say. It's not even true. I don't want to hear you say that in public, Lorne."

"Of course, I'd deny it."

I laughed. "Are you going to kill her, too?"

Lorne didn't laugh. His fat round bald head bobbed like one of those bobble heads in his tacky old Ford. I thought it was funny and smiled again. He hates you. I didn't need my voices to berate me. I could do a fine job of punishing myself.

"I know," I said out loud.

Lorne looked at me real funny. "You still crazy, Annie?" he asked.

"Sort of," I said. "Now why don't you give Constable Tom and the sergeant a call and suggest they send a scuba diver and look for an item of interest in the bay?"

"That's what I thought I'd do," he said.

He was on the horn for about ten minutes, bringing the local cops up to speed.

"They're delighted someone is updating them on the case," Lorne said, after hanging up. "They've been kept pretty much in the dark by the RCMP in City Hall and our detective Snow isn't much information, either."

"Actually, I don't think anybody knows anything much more than Tom and Sergeant Ross do," I said. "We're waiting for a break in the case."

"They're going to send a scuba diver down there later today," Lorne said. "Thanks for the tip, Annie. That's what we pay you for."

"Pay?" I asked. "That's an interesting concept. I been living on a pension since you guys took me off the case."

"How much do you need?" Lorne asked. He peeled off a few twenties from his wallet and passed them to me over the stained surface of his desk.

"That's enough," I said, satisfied. I sat back in the ripped leather roller chair that I had always enjoyed as my portion of the room. I tipped my shoes up on Lorne's desk and pinched my bottom lip with my thumb and index finger.

"Who do you think dunnit?" I asked. "Seriously, Lorne."

"It wasn't me."

"I didn't say it was." Although I had.

I missed my little colored animals peeking around the waste baskets in Lorne's office. I missed my voices, harsh though they were at times.

"I think…" Lorne began. Then he chuckled and his whole body jiggled. "I don't have a friggin' clue who dunnit. Do you?" I stared at his four chins, fascinated, and counted the liver spots on his forehead.

"Yes," I said. "As a matter of fact, I do."

He looked worried.

Chapter Fifty-four

The Red Ox Inn squatted on a hill in the Upper Heights at the end of a curving concrete driveway. Mark's black Kia Sportage purred up the incline and we parked in front of the glass windows that looked out over the town.

"They're expecting us," he said, and leaned over to open the door for me. I huffed a bit, and shoved it out myself.

"You look nice," I said as we strolled to our table. He did, in a smart grey suit with a blue shirt, open at the neck.

"You look pretty spiffy yourself." Mark raised a thick brown eyebrow and winked. "New lipstick?"

"Boy, are you observant. This is *brand* new."

I kept tripping on the broom skirt. My gladiator sandals click-clacked across the terracotta floors on the way to our table by the window. My beautiful hair was caught up in waves by a crimson headband.

"You got changed in record time," he said. "I'm impressed."

"Most women take far too long to get themselves ready," I said. "I'm not most women."

"No, you're not."

The waiter pulled back a leather chair for me. I thanked him and dropped into the seat. My sandals were sensible. I was glad of that. I never wore heels. Mark smiled at me over the fancy menu.

"Drink?" he asked.

"Sure. A virgin Caesar, please. The tomato juice is good for the complexion." He smiled and of course, complimented me on my complexion. I grinned.

"My plan worked," I said. "I got a compliment."

"You're a bit smug today, Missy Anne."

I stretched like a cat. "Celebrating the loss of ten pounds," I said. "Had you noticed?"

Mom always said I needed to be more discrete with men. How, I wondered? Weren't they a lot like women, liked to talk about things open and all? Come to think of it, I didn't know many women like that either. Just me. Maybe Mark was different than most men, I could be honest with him. You think?

He looked surprised. "I hadn't noticed. I didn't think you needed to lose weight."

"Liar."

He smiled. "In my eyes you're perfect."

Nope, he wasn't any different and I told him so. "If we can't be honest with each other, I don't want to be friends," I said. "I'm trying to lose weight and it would be great if I had a weight loss buddy or an exercise buddy who kept me honest."

"I know you've been looking at yoga lessons."

"Yeah, I can drop in on Friday mornings for the price of a food bank donation."

"That's great." He ordered drinks, a virgin Caesar for me and a rum and coke for him. Nothing fancy and that surprised me. He seemed like a fancy guy, to me. Unless he was trying to fit in with plain ol' Annie. I swirled the celery stick in the crimson liquid and sipped. It was very good. I asked him how he liked his rum and coke. He ordered lunch for both of us. I didn't like that much because I'd already eaten, but wasn't familiar with the menu either.

"The lady will have the beef Wellington, medium rare, with a mixed salad on the side," he said. That sounded okay by me, though I didn't know what beef Wellington was.

"You'll like it," he said. "It's English."

"I'm not English. I'm a Canuck from way back and before that a smattering of everything, mostly German and Nordic, from way back some First Nations."

"I was wondering about your ancestry. You have marvelous eyes, that violet's definitely not native."

"Like Lord Greystone, maybe, I have blue eyes in a tanned native face?"

"He was a bogus Indian."

"Maybe I'm bogus, too."

"You're not bogus anything, Annie. That's what I like about you."

"Balderdash. You're a man and men like this…" I batted my lashes and put my face up to his like a French coquette.

"Oh, that's nice." He smiled and ordered a steak sandwich for himself, with baked potato. The waiter fluttered around our table for a few minutes, refreshed our water glasses and finally left us alone so we could talk.

"What was so secret about your visit with Lorne O'Halloran?"

"Not secret exactly. I suggested to him that they send a scuba diver to dredge the bay under my float house. Look for a poker that might have conked old Doc on the head. You know, my neighbors in the big boat to the north saw a black man drop a poker in the ocean outside the door there, in that space between the dock and the front door. Lorne called Constable Tom and the sergeant to retrieve it. The bay isn't that deep in that area so it should be pretty easy to find."

"You think it was the murder weapon?"

"If that didn't kill the doctor then drilling his brains out certainly did."

"That would pinpoint either Pepsi or Samir as the murderer, wouldn't it?"

"If we found Doc's DNA or blood smears on that poker, and fingerprints, that would cinch it, I think, yeah."

"We were missing the blunt instrument."

"Looks like we found it. Simple me, I didn't think of a *purloined poker* as the murder weapon."

"Purloined poker?" He smiled and sipped at his rum and coke.

The waiter brought a basket of dinner rolls. I helped myself to one then thought better of it and put it on the edge of my plate. I'd already lost ten pounds, no need to have any extra bread at what could be a great meal. Beef Wellington, eh?

When our meals arrived, I was ready with fork in hand. I could smell, and imagined I could already taste, the succulent beef tenderloin wrapped in tender puff pastry as the waiter settled it into place in front of me. I grasped my fork with my left hand, the way mom had taught me, and sliced into the steaming flesh with my knife.

"What is it, exactly?" I asked and took a dainty mouthful.

"Filet of beef tenderloin, madam," the waiter murmured, grating pepper on the dish as I asked. "It's assembled with liver pate, mushrooms and onions, then wrapped in puff pastry. Enjoy, madam."

"Liver?" I gagged.

Mark blanched. "I'm sorry," he said. "I didn't think you might not like the liver pate."

"Liver pate?"

"Is madam not pleased? I will remove the dish," the waiter was smooth as a shaved pig.

"Please," I said. "I'm so sorry. I just can't abide liver."

That sort of set the tone for the whole meal. Mark was sorry, I was appalled, the waiter was all deference. *Liver,* my voices said. *He's trying to poison you.* At least it brought back my familiar friends, the voices. So I had the seafood chowder with dill, lots of fresh baked rolls, and crème brûlée for dessert, at Mark's urging. Diet be damned.

We talked some more about the poker and my neighbors, Brent and Catherine Hoffman, my mother Blossom and my father Albin, who made me what I am today (Mark seemed interested) — and especially Lorne O'Halloran, who believed in me but could have murdered the mayor and maybe the Doc, too.

"Do you think he did it?" Mark asked, sipping on an after dinner coffee.

"You think Samir did it?" I countered.

"Yes," he said. "I think he did. But we have to prove it."

"We have to prove anyone did it," I said. "I have no proof of anybody. A lot of suspects, though."

"We have to wait and see what forensics says about the poker. If it's recovered."

"Yes," I said.

"You have your own thoughts, don't you?"

"Yes, some thoughts."

"You're keeping this close to your chest, Annie."

"I'm hoping you're wrong about Samir but it's looking bad for him."

"I think it's a strong wish on your part. You don't want Samir to have done it." Mark rolled his eyes and almost spat. "The SOB knows he has you on his side, too. Manipulative bastard."

I changed the subject as tactfully as possible for Annie Hansen. "What do the boys at City Hall have to say? I understand they recovered the bullet that killed the mayor."

"They've identified the bullet. It matches the gun they took from Lorne. It was a SIG Pro semi-automatic, a gun commonly used by law enforcement when Lorne was part of the force."

"I didn't know that Lorne was ever on the force," I said.

"Oh, yeah. He was fired from the Edmonton city police for unbecoming conduct in 1998. They could never prove it and he says he was railroaded, made to take the rap for a fellow officer. But it concerned the unauthorized discharge of a firearm. Interesting, huh?"

"Yeah, but I don't think he did it, either."

"You don't think anyone did it, Annie." Mark frowned. He sounded frustrated.

"You know what, Mark?"

"What?"

"My Avon rep got my order right."

He was silent, forehead wrinkled.

"She seems real ADD, you know. Attention Deficit. I doubted her. But she got my order pretty much letter perfect."

He paid with a plastic card. "This is deductible," he said. "I'm on an expense account."

"You didn't have to tell me that."

"Does that have anything to do with you? ADD?"

"OCD, for sure. Obsessive-Compulsive Disorder. I'm trying to say…"

"That you can still get it letter perfect."

"That's what they hire me for."

"Why do you think they took you off the case?"

"I'm too close to one of the suspects."

"And now? You're too close to the main cop on the case."

"I have a way about me," I said as he let me go ahead of him to the door. His SUV stood in a drizzle of rain from a grey sky. Dang, I left my slicker at home.

Chapter Fifty-five

Later that week, Tom and Sergeant Ross came to visit me. They had the poker wrapped up in plastic, and drew it out to show me. It looked like it always did, and they asked me to identify it. I turned it over in gloved hands, like they asked me to, and nodded.

"Looks like my mom's old poker," I said. "Got the blacksmith's mark on it, JB, just like always. Cleaner than I usually seen it, Tom."

"Don't you think this dark stuff looks like dried blood, Ross?" Tom asked. He handled the poker like it was still hot.

"The lab in Victoria will tell us soon enough," the sergeant replied. "All we got to do is figure out who dropped it in under the float house. You say your neighbors in the boat saw it?"

"Yeah, you can talk to them. The Hoffmans, in the big boat *Catherine* to the north of me. But I don't know if they'd like to be involved. Keep to themselves. We all keep to ourselves on that marina. We're not popular with the townsfolk as we don't pay property taxes. They think we're spongers."

"Boats, too?" Tom said.

"Yeah, and the float house counts as floating on pontoons, no property there, just the dock fees I pay the marina for power, garbage and moorage."

"Still, your neighbors are number one eye witnesses where this here poker is concerned. You're sure they saw it dropped in the drink?" Sergeant Ross put a beefy hand on Tom's big shoulder and turned him around to point out the bay window where Catherine and Brent Hoffman peered from behind their curtains, with a light behind them.

"That's how I knew it was there," I said. "They told me."

"We're going over to make a little visit," the sergeant said. "You're sure this is your poker, Annie?"

"Sure. It's my mom's poker. But I'm not sure it's the murder weapon."

"It could be what knocked ol' Doc out before they made sure he was a murder victim, brains all piled beside his skull." The sergeant almost gagged.

"Let's go hear what the neighbors have to say," Tom said.

I watched as the two cops trudged across the slippery dock to the Hoffmans' boat and knocked. After a while Brent answered the door. I saw him nod and the two cops entered. Both officers ducked their heads as they lumbered below deck, looking a bit out of place, I thought. Brent and his wife were more petite, suitable to living below decks on a boat for the year. Tom and the sergeant were both big, beefy men in uniform, probably scared the heck out of the couple.

They got what they came for, weren't gone long. I watched from the bay windows as the sergeant tromped around the deck of the Hoffmans' boat, peering at my float house, no doubt trying to figure out how my neighbors seen what they seen the night that Samir (or his cousin) had dumped the poker in the water outside my door.

I stopped Tom and the sergeant as they passed by my front door on their way to the hill and the parking lot where they parked the police car.

"We got nothing to say to you," Sergeant Ross growled, but there was a twinkle in his eye, and Tom nodded.

"You seem happy," I said. "First break in the case?"

"Looks to be a cinch, but don't you tell nobody, Annie." Constable Tom held the poker wrapped up again in plastic.

I sighed. It wasn't looking so good for Samir, I thought. "You still have to send it to the lab."

Tom nodded. This was a coup for him and the sergeant. The sergeant was grinning like a dog eating cat turds.

"Guess you put one over on the new detective," I said.

"Your friend," Tom smirked. "Yeah, I guess we did. Thanks, Annie."

"The Justice Department hired me for a reason," I said.

"There's a reason they took you off the case, too. You're too close to the main players," the sergeant said. I always thought he was the shrewd fellow of the beefy pair. Tom wasn't married whereas the sergeant was married, maybe why Tom was out on his own a lot of the time, didn't have the benefit of the sergeant's excuse to take it easy at home.

That was unfair. Sergeant Ross was Tom's boss, though. Technically, Mark Snow was the boss now, or the RCMP at City Hall. Technically, the sergeant was right, I was off the case.

"You're pretty valuable, Annie," Tom said and continued to smirk. The sergeant nudged him when he didn't think I was looking, but I saw. They didn't want me to think too highly of myself. I might ask for a raise.

I owed Lorne O'Halloran a couple hundred dollars. I thought I'd bring it up with Erna the next time we emailed or phoned. She was our Head Honcho after all, next to the Deputy Minister. My new clothes and make-up were expenses I didn't have before, but they didn't count, I was pretty sure of that. I'd have to think of something else, like the new meds and the trips to Campbell River. Yes, that would do it.

I was worried about Samir's leg. The painkillers and brace were a big improvement for him, but he was due for surgery as soon as he got the call from the clinic. We knew he was on a wait list, and they could move him forward if they thought there was a rush, like maybe he would go to jail soon. Oh, that's real funny, Annie. Yeah, and it's looking likely, too, that there'll be that kind of a rush, either for him or his blood brother Pepsi.

"You're pretty sure of yourselves," I said and indicated the poker. "It could have somebody else's DNA on it, like that big salmon that lives down there in the salt water, or maybe a bunch of ash and my fingerprints?"

"Could," the sergeant agreed. They lifted their hands in salute to me and continued up the dock. I watched them climb the hill by the marina headquarters and get in their black and white car with the big "eye" on it. *They're watching us.*

"Will take a week or two to get it back," I said to my voices, who weren't as vocal as usual now I'd had my previous injection.

That Flupenthixol was good stuff. Kindly old Dr. Blanche knows his meds, I thought. I never gave him enough credit, actually. He was the first psych I'd ever had who didn't hurt me in one way or the other. Maybe I was learning to cooperate and then the therapists wouldn't hurt you or misunderstand somehow on purpose. I remembered the psych nurse, who didn't like me and made the appointments eight months apart, told me she only took the patients who were "low maintenance". I spat at that, spat right into the drink, and laughed. I wished I'd reported her to her association but I was too soft. Too soft and too scared of the authorities. They'd always hurt me and bucking the establishment didn't get a patient very far in those days.

It had changed since then. I also remembered the security guard who had tried to corner me in interrogation one morning, and the administrator who had asked me out on a date. All too ready to take advantage of a psycho on the street. Until I met Erna in the Justice Department, and worked for Lorne O'Halloran (whom I might send up the river), until somebody believed in me. I thought of dried blood and blood brothers.

Erna Sobey didn't know I was still on the case. Maybe I should tell her. This was turning into blood island, and I couldn't escape until the case broke or I did, whichever came first.

Chapter Fifty-six

Far out on the ocean that same night, I could see the big ships coming in, passing by on their way from exotic ports. The Modge Bay Lighthouse swept its yellow lamps across the blue-grey surf, a rhythm of music from the foghorn like Swiss buglers on a lonely mountaintop. I imagined I could see the tall ships tossing in *Tales of Narnia*, on the wild, black waves, the water pouring from my walls into a magical land of talking lions and fierce friendly pirates.

It could be my future to ride one of those ships one day, into Vancouver and then out again to Taiwan or Thailand or Burma, maybe, the new land of Myanmar where Muslims are killed because they refuse to eat pork, where human rights violations don't concern us here on our safe and secure islands in the Georgia Straits, and our safe and secure North American continent. I thought of my mother and how she had taught me to love and protect all creeds and all races. She would be so proud of my Samir. *Proud of me.*

What of blond, tall, paunchy Mark Snow? "A lot like your father," my mother would say, and then smile that distracted and distant smile. She had fallen for a handsome entrepreneur who left her when her ovaries dried up and she didn't dance at midnight for him or his friends anymore. My mother was more attractive in middle age, I thought, a wiser and browner and more aged companion who had sloughed off the ties of conformity. My father didn't think so. He had left with a woman half his age and a daughter younger than me.

I didn't like it. He had come back only once, when he heard I was crazy and in trouble with the courts, on the street, his daughter a shame and disgrace. I had sat there across from his girlfriend and her daughter in the corner, playing with their hair, waiting for him to dust his true daughter from his hands and return to Curaçao with them, which he did the next day. But he was my father after all, and I wished he had stayed for just a few more days. I wished he had told them to go on ahead without him, and talked to me, really looked at me as though I existed. I wished he had loved me more, but maybe he did as far as he could, and I was asking for too much from the man.

My mother always told me I was asking too much from my father, and she gave me, too, what she could, but I asked too much always.

This night was one of solitude, not loneliness. I pressed my face against the cold glass of the bay window by the settee. The lamps of the lighthouse swept the bay and inland. I could see the old shack where I'd seen Firewall Eddie and Firewall Eddie Raven smoking and drinking vodka this winter at the end of my hike through the rain forest and down again. I couldn't make out if there was smoke from the chimney tonight. A flicker of yellow lit the panes that I could see from here. I imagined Eddie and Firewall Eddie lighting candles or maybe an old kerosene lamp. The shack didn't have proper power, I knew that, it had been turned off years ago.

Probably they'd been smoking up in the old shack the night Doc was murdered. The night Pepsi was working alone in the Doc's building, and the women were coming over from the Indian Nation to visit Doc at midnight, the night MASER's name was written down to see Doc then. Maybe an Indian name, maybe a code... SAMIR?

Or short for Margaret Schneider (MS)... my mind was ratcheting ahead, putting together codes and algorithms of code. It was impossible for me to retire from my job.

I loved my job. I loved being a private eye. I liked the challenge and the new clothes I bought, liked what I was wearing then, a pair of flannel pajama bottoms with footballs on them from the Toronto Argos (I'd prefer BC Lions but the thrift shop didn't have those). I felt real special and spiffy, like Mark would say, in my red pullover and plaid sneakers. I'd ordered a Brilliant Ruby lipstick from Avon to match the red duds.

Tess Russell had thrown in a bottle of body lotion last order, so she might do the same thing again, maybe a sample of nail polish? I liked the clear nail polish but she was right, pink paparazzi or blue would be trendy, maybe at the fingertips. *Or coral.* I smacked my lips.

The light in the shack flickered. I saw a snake of flame licking at the corner of the cedar shakes. Fire! Engines and sirens screamed closer, closer...

I sat like stone as the volunteer fire department scrambled down the hill from the parking lot and set up their hoses, pumping saline water from the bay onto the flames sparkling like the First of July. Someone must have called 911. It wasn't me.

The flames cast light onto the faces of two very familiar Sudanese and two very familiar First Nations gentlemen. All four of them tumbled out of the door x-rayed against the hell inside. The shack burned to the ground as I watched. My heart thudded in my chest. I felt my breasts beneath the red pullover. The nipples were hard.

The fire department must have called the cops, who were suddenly there to arrest the four trespassers.

Far out at sea, the ships churned by, majestic, slow, careful of the shoals and the breakers so stalwartly watched by the Modge Bay Lighthouse. Its automatic lamps swept and its alpenhorn boomed like I imagined the Swiss Search and Rescue corps would do on a night dark like this and in the midst of orange-tongued flames.

"Over here," I called. "Tom, I saw it all."

"The fire's under control, lady," a smoke-blackened captain said. "It didn't reach the lighthouse."

"Or the boats and my float house." I took a deep breath and tried to calm myself.

By the lights around the dock, I could see Samir dragging his poor left leg up the hill to the parking lot. Constable Tom twisted Eddie's ear and the sergeant snapped the handcuffs behind Firewall Eddie's back. None of the four seemed to be resisting arrest.

They'd be free by morning. They hadn't done much wrong in the eyes of the town. Nobody here was racist, but that would be the connotation if those boys were kept overlong.

I knew them guys. They were mighty clever, mighty convincing, and mighty dangerous in the wrong situation. This was definitely small potatoes. The fire was out and there were bigger trout to grill. We had a murderer loose on this island, and our cops were about to arrest the wrong man.

Chapter Fifty-seven

Samir told me later what happened the next morning. "Tom and Sergeant Ross took us down to the station..." (actually it was *up* to the station as the station was in the Upper Heights more or less). "They talked to your Samir as a 'person of interest' and let the other three go." He rubbed his sore leg.

"I think that was a mistake," I said.

"Yeah. I need to see a lawyer in Campbell River. Want to talk about false arrest and harassment. Maybe racism." Oh, oh. I knew it.

Never lock horns with a mad Sudanese, they know how to fight back.

Apparently the four renegades had spent the evening before in the shack, smoking ground-up peyote powder and drinking distilled alcohol. Someone had upset one of the kerosene lamps and set fire to a curtain. They'd been too stoned to realize their building was on fire until the fire department got there. Lucky for our boys, the evidence was burned up in the fire.

"The cops didn't press charges for petty trespassing but they questioned me again about the murders last November."

"You must have been drugged pretty good," I said, remembering the circumstances of the fire and the bust.

"I managed to hide most of it from Tom and Sergeant Ross."

"They're pretty naïve, then."

Samir said when they booked him at the station the sergeant wrote "NHE" on top of the warrant, sort of scrawled it there, and Samir was livid because he knew that meant "Non Human Entity," which was the term the cops used when they're dealing with schizophrenics, let's say, or the homeless, or people off the street. Very bad word.

I was surprised that Constable Tom and the sergeant would be so stupid as to use it where Samir was concerned. He'd talked to me, you see, on many an occasion, and I knew very well what that meant.

They didn't exactly book him any longer because after he threatened to sue the Town of Serendipity and the police force, and each officer individually, he talked to the warden and walked out. They couldn't stop him.

"Did they tell you what they found when they were poking around looking for a murder weapon?" I asked him, as he sat brooding in my wicker chair in the kitchen while I cooked up a mess of shrimp stir-fry.

"Yeah, it was a poker," he said.

"They tell you where they found it?"

"Yeah, in the soup in front of your door on the float house." He rubbed his good right leg. "I never dropped it there."

"The Hoffmans saw somebody of your description throw the poker into the water. They told me about it and I told Lorne. He called Tom and the sergeant. A scuba diver brought it up."

"Water's pretty shallow right there," Samir agreed. "Would have been easy to do. But I didn't do it."

"Who would it have been that they saw?"

"I don't know. Can't think of anybody."

"Would it be Pepsi? They described dropped waist pants and a baseball cap."

"Sounds like my cuz, all right. But it weren't him, neither."

"How do you know?" I asked.

"It's discrimination. Just because we're black."

"Just because you're Afro-Canadian? The cops use race to identify suspects. Samir, my dear, you are a very black Sudanese man. Pardon me, my mama taught me to be respectful of all creeds and races, but I'm also a very honest woman. You and Pepsi are not blond Caucasians and if the Hoffmans saw a black man drop the poker in the pond, then there aren't a lot of black men here in this community. You and Pepsi are two, and you're already suspects. You know that?"

"I know prejudice when I see it. I'll sue the Wellingtons off those two dicks."

"I can tell you the Hoffmans tried to identify you from a picture but were unable to do so." I didn't tell Samir that Brent had said, 'All those troublemakers look alike.' "They do describe how he was dressed, the fellow who came out of my door and dropped the poker in the drink."

Samir was silent.

"We all know who dresses that way, and you're right, it isn't you."

"It isn't my cuz, either. We're innocent. They're after us because we're black and poor. I'm going to the papers about this."

"The papers already got hold of it. It's national news, silly."

"I know that."

"The *National Post* did a story on it just the other day, Monday I think it was, berating the cops. Bet that made the officers antsy, to be ridiculed on national media."

"*Global TV* did the same thing in January."

"The RCMP are under a lot of pressure to solve this case," I said. "They're putting pressure on Mark and the local cops. I think they might bring in the bigger guns soon if nothing breaks in this case. Doc Hubert and Mayor Spacey were pretty big fish in a small pond. The killings were gruesome, got a lot of media attention and outcry, a lot of folks slavering to hear the details. I'd look behind me if I was you, Samir, and watch my back. If I were you."

"Don't threaten me, Annie."

"I'm trying to help you."

"What do you hear from lover boy?"

"Mark?"

"You got it, sis."

"Don't dis him, Samir. He's a smart cop."

"Yeah, smart enough to cover his butt."

"Now you're saying Mark's a suspect?"

"Why not?"

"You're being silly," I said. I rolled my eyes. Sometimes this guy could be so childish. I wondered if he'd been stunted or something growing up.

"Mark investigated the time clock records of the night of November seventeenth. Eddie wasn't working that night."

"So?"

"So he's Pepsi's alibi."

"Why are you telling me this?" Good question. Was I protecting Pepsi or protecting Samir? And why?

"Why did Eddie want to give him an alibi? You have anything to say about that, dude?"

"No."

"Go ahead and sue."

Samir put his curly dark head into his hands and sighed. I thought I was the only one short of breath. Guess I'd knocked the wind out of my main squeeze.

Why did Firewall Eddie want to give Pepsi an alibi? That puzzled me. What would be the point, if Eddie wasn't working that night, unless he was covering his own ass. So Pepsi's alibi was false. Maybe Eddie wanted an alibi for himself to say that he was there so he didn't get fired and Pepsi backed him up.

"They must have worked it out together," I said. "Pepsi knew Eddie would give him an alibi, but Eddie didn't think Pepsi did it, so he thought it was okay to tell a little white lie and let both of them off the hook, the force would think Eddie was working that night and that Pepsi wasn't at the scene. But now Pepsi seems to be implicated." Samir stared blankly. He fidgeted in his chair and tapped his fingers on the side of his right thigh, the good leg, I remembered.

I continued. "It could even be Crazy Leroy or Firewall Eddie. There was no record of a security guard that night other than the guard who came in early in the morning."

Samir pinched his lip and frowned. Obviously that hadn't occurred to him. Dimwit.

"Here, you want some dinner?" I served up the stir-fry on paper plates with chopsticks. Samir ate like a wolf who'd just killed a cow, held the plate close to his face and devoured his meal. He looked up and licked his chops. I knew he didn't like to eat in public, but was used to it since living with the Powolskis.

I wouldn't have felt safe or right confiding in Samir if I wasn't sure neither he nor his cousin had done the foul deed. I was giving them both the chance to get themselves off the hook and was taking a chance myself by telling him all this, the bastoid who'd framed me with opening the birdcage at Mrs. P's place, and might be trying to frame me now. I thought I'd call Mark and tell him what I'd done. My conscience bothered me, taking a suspect into my confidence like this.

Mark wouldn't like it. He'd think I was soft on Samir.

That night I watched old-time movies on my laptop. I remembered my dream and the funnel of red flowers that threatened to swallow me whole. Perhaps Annie could leave a calling card like the *Scarlet Pimpernel* and astound and confound the world. If I could solve this case I'd be set for life. Erna Sobey would get me a pardon for sure and I'd be back in Lorne's good graces. Samir and I would be old pals and his blood brother, Pepsi, would be *exonerated*. I got that word from the movies. I got a lot of information from old movies. And old books.

I was sure learning some big words, I thought. I was sure getting smarter every damn friggin' day, like my mom said I would if given a chance. If my daddy could see me then he'd be so proud. I think he would, if he could pull himself away from the fat Dutch woman and her daughter. My fingers flew on my lap under the keyboard shelf as I counted the icons on my desktop.

First I had to talk to Mark, the Warren Beatty of Serendipity Island. I brought up the Monday *National Post* on the library website. Sure enough, my name wasn't mentioned at all, but Mark's name was there, and Erna's. The RCMP were mentioned and the local cops.

My moment of glory had not yet arrived.

Chapter Fifty-eight

I thought maybe the increase in meds wasn't enough to take care of the break-through voices, though I hadn't seen visions for a couple of months until fairly recently. I still counted, but that was OCD and not schizophrenia, so maybe the antipsychotic didn't do well for the counting. I thought Dr. Blanche might be able to figure something out, so the next day I phoned his office and made an appointment to come in for some fine-tuning.

A couple days later I was on the ferry again, headed for Campbell River and my psych's office. He was real good about seeing me when I needed it. Guess he wasn't too impressed with my stint on the streets when my mother was alive. So now that I was a contributing member of society he seemed very happy with my progress, and would say so now and then. I'd stuck with Dr. Blanche for longer than any of my other therapists, mostly because he was pretty laid back about my life. Guess mom didn't know what to do with me when I was home and she enlisted Dr. Blanche's help. I don't know how she knew him but mom knew a lot of important people. My mom died without knowing how well I could be, and my dad didn't seem impressed even now. I sure did miss my mother though, and wished she'd known me now that I was better. <snuffle>

My middle name was my mom's, Annie Blossom Hansen. I always thought it sounded exotic and sort of First Nations, you know, like my mom was, part Cree from the Samson Reserve in Alberta. She was a prairie girl just like I'm a west coast girl. Marks a person, and molds us, I think, where we're from, like my mom always liked the wide open spaces of the prairies, I think it was in her eyes, and only moved to the west coast when she married my dad.

They met the traditional way, not online like how my father met the big bosomed Dutch woman from Curaçao. Dad was a young lawyer and mom was an admin assistant in a legal firm, one of her first jobs out of school before they moved to the coast and she became a well-known artist. Dad had got involved in something marginally shady, I'm not too clear what, but he made a beeline for the coast and the BC bar before they caught up to him in Alberta. That's the story I heard years later.

I reminisced like that while I waited in Dr. Blanche's office, stuck against the wall staring at his admin assistant's feet under the L-shaped desk.

"Good morning, Anne," the doc said when I finally was allowed in the big office. His assistant smirked and left the office. I didn't think she liked me. I didn't care.

"What can I do for you this morning?"

"Maybe a change in meds," I said. "Still hearing voices."

"I'll increase it to 70 cc but that's all I can do for you for now. It might make you sleepy."

"I don't care. I don't like hearing voices."

"This might not do it, Anne. But we can try." He made a steeple of his fingers and peered at me over the top of his hands. "How is the case coming along? The double murders on Serendipity Island? Any breakthroughs?"

"I'm working on it, and so is Mark."

"Mark?"

I told him who Mark was and he seemed interested. Perhaps Dr. Blanche was a professional voyeur, interested in the sensational news from Serendipity and my part in it?

"I can't say much about it," I said. "I don't know any more than the media is guessing, though I have some ideas. That's what they pay me for. I want to be optimal, right on top of things, I don't want to be that crazy Annie Hansen who's off the case because she can't cope with the stress."

"Is that what they think?"

"I don't suppose so. I'm pretty handy. Handy Annie." I grinned. He smiled back.

"You're doing well. Go in and have your injection. I'll tell the nurse. Let me know how you're doing with the increase. We can always give you a pill to supplement the injection, too."

"Like diazepam?"

"Perhaps."

"It's addictive."

"Would you like to try it?"

"Maybe I'll try a pill. I don't like to be sleepy. Don't you have something that will make me alert?"

"We could try something like Zyprexa."

"Okay."

The nurse slipped the needle into my butt with the usual alacrity.

The Flupenthixol had already been increased to 60 cc and I thought that was about enough, as I slept the first day straight through after every injection now. I didn't want to sleep for a week.

So I didn't take the increase in the Flupenthixol but took a little white tablet at bedtime instead. It ended up working like a hot dang. The Zyprexa kept me from hearing voices most of the time. As it was, I seldom saw my little colored creatures, though I missed them.

I was getting so darn responsible. I sometimes missed the old irresponsible Annie who'd skip a dose of feel good pills just because she wanted to be 'normal' and like everybody else. Not have to take the pills that made me drowsy and gave me a dry mouth and tremors in my hands. I was already on antidepressants for the OCD and they didn't seem to do a heck of a lot of good, but at least it kept the Seasonal Affective Disorder at bay during the rainy months on the west coast. Boy, I was a mess. Just thinking about all my problems made me depressed.

I crossed the strait on the ferry for the second time that day. The ride was only ten minutes, as usual, but seemed longer. I got thinking about how I could make my life more interesting without actually being insane about it, in more ways than one. I was stuck in what would be called a rut and although a rut might be comfortable, so might a grave.

I thought Samir and I had made a good pair at the Powolskis and I seldom got bored then. What was the difference now?

Mark? Or the fact that I wasn't officially at work?

It might be Mark. He was the wild card. I thought about how I could mix things up with Mark, and then yawned, because the injection was getting to me.

I had more fun on the street. Being with Samir was next best thing to being on the street, the wild, crazy Sudanese dude and his wild, crazy cousin, Pepsi.

I wanted to break away and do something really crazy, really wild, less conservative and placid. What would that be, and still be on the sane side of the law and on the side of... well... 'normal'?

Something occurred to me, not for the first time. I missed my visions. I missed my voices. I wasn't happy with counting but that was a constant. I considered skipping my evening pills that Dr. Blanche had kindly given me. Then I thought, Annie, you truly are a magpie in a robin's nest.

Never satisfied with the status quo, and it's not because I'm crazy. It's because I am that kind of personality and my character is such that I would have made a good pirate, back then when my Viking forebears were pirates. I would have clung to the masthead and bawled the hell out of the Germans that came down from the north, and punched out the mighty Norsemen who tried to mess with the Hansen Valkyrie.

That's what I would have done. Maybe my trouble wasn't the mental illness they tried to hang on me, but the fact that I was a Viking Valkyrie, surrounded by white mewling pussies who made me want to throw up.

That decided, I crawled home and went to bed.

Chapter Fifty-nine

Mark googled the local news on my laptop as we sat in the Golden Arches two days later, drinking inexpensive but excellent coffee and nibbling on breakfast burritos.

"Just as I thought," he said. "Nothing there about the case."

"They must have got tired of it by now," I said, doodling with my wet finger on the side of my cup.

"No, the prosecutors called a media blackout and the media went home," Mark said. "Too much publicity isn't good for the eventual trial and it's prejudicing the case."

"They've already broadcast the case all over Canada and the US because it's so macabre. Not everyone will be glad to see the media's no longer involved, I expect. Lots of folks hang on every pukin' word and video footage of the murder sites. Whose idea was it for the blackout, Mark?"

"Mine," he said with modest demeanor. "The reporters were very understanding, and Global News wrapped it up at City Hall for the last time before they went back to Vancouver."

"I'm glad about that," I said. "I was getting tired of the dirty looks and innuendos that we're not doing our part to solve the case. Just the other day my hairdresser said it looks political."

"Which it is."

"Yeah, well, the new mayor was voted in and Lorne didn't get to ride on the coattails of a successful conviction."

"Lorne's small cookies."

"I don't know. I still think he knows more about this than he lets on. You know, he had a lot riding on the hole left by Mayor Spacey when Hizhonnor was blown away. If he'd been successful with his race for new mayor, and not the alderwoman who got in, then he'd be sitting prettier now than he has for a long time, the dirty little gumshoe."

"How can you talk like that about your benefactor?" Mark asked.

"He took up with me because it benefited him, he wasn't trying to do me any favors."

"I think you used to like Lorne. What happened?"

"I stopped hearing voices and seeing little furry purple snakes in his wastebasket. I got better and my friends are better people now. I can see that my gratitude for rescuing me from the street was really the court's compassion to send me to Lorne, and not Lorne who tried to help me. He took advantage of my knowledge of the street and the local hoodlums, while he sat there and counted tokens he'd won at the casino the night before, and took half my wages while doing it."

Mark raised his eyebrows. "He did? He took half your wages?"

"Found that out when I did the bookkeeping the other day. Got my time sheets from Erna. Lorne had fixed them to make it look like I worked longer hours than I did, then he took the extra plus more. I get paid through the Justice Department, not Lorne, and he was bilking both Erna's department and me. I don't know who to tell."

"Start by telling me. Then I'll talk it over with Erna."

"Yeah, she might not believe me. I'm not too credible."

"Oh, I don't know," Mark said. "I think you're pretty darn credible with the people who count."

"Thanks."

"I'll get your money back."

"I owe Lorne two hundred dollars."

"Why?"

"I borrowed a couple hundred from him about a month ago."

Mark grinned. "That was nice of him."

"Guess he didn't want me to go to Erna and tell her I was short."

"I don't know what makes people like Lorne O'Halloran tick. I have a psychology degree yet it only makes me more clueless about human nature."

"That's the impression I get about people with psych degrees."

"I guess I wanted to know what made *me* tick. Or what makes the world go around in general," Mark said.

"Typical." I finished my breakfast and drank the rest of my coffee.

"I was pretty young when I finished university," Mark said.

"A child prodigy, were you?"

"Something like that. I graduated from high school when I was sixteen, started university the next fall."

I made an 'o' with my pretty painted mouth. "So that would make you twenty when you finished your degree?"

"I got involved in the undergraduate party scene. Took two years to finish my first year," he said.

"Still. You went to police academy after that?"

"Traveled a bit. Went to Spain, the rest of Europe, backpacked in hostels with friends." His eyes grew dark. "Fell in with bad company but never got arrested. Had a clean record when I applied for police academy. Was lucky, they were looking for White Anglo-Saxon Protestants at the time, and I got in right away. Now if you're a minority or a woman you got more chance of getting in."

"I heard that."

"I like police work. I was on the beat in Edmonton for five years, then had a rock climbing accident and hurt my leg. I couldn't run anymore. You might notice I walk with a bit of a limp even now, especially when I'm tired."

I crumpled up my napkin and took the tray to the counter. Mark walked with me and ordered another coffee. "No, I hadn't noticed that," I said. "You want to stay here for a while longer?"

"Yeah, I'm enjoying our chat. I don't know a lot of people here in Serendipity. You're almost my only friend."

"I get the impression you're a bit of a loner anyhow." *I'm a loner myself. Maybe that's why I like you*, I thought.

We sat down again and got to talking about the case. It was good for both of us to do that, got the details sorted out in our heads a little better. I didn't have a lot of people to talk to, either, now that Lorne was in my bad books. I just didn't trust him. I thought he could have killed the mayor, and the thought of that fat badass private eye blowing the mayor's balls away the way someone did, well, it just sickened me and yet I could see Lorne doing something like that. I was ashamed to admit it, but I could see him enjoying it. I knew Lorne pretty well by now.

So I shared my suspicions with Mark.

"More suspicions?" he said. "We've got enough red herrings on this case to feed Norway."

"I know. But I think we should pay Mr. O'Halloran a visit tomorrow."

"Should we tell him we're coming?"

"Sure. Why not? I won't tell him I have a backup, though. I'd like to see what he's capable of if he thinks I'm vulnerable and alone."

"I'll stay in the outer office." Mark got out his iPhone. "I'm going to take a lot of pictures and record what I can hear from his office. That should intimidate him, if nothing else."

"Yeah, good idea," I said.

Mark peeled off four fifties from a roll in his wallet. "Give this to him," he said. "Take it from Erna. I'll put it on my expense account. I don't want you owing the son of a gun anything more than you do."

"More than I do?"

"For his supervision. He did you that favor, you got to admit it, Annie."

"I guess I'm an ungrateful witch. But Mrs. Hansen didn't raise no fool," I said.

"It seems to me that you and Lorne are quite symbiotic."

"What's that mean?"

"You depend on each other," Mark said.

"Co-dependent, you mean?"

"You, Annie? No. But life and people are more complicated, and more interesting, than you might have suspected. You got street smarts, I know that, I'm not saying you're not a very bright young lady."

"You got street smarts and a college education. You win." I smirked and took the cash. "Thanks."

"Give Lorne a call. We'll go pay him a visit in the morning."

"Okay." It didn't take long. I told him I was going to pay him back. In more ways than one.

The Valkyries had landed.

Chapter Sixty

Lorne O'Halloran, my erstwhile (what the heck does *erstwhile* mean?) supervisor and acquaintance of dubious lineage, sat like I'd shot him in his office on Port Street and stared at me from bulbous eyes. I'd just paid him back his cash and accused him of murder. Mark sat out in the anteroom, unknown to Lorne. I felt powerful and clever, and was enjoying the feeling as I sat in the office of my former associate and bully.

"I admit I needed the money," he said. "Gambling debts, we all know that. I'm not the only man in this town who needed money. Not the only man in this town who did drugs now and then." He took a deep breath. "You know too dang much about me, Annie."

"Was it coincidence that Doc was killed the same time the mayoralty race was on?" I asked, biting my nails. "Did you think the mayor was involved with Doc and the doctor would get the blame, or his killer? So you killed two birds with one stone, so to speak."

Lorne chuckled. "Who did it? Okay, I shot the sheriff but I did not shoot the deputy. You know that song?"

"I'm saying you could have shot the mayor but maybe you didn't kill the doctor. They could be two separate murders. We've been assuming they're by the same madman."

"I taught you well, little girl. Never assume. Makes an ass out of you and me."

"Somebody might have tried to make it appear that the same person who killed Doc Hubert shot the mayor. Modus operandi was different, only thing the same was the bizarre methods and the fact that they were close in time. Maybe we should start thinking out of the box. Lorne."

"I always think out of the box."

"When Doc was killed first, you had to act fast. Needed money for gambling debts, wanted to sell the drugs on the street in Campbell River but someone had got to Doc first. Doc was dead as a salt cod, his drugs and cash were gone when you got there."

"Got it all figured out, ain'tcha, Annie? If you're so smart, why are you confronting me and not telling this tall tale to your detective friend Mark Snow, or to the RCMP down at City Hall? It's because you're whistling through your teakettle, girl."

"Mark's right out there, Lorne."

"Is he now?" The private eye heaved his bulk out of his torn leather chair, opened the door a crack, and peered at the lone figure in his waiting room. He returned with a smile on his face.

"I'll be danged. Mark *is* out there, and he's taking pictures and apparently recording something."

"Nurse Molly likes to garden," I said.

"What you talking about?"

"Nothing. Just an observation."

"You're the strangest woman I ever did meet. I'm almost sorry I took you off the court's hands and gave you the education I did."

"I got my education long before I met you."

"Are you going to call that detective in here or do I have to do it?"

I took my feet off Lorne's desk and swung around in my roller chair. "Mark," I called. "Come here."

Lorne was a good four inches shorter than Mark. He stood up and stared at my friend, eyeball to chin.

"She tell you what she knows?" Mark asked. "We're here to arrest you, Mr. O'Halloran."

"'Course I'm not under arrest. That's the most ridiculous thing I ever heard."

"We thought we'd present you with the evidence, see where it takes us."

"It takes you nowhere, that's where." Lorne sat down again with a *huff*. He seemed out of breath. I sighed and my fingers flew in my pockets, counting the butts in Lorne's ashtray. There was a no smoking ban in this guy's office.

"Did you know she was gonna barge right in here to my office and accuse me of the mayor's murder? I should throw you both outa here right now."

"Not so fast, Lorne. You know what a fishing expedition is."

"Yeah, but I don't like it when it's me you're fishing for. I'm an innocent man, I'm bonded and everything."

"Got a gun and everything," I said. "And a license to kill."

"Where is that gun?" Mark asked. "The SIG Pro semi-automatic that killed the mayor?"

"Danged if I know," Lorne said. "I haven't seen it since last October when it went missing."

"A licensed firearm went missing six months ago and you didn't report it?"

"Never thought it was important until you mentioned it just now. Thought I'd just misplaced it. I always kept it in this here case in a locked drawer of my desk. It ain't here." He sounded pathetic, almost whining. The key creaked in the lock. He opened the case with a flourish, showing it was empty.

"We know where the gun is," Mark said. "It's with ballistics downtown in Victoria."

"Is this your usual method of ferreting out information?" Lorne asked. "Intimidating witnesses?"

"No." I winked at Mark. "We thought it would be a good idea after I told Mark how I confronted Samir."

"You're just too open and gullible to be counted on, girl," Lorne said. "You spill all the beans about everything and everybody. Don't know how I ever trusted you with one of my cases."

"I get the job done in my own inept and incomprehensible way," I said. "Even being as naive as you say I am. You have to admit that, Lorne."

"That's what Erna hired you for," Lorne agreed. "You're good on the streets, I'll give you that."

Mark smiled.

"You get anything out of Samir with the same tactics?"

"Nope."

"You won't get anything out of me, either. I admit I shot the sheriff but I didn't shoot the deputy, hee, hee."

"Don't get smart with us, Lorne."

"Oh, so now it's *us*, is it?" he said. "You and whose woman's army?"

"Sorry, a slip of the tongue."

"If you were a man I'd give you a fist right in your smooth, smiling little chops."

Mark shut off his cell phone, and stopped the recording. "Why don't you address *me*, bacon lips?" he asked.

"You're just a minion," Lorne snorted. "You got no mind of your own, Detective Snow, since you come here. Just snoopin' around and taking advantage of your position to throw up sand in all the wrong places. Obscuring evidence, that's you, and if you want to know who MS is, I'd say look no further. You got to the island just as Doc's blood was cooling and the mayor shot with a regulation gun, which you possess too, don't you?"

Mark shook his head. "You're a cool one," he said.

"Is that right, Mark?" I said. "Do you have a SIG Pro semi, too?"

"Old stock," Mark said. "I happen to have the new issue. But good try, liverwurst chin."

"Just trying to say," Lorne said. "I ain't the only one under suspicion here, and my initials aren't MS, and I'm not known as MASER or Samir, which that could easily stand for, turned around, and you know it very well, little girl."

"So you're denying you had the murder weapon in your possession?" Mark asked, sitting on a corner of Lorne's desk and swinging his shiny shoes.

"Dang rights I am. Never knew what it was knocked the mayor off, or where it was, or that my piece was really missing until now and not just misplaced. I don't carry firearms as a rule. Keep it all locked up legal like. Now I see it weren't ever here at all."

"Very convenient for you," Mark observed. "You're under arrest."

Lorne started to bellow and pounded his fists on the desk. "The citizens of Serendipity are after your cop's hide to get an arrest. This won't last any longer than booking me down at the station with the RCMP and letting me go for lack of evidence. You and Annie here are making a big mistake. A bigger mistake than your head is for allowing this to go on as long as it has, just to make you look good. So you got a suspect. You'll be sorry."

"I think I may be sorry," Mark agreed, bringing out the cuffs and snapping them behind Lorne's back. "But not as sorry as you'll be if you keep resisting arrest."

"What's the charge?" Lorne blustered, throwing his weight against Mark and almost knocking the big detective over.

"Predetermined murder in the first degree," Mark said.

"I'll be out before you turn around in the sergeant's cubicle," Lorne said. "You got the wrong guy."

Lorne was wrong about that. We never even got him down to the station to book him. Mark got a call from the Mounties as we were leaving.

The report on the poker had been faxed to the boys at City Hall. It had been wiped clean but they found Samir's thumbprint on one end. Now all we had to find was a piece of Doc's DNA. We had to let Lorne go because we had bigger fish to parboil at that moment than doing paperwork on a pathetic suspect like him. We had to find Samir, and my heart was somewhere down south in my shoes at the thought of it.

"You warned him off," Mark said. "Congratulations, Annie."

Did that make me an accomplice? I was afraid it did.

Chapter Sixty-one

I didn't mind when April twenty-seventh came around and it was a Saturday and my birthday and nobody remembered. I stirred the embers of the fire in the Franklin stove. I'd long since replaced the missing poker with a stick and then a wrought iron beauty. It seemed to me that Mark might come over later. I couldn't remember if I'd invited him. It wouldn't be like Annie Hansen to blow her own trumpet like that, inviting a friend on my birthday, but I wasn't myself lately, did a lot of things I never thought I'd do, and a lot of it had to do with stress. Or wanting things to be different than they'd always been.

Mom would be proud of me, not because of the stress, although she often said stress was good for her, it kept her on her toes. She'd be proud because now I'd accomplished something with my life, I'd confronted my demons and almost won. Erna Sobey was proud of me, too, I knew, there in the Justice Department in Victoria, hopefully working on a pardon for ol' Annie.

I thought now about what had happened that morning in November when Brent and Catherine Hoffman had seen Samir drop my old poker in the water. I sometimes heard a ruckus next door at the boat and peeked out the front door. It could have happened to me, too, if I'd had something in my hand. Easy to drop something in the space between the door jamb and the dock.

I thought I'd talk to Pepsi. I'd given him a call earlier in the morning. The description seemed to fit Pepsi more than Samir and the two of them were blood brothers, after all.

Up on the hill, near the parking lot, I could see the cherry blossoms, all pink and white and lovely. Spring was so pretty in this part of the world. Long before that, the hyacinths and crocuses had thrust their bright faces out of the mud. Thinking about Samir, I thought about a short story I'd read about a woman on death row, sentenced to death for the murder of her lover and his girlfriend. "To see the cherry hung with snow…" She could see a cherry tree from the bars of her cell. She was going to die. Did Doc Hubert know he was going to die when the murderer walked into his office at midnight on that Saturday in November?

My phone trilled *Dixie*. I looked at the call display. It was Pepsi, calling back. Don't say anything bad about the dead, I thought, thinking of the mayor and Doctor Hubert. They were dead. Good.

It could have been me, MS or Maser, standing at the counter in Doc's office and striking him again and again on the head, then drilling a couple holes the size of a ping pong ball in his skull and emptying his brains.

Was it me? There were things I didn't remember. It could have been me as well as my friend Samir. I had a clever little subconscious but no motive other than sheer contrariness. Was I capable of murder? It seemed to me that anyone could be capable of murder if pushed far enough. Had Samir been pushed to that extent? Was he after drugs to calm the constant pain in his leg?

I asked all these questions of Pepsi when he called.

Then I told him about the forensics lab and what they'd found with the poker, Samir's thumbprint and the rest wiped clean as though he'd tried to hide the evidence, otherwise why would he have bothered to wipe it clean? I told him about the Hoffmans seeing a black man drop the poker in the drink.

Pepsi surprised me with his answer. "My cuz didn't do it," he said. "I did."

"You did what? Wiped the poker clean or cleaned the Doc's clock?"

"Samir and I come out that day to the float house. You weren't there, Annie, but Samir and I got to talking and he seemed awful upset about something. Neither of us could get the fire going. Samir was banging that poker around the front of the stove, trying to poke some fire into the logs. I started thinking about somebody hitting ol' Doc over the head with a blunt instrument, and looked at Samir's cane. I thought he done it, Annie, I thought my cuz had drained ol' Doc of his brains and took the cash and the drugs. So I planned in my noodle head what to do to throw suspicion off him. He went to have a shower in the stinky ol' bathroom in the float house that morning, and I took the poker and wiped it clean, then looked out the window and saw the neighbors in the boat next door walking around their deck, lookin' over there, real nosy they are. So I opened the door and dropped the poker in the drink so they'd see me, throw suspicion off my cuz. I didn't know they'd think it was Samir. I was wearin' my Blue Jays hat and my drop waist jeans, Samir didn't look anything like me at all, I thought. I forgot what white folks think of us Africans, they think we all look alike. I made sure they seen me drop the poker. I thought it had been wiped clean, if anything, I thought my fingerprints might be on it, but I made sure I was wearing gloves. I didn't know I'd left Samir's thumbprint." He snuffled on the other end of the phone and coughed. I felt my breath catch in my throat with relief.

"I knew I had an alibi but I thought the cops were getting too suspicious of my cuz, and his only alibi was you, Annie, and I knew you weren't going to cover for him if it came to that."

"He stuffed his bed with pillows that night and was off drinking in the Serendipity Hotel with you, wasn't he, Pepsi?"

"Yeah, and it was raining. When he come back, his shoes was covered with mud. I figured he wouldn't get away with it."

"You didn't figure on my naivety."

"Neither one of us killed the Doc, I swear, Annie. We covered for each other that night, but we each split up before midnight and I went to work."

"Eddie covered for you."

"Yeah. Firewall Eddie wasn't there that night, you know. Am I in trouble, Annie?"

"Could be, Pepsi."

"I figured Samir had more to live for than I do, his parents might still be alive, he's got you, might get his legs fixed, has plans and if he did it, Annie, I wanted to get him off the hook."

"You didn't do it either, Pepsi."

"It don't look good for us, I know that."

There was silence on the line. Then I sighed. "I'll do what I can for you both, Pepsi. We'll need you to come in and make a statement."

"We're blood brothers, Samir and I. Two for one and one for all. The two musketeers. Where he goes I go."

"It doesn't look good that you tried to cover for him."

"I guess I made things worse."

"The Hoffmans will try to identify you from a police line-up."

"That's all right."

Mark? I need you. My friends are in trouble. Now I got to think things through. Pepsi tried to help his cousin and made things worse. An innocent man, or men, might go to jail.

"Sorry we took your poker, Annie. Sorry we went out to the float house when you weren't there."

"I told Samir he could come out any time. He needed to get away sometimes. Like I do, by myself, I don't mind that.You both knew where the key is. No problem."

"You're a good friend."

It was my birthday and nobody remembered.

"I'll go down to the station," Pepsi said.

I saw Mark through the small window at the side of the front door. He was carrying a large plastic bag that said, 'Support your local library' on the side. I was poking around with something in the oven, thinking of the Sudanese and their vulnerability. Mark pushed the door open and I turned around. He was carrying a huge bouquet of red roses. He placed them into my arms. "These are real, Missy Anne, they're not an illusion like the Scarlet Pimpernel."

Mark remembered. I put a rose into the buttonhole of Mark's suit jacket. He came in and sat in the wicker chair by the kitchen counter. I gave him scones, fresh out of the oven. They tasted like raspberry air freshener, but he enjoyed one, or that's what he said. Mark was a gentleman.

I put the roses in a large crystal vase my mother had left in the cupboard. I was twenty-five that day, April twenty-seventh, and Samir had turned twenty-two last winter. Mark was at least nine or ten years older than me, I figured. I wondered if my mother would have liked Mark. I thought she would.

"Pepsi called," I said.

"I know," he said. "I saw him down at the station."

"Do you think he was trying to protect Samir or trying to protect himself?"

"I'm thinking this is an awful convoluted case and I don't have a clue who the hell did it."

"You do."

"Yes. It was Samir and this clinches it. Even Pepsi thinks Samir is guilty, this proves it. We'll go pick him up tomorrow. I want to give him time to give himself up."

He's an aristocrat and so am I, I thought. I counted the roses (there were two dozen plus one) and spread butter on another scone.

Chapter Sixty-two

I found out the next morning, when Mark came calling at my float house before breakfast, that Samir was in a hospital in Vancouver getting his leg operated on. Pepsi had gone with him on the morning ferry after they got the call from the Civic Hospital. He'd seen the specialists in the clinic weeks before and they all agreed it could be done. I knew he was excited about the surgery to straighten his legs. They'd do the left one, the worst leg, first and then the right one was scheduled for surgery in six months when the left leg should have healed and be mobile with physiotherapy. That was the plan and I knew the plan. Just didn't expect him to be off the island right now with what seemed like a perfect excuse.

I didn't miss Vancouver. I knew I had to go see Samir though, and Mark and I, maybe Tom or the sergeant, would have to stand guard over the hospital bed until we could bring him back here under suspicion of the Doc's murder. I hated going to the mainland. I was an island girl at heart.

"Why don't you let me go?" Mark asked, always the gentleman. He acted like a cop around me a lot of the time, but would soften quickly when I got all vulnerable like.

"Samir's my friend," I said. "I think it's up to me to bring him back. He wouldn't make a lot of trouble if I were by myself there, guarding him in the hospital room, and then making sure he gets an escort back to the island."

"I disagree," Mark said. "He could be dangerous, and so could his cousin."

"I don't think he's trying to get away. He got a call, like he was expecting, and had to pack his bags in a hurry and leave. Pepsi went with him to give him a ride, because he and Samir are like two bean pods on a vine."

"He would have let you know, Annie, if he didn't have something to hide. I don't think he plans to come back."

"How long will he be in the hospital?"

"Less than a week, they said when I called this morning."

"He won't be able to walk," I said.

"No, he'll have a cast and crutches. Then later physiotherapy."

"How do you know so much about it, Mark?"

"I fell off a mountain ten years ago and broke my leg."

"Wow. I didn't know that."

"It still hurts sometimes when the weather changes."

"That's such a cliché. Tell me another one," I said.

He grinned and rubbed his thigh. "Really. I can't run like a cop. That's why I'm assigned to desk duty most of the time, I'm no good on the beat. Might have been the reason for my promotion. They promoted me beyond my level of capability. Murphy's Law."

I thought about that some. Mark was not the super cop I'd taken him for, he wasn't assigned to the case here because he was the Green Hornet or something. He was here because he couldn't *run* proper and therefore was useless as a cop on the beat or someone who caught active criminals.

"Wait a minute. That means you're here because of your brains. Right?"

Mark's mouth twitched. "I have a university degree," he admitted. "I use it to help me think."

"Psych," I said. "Do you know what I think of psych degrees? Dr. Blanche notwithstanding."

"I took criminology at the Police Academy. Forgive me?"

We were sitting in the sunlight on the settee, together on the orange and gold blanket, with mugs of steaming tea on the floor between us.

"How'd you find out Samir and Pepsi were out of town?"

"I went around to the Powolskis this morning and Meredith said they'd left early. She knew all about it. They'd taken the ferry, Samir packed his bag before they left, Pepsi took a leave of absence from his job in maintenance so he could be with Samir. It didn't seem to be any secret. I don't know why he didn't call you, though."

"I guess he was still mad at me for confronting him," I said.

"Oh, I suspect he's pretty deep when you get to know him." Mark traced a line of moisture down the side of his ceramic mug.

"What are we doing here? We're wasting time."

"Samir's in surgery this morning, the unit clerk said on the phone," Mark shared. "He isn't going anywhere. Constable Tom left a few hours ago to catch the *Island Queen* to the mainland. He'll be standing outside the OR with a gun in his holster."

"A SIG Pro?" I thought I was being clever.

"Nah. We're more modern than that. I carry the M&P40 semi-automatic pistol. We used to carry revolvers. Lorne has brainwashed you."

"He taught me all I know. Now he's under suspicion for a horrible murder. I feel like my guts dropped out of my skin."

"You figured it out."

"Sometimes I'm too damn smart," I said. But I didn't feel smart anymore. I didn't feel anything at all, except maybe depressed just sitting there, with Mark, talking about Samir and Lorne as though they were bugs on a griddle.

Chapter Sixty-three

The Attention Deficit Disorder Avon rep, Tess Russell, came by later that day with my coral lipstick and the blue nail polish. She bent to get through the door and stood there, looking awkward, with her stupid Avon bag in her hands and her order book all filled in from last time. I looked at it. Perfect. Amazing.

"Thanks," I said. "I'll give you a call. Busy now. Murders all over the island, it's all up to me and Mark."

"Really? I sure like that Detective Snow. He's real handsome, isn't he? Does that scooter outside belong to you? Oh look, the sun is shining and yesterday it rained." She was priceless. She was young, so that was some excuse for being scatterbrained. I knew ADD when I saw it, though. Sort of like me.

Except I'd learned to live with it. The Zyprexa took care of the voices and the Flupenthixol took care of the visions. Nothing could treat the OCD very well, but I didn't ruminate now the way I used to. That was an improvement, because nobody can work worth a squat if they're obsessing about something that can't be helped, maybe something that happened before, like Samir's past or when I first met him.

I remembered meeting Samir. Pepsi was there but it was Samir I noticed.

I always loved to teach, though I didn't think I was very good at it. It tickled something inside me though, to know about something, like a little precious stone I could hold next to my heart and warm, and then give away to somebody who might love it too, and need as much as I did. So when I came off the street when I was seventeen and my mom died, wasted away with stomach cancer, I lived at the float house for a couple of years and then decided to volunteer to teach. Tickled my fancy. That was before I come to the Powolskis through Social Services and the court system.

Between stealing cigarettes and booze, and living off the proceeds of fencing stolen property, I thought I'd like to volunteer with classes in English as a Second Language, or ESL for short. You know, teaching English to those immigrants unfortunate enough to end up with me as a teacher. Even in those days I wanted to make more of myself than I was.

One of those dudes I taught was a long lean drink of soda water from the Sudan. He sat in a group of tall, thin, good-looking Africans who all looked very handsome but just the same, to my eyes. To the eyes of the immigrant officials, too, presumably. Because practically all of this group had come into Canada on somebody else's passport and with somebody else's name.

They were quite mannerly on the surface but I felt them mocking me under their cool exteriors. Some of them went to a Christian church down the block. They all lived in the same area, in a sort of Sudanese ghetto just off Hoyt Street near the intersection of Port and Livingstone. They had quite a bit of money from the Immigration Department. They'd come here from Toronto where they'd learned some English, got their dental work done, got requisitions for furniture and apartments, and some of them sent money back home. They were all well dressed.

I noticed after a couple of weeks that one of the black dudes was different from the others. Whereas most of my students picked up the work rather quickly, they exploded into different directions when the bell rang for the end of class, and only a few of the women stuck around to collect the papers I'd marked at the beginning of class. The men worked in the lumber yard for the most part, prime source of employment here on the island. They'd be anxious to get home to their walk-up apartments and watch TV, drink a bottle of beer, play with their children.

Samir was different. He stuck around after class to collect his papers and asked questions if he didn't understand something I'd written or said in class. I was careful to be professional but gradually this quiet, crazy guy with a limp piqued my curiosity and I started spending more time with him after school finished at nine p.m. He seemed okay with that. Pepsi usually went directly to his job at City Hall and the medical building after class. I came to know, however, that Samir and Pepsi were connected at the hip, and I was careful to include Pepsi in any conversation I might have with Samir.

Even at that time, I was feeling an attraction for Samir that went beyond sympathy or even pity.

So when I got caught for the last time shoplifting and fencing stolen property, and was given a break with Lorne O'Halloran doing community work, I was forced to apply for Social Services benefits to keep me off the street and give me some income. Understand that the ESL teaching job was voluntary. Nobody would really *hire* somebody like Annie Hansen to teach their new citizens. I knew that and accepted it. When I went on Social Services benefits and was sentenced to two years' probation and community service work, I needed a safe place to stay as the court system didn't want me on my own. Not responsible, they said.

So they sent me to the Powolskis' and Samir was there, too. That made our living arrangements a bit iffy because there was only the one spare room upstairs. So we pretended we were married. Nobody really caught on. Except of course, the Powolskis guessed. But Samir and I worked it all out after class before we ever moved in together. Social Services hadn't figured out there was only the one room and the Powolskis never told them. They got paid for two rooms. There was two beds, which Samir and I didn't share.

So he limped and wanted to kill himself a lot when I first moved in. I like to think I trained him not to think that way anymore. He hasn't talked about killing himself since the cat ate the pretty bird that day before Thanksgiving when Samir left the cage open and blamed me.

Maybe that did something to his brain but he seemed to get a lot wilder after that, and a lot more outgoing. It might have been something to do with me moving out, or him getting settled into Canadian society and not being so homesick for his parents and friends, the Sudan and what had happened back there. He had no choice, of course. I knew he sent money back with the missionaries. Who knew if his parents ever got it? Some word always leaked out, though.

I felt secure in thinking that his parents were still alive. I didn't know what Samir thought, though. His touch was gentle, surprising in a man like that who often swore, took drugs, drank too much, and limped with a simple ferocious gait at my side to the ESL office until I had to quit and do community work instead.

We seemed to fit together like two spoons at first.

Something went wrong but we were too intertwined by that time to realize the other's manipulative behavior or the resentment that soured and bubbled below the surface.

Samir might have tried to make me believe I was crazier than I am, and he might have succeeded partially. He might have been manipulative but he'd learned it as a survival skill.

I forgave him for that. I hoped he'd get his leg fixed. I hoped he hadn't killed the doctor, but it didn't look promising for Samir right now. He'd turned twenty-two, and he'd already lived more than most people three times his age.

Our history bonded us. I felt like my intestines were being squeezed up my belly and out my throat when I thought about Samir in jail, or on death row if the death penalty came back to Canada.

Dr. Hubert, of course, was a hero in the media's eyes. Nobody else knew the truth. The mayor too, a hero in the eyes of everyone not connected with the island.

To me, the motive seemed thin; drugs and money, and why the horrid method of execution, but the story wasn't over yet.

I didn't believe Samir had done it.

I had no reason not to believe. I just didn't believe it and I think it was a very powerful wish, but it was more than that, it was a primeval and gut knowledge.

I thought I knew who murdered Doc Hubert and the mayor, but I'd have to prove it. My hands were already soiled with knowledge of evil beyond my twenty-five years. I felt that was a strength.

Chapter Sixty-four

I didn't know the day would end with another shooting, that Friday that I dropped into a yoga class at the community league where nurse Molly took karate. Good thing we don't know the future.

I had brought a couple cans of tomatoes and beans for the Food Bank and got in free. I had a reason for wanting to attend but most of it was because I thought it would be good for me to relax and stretch. Little did I know the yoga class was hatha yoga and taught by a wild and crazy student who didn't know the meaning of gentle stretch.

After an introduction to Sun Salutation and the camel, the child's pose, and the Warrior's pose and shoulder stand, we started the hard stuff. I found that the rest of the class had been attending since September the year before and were well versed in more advanced asanas.

I enjoyed stretching my limbs and the balance. I found at the end of it, when we lay flat on our backs in the Dead pose and listen to the singing bowls and the student chanting, that I felt more energized than I had for months. I was interested to note that I enjoyed the physical stress and the visualization that came at the end in the lotus pose like sentient pretzels.

I made a new friend, the girl next to me who stretched like a lioness and helped me with my balance when the student teacher wasn't looking. It was all very nonjudgmental and supportive.

Covered with a cotton blanket, I lay still in the Dead pose as the student teacher played the singing bowls. *Namaste*, I repeated after her and bowed, then gathered up the borrowed yoga mat, blanket, and rolls, and stashed them in the closet at the side of the large room. The teacher stayed after class, answering questions, but I was too shy to approach her. Not now. Maybe next week. I vowed to myself to come back the next week, and maybe bring some better food now that I knew it was worth the small price of admission.

I stopped at the desk outside the room and signed up for more classes: a karate class on Tuesday evenings for the cost of a large latte, and indicated my willingness to learn meditation with Serena before yoga classes next Friday. The classes were mud cheap because they were subsidized by the community league. As a recipient of a disability pension, I got a free pass to most of them.

I was very happy and relaxed when I started my Vespa scooter and put-putted back home that afternoon. Life could only get better.

That's why I was totally blown away to Oz when I saw who was standing on the dock outside my float house waiting for me to come home. The skin on the back of my neck began to prickle and fear crawled between my shoulder blades. Anyone who could blow away the mayor's balls at six o'clock at night in his own office, well, anyone who could do that or suspected of doing that wasn't my cup of mocha right then. I might need that karate course, but I didn't even have my white belt yet and this man had a revolver in his hand.

I was out of my depth and I knew it. Mark wasn't in the next office waiting for me to call out that I was in trouble. Samir was flat on his back in Vancouver Civic Hospital and Constable Tom was standing guard outside his room. My heroes had deserted me. I had to be my own hero.

I saw Lorne O'Halloran standing on the slippery grey boards of the dock outside my float house. He staggered a little and gulped from a flask he'd taken out of his jacket.

I didn't have to hear the click of his revolver to know that it was loaded and pointing at me. He'd obviously replaced his missing weapon. Lorne was big, drunk, mad, and tough. So I kicked the accelerator on my scooter and roared out of the parking lot.

"Come back here, you bitch!" he blustered. I floored it.

I was going for help. Discretion is the better part of valor, mom had always said.

Bam! A bullet whined near my back tire. *Bam! Bam!* The next bullet flattened the tire. I skidded out of control and scraped my leg along the gritty asphalt. Sparks flew as the Vespa screeched along the pavement and came to a smoking halt at the edge of the road.

"You've done it now, Lorne O'Halloran!" I shouted. *One should never mess with a Valkyrie.* "You're burnt cheese toast at the end of the line in the soup kitchen. You're dead animal meat hung up to rot. I'll stand up in court and see your sorry flesh putrefy in jail for the next hundred years." *That is, if you can get out of this alive.* SHUT UP, VOICES.

Chapter Sixty-five

I heard Lorne laugh and feet scrabbled on rocks up the trail to the parking lot. The edges of my vision glowed and the sun came up in the west just before a flock of blue dodo birds escorted my former supervisor to the top of the hill. I had to think fast. The next Flupenthixol shot was due. My Zyprexa was back in the kitchen cupboard. My stress level was over the top of the mountain. My brain was full of shredded confetti like in New York on St. Patrick's Day.

St. Patrick's Day. The Irish and their pride and booze, and this man's name was O'Halloran. This was May, not March seventeeth, and the cherry trees were in blossom. But I had to confuse him. 'To see the cherry hung with snow.'

"Up the Irish!" I shouted and lifted an arm in greeting. He hesitated, gun in hand.

"Buy you a drink?" I asked and stumbled to my feet. Lorne looked puzzled. The Vespa lay smoking, dead on the tarmac.

"Ever see the sequel to *Gone with the Wind*? It's called *Scarlett*. Excellent movie but the critics panned it. What do they know, eh, Lorne? It was set in Ireland, beautiful green land of shamrocks and faery people. You know the faery people? There's gold at the end of the rainbow. Let's talk, big fellow."

"Talk?" He stumbled and almost dropped the gun.

"Yeah, no harm done or offered."

"I think I might have a drinking problem," he mumbled. *Yeah, I'd always thought so.* He shoved the gun into his pants pocket. "I'm sorry I shot at you."

"You did," I said. I wiped my hands on my khaki pants. My brown plaid shirt was ripped.

"I got tired of drinking coffee," he said. "Alone."

"You had a slip. No big deal." My hands were sweaty and covered with dirt.

He dropped to his knees and covered his face with his beefy hands. "I didn't do it," he sobbed. "I didn't kill the mayor."

"I know," I said. "We won't mention this little incident. You just go home and get cleaned up."

"You know?" He peered at me through his interlaced fingers. "But I thought… you and the detective… the arrest."

"We were bluffing."

"You can't bluff like that. It isn't right."

"I know. I'm sorry. We all make mistakes."

"Have you got it figured out yet?"

"I need your help, Lorne. First sober up, get some hot coffee in your belly so you're a wide awake drunk." I smiled. He would pay. He would pay big time. First I had to disarm the son of a beaver bitch.

A silver SUV whirled around the bend in the road going down to the marina. Mark. Never was so glad to see a cop of any complexion in my life. Crumb, my leg burned. I had major road rash all the way up to my thigh. I hated myself for being a weak sister, but I sort of collapsed in Mark's arms when he opened the car door.

"What's this?" he said.

I noticed the cut-off rose in his buttonhole. I noticed the yellow halo around the sun rising in the west. I noticed Lorne reach for his revolver in slow motion.

Mark shot him. I heard Lorne scream. *There you've done it, stupid,* roared the voices.

Chapter Sixty-six

What I heard from Sergeant Ross, who got the message from Constable Tom, was that Samir cooperated fully. "So did Pepsi, to his credit," the sergeant said. "Samir's surgery went very well. He's resting with his leg in a cast. The hospital put him in a private locked room and Tom's outside."

"The constable took Pepsi's and Samir's statements and got them sworn to on an affidavit by a Notary Public. Both statements were consistent."

"Good," I mumbled. *Goody two shoes*, whispered the Screamer, not screaming now.

I remembered the muddy shoes in the morning and how Samir had showered first thing, that morning we found out the Doc was killed. Pepsi and Samir had parted ways before midnight so Pepsi could go to work. That gave Samir the time and opportunity to do the deed and get home, sneak into bed before I woke up. "Putting pillows into a bed to make it look slept in is the oldest trick in the schoolboy's box of tricks. I fell for it," I said. "We had a curfew at the Powolskis and he knew it. It didn't look good for Samir. Hence he tried to cover it up."

"Looks that way," the sergeant said. "Anyway, you're cleared, Annie."

I wondered if the police had been around to question Meredith and Henry Powolski. What they thought about it all. I guess if they opened up their house to cons and crazies they should expect some police activity and questions about their residents. I wondered if Meredith was expecting Pepsi and Samir to come back. Of course they would. There was no place else to go that they could afford. And they loved it there. Mrs. P treated them real good.

I got a prescription for my meds and had them filled at a local pharmacy.

"You'll give me the injections here at the pharmacy? Just call Dr. Blanche. He's set it all up there in Campbell River, too far for me to travel every two or three weeks for a shot."

"That's fine," the pharmacist said. "We do it all the time. We know Dr. Blanche. I'll give him a call."

"I'm not supposed to leave the Island."

"No one can leave the Island. These are bad times." The pharmacist began some paperwork, at the back where I couldn't see.

"I can see Dr. Blanche when I need him." I hoped that wouldn't be often. Intent on his paperwork, the pharmacist smiled, dismissing me.

It took a few days to fix my scooter almost good as new. After that, it wobbled a bit though, and I had to be real careful. Probably shouldn't have been driving the thing after Lorne shot the back tire out and it skidded on the gravel. Oh well, my Vespa and me were a fixture on the island and everyone knew it. So I got it repaired.

A week later, I went down to the landing at Modge Bay and welcomed Samir and Pepsi home. They were escorted by Constable Tom, but not in handcuffs, to Tom's credit. The RCMP and the sergeant met them at the pier, too, as the ferry chugged in, spilling water from its engines and maneuvering into the dock. Mark was on board as someone who'd met them at the mainland off the *Island Queen*.

Mark was on supervision for firing his police gun but hadn't been given a leave of absence. He'd seen a counselor a couple of times. I didn't detect any guilt or regret for firing at Lorne. It was clearly self-defense and I was a witness.

"Poor Lorne," I said to Mark as we walked to the police paddy wagon. "He has a broken shoulder, bullet went clear through the bone, but other than that he's physically all right except for the drinking problem. I saw him down at a twelve-step meeting a few times."

"Almost anyone would do anything, if full of too much booze, especially an alcoholic like Lorne with a bad history," I continued, trying to match pace with Mark, my hero.

"I found out that Lorne came from a military background too, and was dishonorably discharged for assaulting a superior officer," Mark said. "Funny how those pseudo-cop occupations find the right people."

"Or the wrong ones," I said. Mark pushed Samir and Pepsi into the back of the police van and locked the door. "Will Samir be all right?"

"He manages with crutches. I'm surprised how far he's come since the operation. His surgeon is a genius."

"They won't keep him long, will they?"

"They might transfer them to Victoria. I don't know. They'll face the circuit court judge in the morning."

"Lorne's on probation for drawing a firearm against a police officer. He's lucky that's the only charge."

I didn't say anything about shooting at me. I tried to protect Lorne, the gods only knew why, I guess it was old habit. He'd been like a father to me at one time. I was confused about my feelings for authority figures. I generally got along all right with them. Except for when I was twelve and set fire to the living room drapes to demonstrate my rage and frustration with authority at home. *No wonder your father doesn't trust you.*

Behind my back, I counted the vertical stripes on Mark's shirt.

Chapter Sixty-seven

Samir and Pepsi were released the same day, after a closed-circuit TV appearance with a Justice of the Peace. They were warned to stay in Serendipity but other than that, they were free to go.

"Guess the evidence wasn't overwhelming," I said as Mark frowned and drummed his fingers on my kitchen table. The laptop was streaming music but not very loud.

I found out later that Mark had interceded for the pair. Odd, since he'd been convinced of Samir's guilt all along.

"He's not going anywhere," Mark said. "Guy's just out of the hospital and major surgery, he should be at home recuperating."

"Nice of you," I said. "Changed your mind about him?"

"I think too much evidence is stacked against other players in this melodrama."

"Like Lorne O'Halloran?"

"Like that."

"Ever watch Sergeant Preston of the Yukon?"

"Loved it," he said.

"Well, King, this case is closed." He put an arm around my shoulders. I melted a little inside but shrugged his hand off my bones. "It isn't, though," I said.

"I think it's looking pretty clear. It's either Lorne or Samir."

"Not necessarily."

"Why are you protecting them?" Pink was singing *Goin' to California*.

"I don't think either one of them did it," I said.

"You changed your mind about Lorne?"

"Yes, I can change my mind. I'm figuring things out, and Lorne didn't do it. He's a mess, but he didn't blow away the mayor. He couldn't plan something like that, doesn't have the brains or the guts without alcohol, and he wasn't drinking at that time."

"I believe Lorne's gun is in Victoria now," Mark said. "The one he pulled on us in the parking lot. I got a question."

"What?"

"Are you off this case or not?"

"I talked to Erna about that yesterday. She says it was Lorne took me off the case, and she's put me back, with retroactive pay."

"Is that a good thing?"

"Yes, Martha Stewart."

"What about the stress? Are your drugs handling it?"

"My meds are fine. No more visions, no more voices." I lied again. *Nobody has to know.*

"I didn't know about that," Mark said.

"What? The hallucinations or the obsessions?"

"It must have been hard to work with all those problems," he said. "I can't imagine that myself. You're a strong woman."

"We're all strong, all us crazy people. Can you imagine how much willpower it takes to get up every morning and face the day when your meds make you feel like crap and you can't get your head off the pillow in the morning because you're drugged out of your mind? To go to work like that, to talk to friends and employers when your voices are screaming and whispering evil intentions on the part of everyone you trust or should trust? To pretend everything's all right when snakes are coming out of the TV screen?"

"I can't imagine," he said.

"Every med has side effects and the psychotropic meds are amongst the worst. Sedation is only the tip of the Titanic. I used to fall asleep on picnic tables. But the worst is the stigma. The worst is the general public's fear and the suspicions of wrongdoing when you're not doing anything wrong, if anything goes wrong and there's a mentally ill person nearby, guess who gets the blame? Guess who gets investigated? Guess the nasty innuendos and the snubs? My dad thinks I have a weak mind. My mom knew better, bless her heart, but my dad wanted to take me right out of the will. My relatives all thought I was stupid not mentally ill, they don't know the difference. Guess who's stupid? They are."

"Yes," he said and put his arm back around my shoulders. This time I let it stay for a few minutes before shrugging off his touch. I felt a pang in my guts and my bowels started to let loose.

"I think you're upset," he said.

"That's a problem?" I asked and grinned. "I *should* be upset. There would be a problem if I wasn't."

"You're right. You should be upset. Prejudice of any kind isn't right."

"You're right, Mark." I felt tired all of a sudden, so weary, so tired of all the fighting and the posturing and the staying strong because there was no choice, it was either that or die.

"Some of us kill ourselves," I said.

"Why?"

"We can't face it anymore."

"You are strong and courageous people. Misunderstood."

"I'm not keeping the truth secret."

"Good for you." Mark tapped his feet to music spilling from the stereo speakers.

"Want to get away?" he continued. "I've been thinking, after this is over..."

"No," I said. "You just feel sorry for me."

"I don't," Mark's breath was warm and very close to my face. I could feel the exhalation of air stir the fine hairs lying across my forehead. "I..."

"What?"

He didn't say it. I was glad he didn't say the word I'd been afraid of all my life. No wonder I never felt safe. There were too many jerks out there using the wrong words to get their own way, and too many saps who believed them. Was I a sap?

Oh, yes. Little stabs of excitement bucketed through my viscera, my guts, my belly, my chest, my brain, where it all begins.

I reached out and stroked the smooth contour of Mark's face. That took a lot of guts but I couldn't stop once I'd started. My fingers traced the outline of his thick broad eyebrows, his brow, his fine nose and... his mouth.

His lips brushed mine. Soft like summer sunshine on a basking hill open to the thrill of exploration. I felt the tip of his tongue and drew back.

"Too soon." He put his face in his hands.

"I'm sorry," I said. "I think you should go."

Pink sang *Lonely Girl.*

Chapter Sixty-eight

Boy, that Samir looked handsome sprawled in my armchair by the stereo. Even his cast and the crutches he'd used to get here looked sexy to me. I liked him vulnerable. I wondered how it would be to crawl into bed with a man with a cast, if there were any complications and who would be on top? I couldn't imagine he would. That was an interesting premise. The guy who always had to be in control. The irresistible force against the immovable object. I smiled to myself at the image of the two-backed beast with a stump.

Memories of Mark two days ago surfaced, his lips brushing mine, his tongue searching my mouth. I felt like a whore looking at Samir the way I did now. If Amy Winehouse sang *Back to Black* that would have been perfect, but instead there was the two of us chatting in my little rooms. The judge had let Samir and Pepsi go on their own recognizance, meant there was a bond but they didn't have to pay anything unless they broke their probation. Meaning unless they left the island or did something else illegal. Like drugs, maybe. I pulled on my lower lip and frowned.

"Cute, honey," my man said, long legs stretched out in front of him. My dark hair was growing out to take the place of the golden brown that had covered up my roots. I'd hacked most of the dark off. "I like your new hairdo."

"How do you know about women's hair?" I asked. It was too short now to tie into a pony tail. The pony tail had shown me what it would look like short in front and on the sides, though, and I was pleased with the pixie cut I'd managed. True, the two colors looked like low lighting, darker throughout the ends. It had grown out fairly nice, and I'd managed to arrange it so you didn't really see the roots. It was almost all blonde now, like it had been when my dad tousled my head and left.

"Got a white friend who does that with his hair," Samir said. "You women aren't the only ones vain."

"Vain, am I?" I took a wisp of hair and pulled it over my forehead. I pranced in front of him and threw my arms back, singing *Wannabe*. "I'm a Spice girl."

"You're a nice girl," he said.

I sobered. "No, I'm not."

Samir smiled and tucked his yellow shirt into his indigo sand-wash Pelle Pelle jeans that had cost him forty dollars at the thrift store. "I know about you and the detective."

"What about me and Mark?" I threw one arm across my eyes in a seductive gesture and wriggled my hips.

"This is so unlike you," he said. "The bastard is changing my funky street girl into a ho."

"I'll show you who's a ho."

He put out his arms and grinned. "Show me then."

"Doesn't it bother you or don't you care that you're not my main squeeze anymore?"

"I think I am."

I moved across the room to the bay windows and looked out at the boat and the inlet. I was pretty sure I saw a dolphin out there. I knew I saw my neighbors peering back from behind the drapes on the *Catherine*. Maybe they were looking at the dolphin, too. Or maybe they were looking at me looking at them...

"Pretty sure of yourself, aren't you? Would it surprise you to know that I've never even kissed Mark back?"

"Would surprise me if you had, Angel pie. You got the best. When you got the best you don't want second best."

"Oh. My. Gosh. How arrogant can you get?"

He smirked.

"Pepsi should be coming back soon. You're lucky to have a cousin who'll give you a ride anywhere, help you down the slopes, and pick you up again. I don't know if you know how lucky you are to have him. What he'd do for you."

Made me think of the case again and I didn't want to think about work. I didn't want to think about Mark and his suspicions. I just wanted to be with Samir and get caught up on our news or lack of it. I didn't even know what made me think of Pepsi just now. Except he was up to his black neck in alligators.

"I know my blood bro is a good man. He's got my back."

"You're right about that. He'd lie for you."

"He'd lie for anybody." Samir threw his head back and chortled. "What you getting at, Angel pie? Pepsi do something he shouldn't?"

"I don't know."

Samir reached for my hand where I stood at the window. He was too far to grasp it. "Come here."

"Are you Maser?" I asked. "Are you MS? I know your real name. I know you used somebody else's passport to escape from the refugee camp. Is that your real name or are you a mystery wrapped in an enigma?"

"What that mean, a nigga?"

"No, no. Enigma. It's a word my mom used a lot. She was always talking about other people's secrets and the mystery of other people's thoughts. My mother was a writer and an artist. She was a genius."

"I don't think so. She was your mother."

"You never met her. She helped my father so much. I don't know how he could have left her."

"I saw his Dutch girlfriend. I think I can understand." Samir tried to lurch to his feet after me. I ducked into the corner behind the stove and laughed at him, but this wasn't funny, so I stopped laughing and hit him on the leg. I took his crutches. He was helpless. I waved a crutch at him.

"Can't catch me, slow foot. Let's see you fall down."

"My cousin will be here soon to take me home. He'll slap you acrost the face, loony tunes."

I gave him back his crutches. "I'd like to see him try. You stop talking about my parents like that."

Samir smacked my butt with a free hand.

"Cripe," I said. "Your leg hurt?"

"The other leg hurts. Not this one. This one's itchy, though. Doctor gave me a scratcher to fit inside the cast."

"Do you put powder in there?"

"Nope. Not supposed to put anything down the leg, not even itch powder. It don't hurt near as much as before they broke it and set it again. Maybe all the narcotics help." He rolled his eyes and grinned. I laughed, dancing away from him.

"I'm so glad you're going to have a normal leg, Samir."

"I'm glad too, but it isn't normal yet. It will be, though, and then I can go back to jail, I suppose."

"No, I don't think so. I don't think they released you because you're just out of surgery. It might have helped, though."

"Your friend Mark stepped in to support us. He said he'd vouch for our honesty that we'd stay on the island. Now why you suppose he did that?"

Why indeed? I chewed on my nails and thought hard. All I could figure was Mark was giving them enough rope to tie themselves in a hangman's noose.

Mark was smart. He thought Samir and Pepsi murdered the Doc but he didn't have enough proof to make it stick to the wall. I was sure some plainclothesman would be following my Sudanese friends. I should warn them but something kept me quiet, something like loyalty to my job, which had been reinstated, and I wanted to respect Erna's confidence in me.

I wasn't sure that Samir hadn't done it. But I wasn't sure he had, either.

One way or the other, I'd find out. I was sure of that.

Chapter Sixty-nine

I missed the Red Ox Inn but decided Mark didn't think I was worth it, what with me being friends with Samir and all. Samir could be thought of as his rival. Ha. Me, Annie Hansen, with two fellows after her, oh, it was rich, but I dared not gloat because it could all go up in flames at any time.

I hadn't actually slept with Samir so I thought I wasn't really a whore to kiss Mark, and I hadn't actually kissed Mark back, so I wasn't a whore to hug Samir. That was all mind games, I knew, and when I sat in the Serendipity Hotel with Samir on that Wednesday after I got my injection in the pharmacy, I knew I would have to make a decision. I wasn't very good at making decisions.

What was really interesting, we were sitting there, me and Samir, with Pepsi in a corner spooning ice cream into his maw with his left hand and drinking beer, and nurse Molly walked in. She seemed to be unhappy and I mentioned that to Samir.

"She wants to get off the island," he said. "Too bad none of us can leave except you and me, Annie, we seem to get to Campbell River often enough."

"We got medical reasons," I said and sipped the pretty bad coffee they served in the hotel. "I don't like going to Campbell River at any time, and so now I don't have to except to see my psych now and then. Every four or five months, that's all, now the drugstore here looks after my prescriptions and shots."

"Yeah, the druggists are getting like real doctors, and they know a lot more about the drugs than the doctors do." Samir had a new walking cast and seemed more comfortable now than when he first had the surgery. I got to thinking this would really fix him up to be a real attractive fellow, so I wouldn't have to feel guilty for maybe leaving him. Then I thought, if he's that attractive, why do you want to leave him, Annie? I grinned.

"Whatcha smiling about, Angel?"

"Just thinking about you and me," I said. "How we been together for more than a year now, and nothing's really changed between us. We're still pals even though a lot of wine has gone under the viaduct."

"What's a viaduct?"

"Something like saying a lot of water has gone under the bridge, but I don't like clichés," I said. "A viaduct is a Roman sort of bridge, I think, made to transport clean water to a city."

"Oh, I see, some more of your fancy history."

Nurse Molly sat by herself in a corner and I noticed she ordered one of them fancy drinks the hotel doesn't really know how to make proper. She should be drinking at the Red Ox Inn with the rest of the fancy folk. Maybe she can't afford it now she don't have a proper job. I stood up and walked over to her table.

"Mind if I join you?" I said and set down my coffee cup. She looked surprised and a bit pleased, so I sat. Samir sipped his beer and stared at us in a baleful fashion. That was a good word. Baleful. I'd have to look it up. It seemed to suit my fellow at the moment, though. He was staring at us. Ha.

"No, I don't mind," Molly said. She grimaced a bit when she moved over and I questioned her if her back hurt.

"My back always hurts," she said. "I have a degenerated disc. Nothing really helps. Doc used to give me something for it. I haven't found anything that relieves the pressure for long, though."

"That's too bad," I said. "Have you had that for long?"

"Ever since my early teens," she said, stirring her drink. I looked closer. It seemed to be a Mai Tai without the little umbrella. I knew a bit about fancy drinks. My mom had liked them. I liked them too much, that's why I didn't drink anymore. Spent the first three years at a twelve-step meeting then weaned myself off the meetings, too. Now I was Annie the free, not a freeloader but free. Annie off the street and onto main street, who would have thought it? My mom should see me now. I thought I should look more serious at someone who confessed to chronic pain, so I frowned.

"That's a long time to have a bad back. Anything the doctors can do for it?" I asked. She looked pained in more ways than one.

"I'm hoping to have surgery at the Vancouver Orthopedic Centre, the best place I can imagine to go if one wishes to have surgery. I'm not sure about that, though. Dr Hubert didn't believe in back surgery. I have to do something, though."

"Yes, I don't know anybody who's had back surgery that was successful," I said. "Maybe you shouldn't do it."

"I know. I just don't know what to do. I really have no one to talk to about it."

"Your doctor?"

"I can't leave the island, you know, right now."

"That's right. Neither can I."

"None of us can."

"It'll be over soon," I said.

She nodded and grinned, and I wondered what was so funny.

Chapter Seventy

Tess Russell arrived on the float house later that day with a new Avon catalogue and some gossip, which I welcomed, because I wasn't really privy to women's gossip very much. I usually missed out on local juicy news that everyone else seemed to know. Nothing important but it was good to be in the loop.

Mark had been seen drinking alone at the Red Ox Inn. A certain older woman had been seen to join him. Nobody I knew, but her name was Olivia and she was a nurse down at the clinic in Campbell River, commuted every morning and afternoon on the ferry because she loved it there on the island.

Firewall Eddie was back at work and sober again. He was missing his gun and they wouldn't issue him another one. Probably lost it in a poker match.

Speaking of poker matches, my old boss, Lorne O'Halloran, was rumored to be in bad financial trouble, he'd had no clients since the mayor was blown away, because he'd run for mayor and lost for the second time. That had about finished Lorne in this town. He was under a dark cloud of suspicion for blowing away Mayor Spacey. Nobody could prove it, not even Mark and I, though we'd tried, but word got out that Lorne was suspected, and City Hall wasn't giving him any more jobs.

Poor Lorne. He tried to make it up in poker matches and at the casino, lost heavily, was rumored to spend his days and nights sitting in his office drinking rum and placing bets long distance to New York online.

"Any *good* news, Tess?" I asked finally, and ordered a set of colored graters for my kitchen. They could hang on the wall or I could pop them into a drawer where they'd be real handy next time I had to shred something like cheese or carrots. I knew just the casserole that would come in handy for, and I hated shredding with my little square metal grater. Always took a part of my fingers off with it.

"I love Avon," I said, and she took down the order then tapped my hand.

"Thank you, hun. You're my best customer. So glad we met. You know Mark, don't you? What do you think about Olivia? Is that a match or not?"

"I don't know," I said. "I don't know Olivia. Isn't she a bit old for him?"

"Oh, he has to be in his mid-thirties," Tess said, perusing the catalogue. "Oh, look, here's a new lipstick, Annie. Interested? How do you like the blue nail polish? I never see you wear it. No, I don't think Mark and Olivia are a couple, they're just interested in the same thing, like why Doc hired somebody who'd change her name and not be able to work in the OR anymore."

"Why's that?"

"Molly has real bad back trouble. Result of a bad car crash when she was fourteen."

"Why would Mark be interested in Molly?"

"Wink, wink, nudge, nudge," Tess said with cheer, flipping the pages. "They've been seen together before."

"I hadn't noticed," I said, then thought, oh yes, the night I ran into Mark and Molly at the Red Ox Inn. But she hadn't looked happy, and neither had he.

"Wink, wink, nudge, nudge," Tess repeated. I hated her.

Chapter Seventy-one

My mother often used old aboriginal or Irish sayings she'd heard from her grandmother, who'd raised her, and I still thought in those terms sometimes, like she did. It was kind of the mother's curse that her daughter would grow up to be just like her. I didn't grow up like that exactly, but as I looked in the mirror today at my nose and mouth (but not my beautiful violet eyes, thank golly), I thought, Mom! and then realized what daughters the world over had always known, we are our mothers. Damn.

I knew I had mother issues big time, but she had died so young and I was only seventeen and out on the street for most of my adolescence, missed a normal growing up with innocent dates, a sixteenth birthday party and so on. My mom had missed that about having a daughter, too, a daughter she could teach to put on makeup (I still didn't know how), a daughter she could teach to cook (though I'd learned pretty well from her books and natural talent), and a daughter she could teach about men and sex, and so on. I'd found those things out pretty much on my own, too, and not having close women friends to rely on either, for information and whispered secrets and gossip, and stuff like other girls did. Right now I had Tess and the yoga teacher down at the community center who sort of took me under her feathers.

Yoga was fun but I was a little disappointed in karate lessons on Tuesday nights. You do get what you pay for, I thought, and I didn't pay anything for those. But I wanted to get a brown belt so bad, a black belt, actually, or any belt above a white, which was rank beginners and which I was told I would have for the next few months, even with hard work.

We spent most of the evening in groups moving around doing moves which I didn't understand. The rest of the students said they would come to me eventually and I'd have to be there for a few months before it made sense. It seemed to me, though, there should be a better way of teaching self-defense. This course was the only game in town, though. I couldn't find anything else here except maybe in Campbell River, and I really shouldn't leave the island.

Technically, I was still a suspect.

So I went through the little dance the karate instructor taught, and learned a bit of Japanese so I could say hello and thank you and what passed for see you next time, I honor you or whatever. I bowed to the instructor and shook hands with the rest of the students when class was over. I was pretty dutiful but two months went by and I hadn't learned any self-defense and I was no more fit than when I started, except for the yoga, which I enjoyed. The yoga did seem to make me more flexible and my balance was better. I was only twenty-five, after all, not an old woman. But I'd been what they called deconditioned for most of my life and that really means I was out of shape and overweight.

I'd lost another few pounds this month. Was looking pretty good.

"Tess," I said, next time I saw my Avon pal. "I notice you sell a lot of clothes and shoes and stuff from the Avon catalogue. Anything that would fit me, do you think?"

"What do you have in mind, Annie?" she asked, turning the pages. "Although, I'd recommend Thrift Village for someone on a budget."

"Just thought I might get something more up-to-date," I said, peering at the pretty bright pictures. "Something orange or pink, or blocked colors like I've been hearing about. Or new shoes."

"You can't afford them," she chided me, and I knew she was probably right, but I was back at work and Erna had given me a raise and back pay for what Lorne had cheated me out of. So I was feeling pretty flush.

"What do you think your fellow would like?" she asked. "You know, that tall black man I've seen you with."

"Oh, you sell stuff for men?"

"I didn't mean that exactly, I meant what do you think he would like on *you*. But yes, we sell men's tees and aftershave and stuff. Say, it's almost summer. What do you think you'd like to do with your holidays?"

"Here, look at this," she continued. "This even has soap on a rope."

"He might like that." I plugged in the kettle and took out two bags of berry tea. "Want some tea, Tess?"

"Sure. I like herbal stuff. Here, this is something that would look good on him." She pointed out a pair of football pajama bottoms. "Everyone in the city's wearing pajamas on the street. Really, he'd like these."

"Oh, I don't think so. We're not at the point where we buy each other gifts."

"Why not, for heaven's sake? Take a leap, girlfriend, get him something...oh, I know! You're holding out for Mark."

I felt myself blush, a warmth that crept up my neck to the top of my ears. She had sort of got too close to the truth. But Mark and I weren't in a relationship either, exactly, and I didn't want to appear brazen and get him a gift. Come to think of it, I didn't know when his birthday was. Samir's birthday had come and gone this winter in December, I thought it was, but I'd missed that, too. He was going to be twenty-three this coming winter, we'd have a big celebration then. The flush continued up to my forehead and I felt myself grow warmer.

Annie with emotions, and thinking about other people? Tess and I sipped our tea.

It was good to have friends.

Chapter Seventy-two

I lay in bed, upstairs in my float house, after climbing the ladder to the bed-rooms, and watched the light sweep across the little window and then out to sea. Every now and then the foghorn would call me to the music of its mourning.

I pushed back the lovely white heavy duvet from my shoulders and tiptoed to the window, looking out at the waning moon and the Modge Bay lighthouse sweep-sweeping its lamps over the ocean, warning the ships off the bar. There was a tall ship I'd been told about that had steered too close to the shore and was wrecked with all hands on board lost, this was back in the 1800s before the lighthouse was erected.

Sad, the tales of the ocean, but brave and strong the sailors who loved it. My paternal grandfather had been one, a sailor from Denmark, a modern Viking who had not touched my stiff and formal father with his magic. The rocks had claimed him before my father was born, but he'd left his family with money and a will to succeed. My father had passed a bar of his own, in a manner of speaking, twenty-four years after my grandfather drowned in the Georgian Bay.

I wondered if I had some of the young sailor's spirit as well as his blood. More so perhaps than the Irish aboriginal blood from my mother, although my mother had touched my mind and heart more in life than my father's family.

I opened the window on its creaking hinges from the top, and leaned out to study the burned remains of the old shack by the lighthouse. The four men had been reprimanded and fined, but let free the next day. I missed the shack and wondered where the homeless now went to keep warm, from Hoyt Street near Port, and whether anyone would think to clear away the rubbish and charred logs. The shack had burned down the night that Samir, Pepsi, Firewall Eddie, and Eddie had escaped in a steam of drugs and alcohol. They were lucky no evidence remained, and the circuit judge and JPs were lenient on this island.

I pondered about my Sudanese friends and how I was outgrowing Samir and Pepsi emotionally and intellectually. Samir was going to be okay with his surgery. In six months he'd be skipping on his poor left leg, and his other leg would be addressed. In a year he'd be off the disability pension and able to work like Pepsi, or go to school in Victoria, or work in Vancouver as a dockhand or maybe ship aboard a freighter headed for exotic places. I wouldn't go with him but I would wish him well.

Right now my heart leaned toward the tall, paunchy golden-haired detective from Victoria. Were we dragging out the process because we knew when we solved the case that Mark would be returning to his job on the big Island? Or that wasn't fair, was it? We were two adults and it was important that we do our jobs. I knew Mark was very professional, and I knew he was hankering to put Samir and perhaps Pepsi behind bars for a long, long time. That wasn't personal with him, he was far too much a pro for that, it wasn't because of my friendship with Samir or jealousy on Mark's part. No, he believed that Samir, and perhaps with Pepsi's help, had killed the doctor and maybe the mayor, too.

I believed myself that Samir could have done it, but so could I in a fit of insanity, I wouldn't put it past anyone not to murder, when under enough stress, and we'd all seen stress this past winter. I still thought of Lorne O'Halloran, and how he'd almost killed me, and I'd protected him. Why had I done that? Was Lorne the father I'd never had, and was I less than professional?

My emotions were getting the better of me. I'd been on stress leave for several months, the whole winter, actually. Erna from the Justice Department in Victoria believed in me. She had arranged a pardon, which in two years would go through with good behavior. I was very grateful, but guilty too, as I wasn't sure I deserved a pardon or Erna's support. I knew that she had spoken kindly of me to Mark.

I decided to tell him the whole story about Lorne. If Lorne was capable of murder then he should be put away. Although I believed in his innocence, since the incident at the float house, I thought that proved he was capable of using a gun for murderous purposes. Mark suspected there was more to it than aiming a gun at a police officer, though that was serious enough. If he'd known that Lorne had shot at me and missed, or that Lorne had been responsible for my scooter crash, then Lorne would be on trial right now. Mark thought my scooter had skidded on the gravel and blown a tire. Lorne had pointed his gun at the detective, and Mark had no choice but to shoot him. There were too many loopholes in the law here on Serendipity. Too many bad citizens protected and let free.

I shut the window in my little bedroom on the second floor of the float house and closed the pretty curtains. The moon had been eclipsed by cloud and the foghorn and lamps on the lighthouse were more necessary than ever. I could hear the chug of a ship passing quite near to the bay. I knew there were logs and flotsam dancing on the surf, which boomed now in a rhythm that was like my heartbeat. I loved the sea and I loved the sound of the sea. I loved the sweep of the lamps on the lighthouse and the alpenhorn that sounded to warn our sailors off the shoals.

It was the Viking Valkyrie that stood at that window now. My heart swelled with the hiss and thunder of the ocean's spume. It was in my blood, my grandfather's ghost stood near me at the window, and I could feel the shadow spirit of that young man who had died too young at sea. Did my father see it? Did my father, in his tight, dry soul, hear it? His soul was not what I remembered, though, his hand tousling my hair when I was twelve, and leaving a year later to fly off to Curaçao with a lover.

Had my mother cramped his style? Did his daughter and responsibilities weigh on him and did he yearn to escape? Maybe he was a Viking, too, a Paul Gauguin of the Danes. Maybe he heard the sound of the sirens where the sea meets the rocks.

Seemed to me like the good guys don't always win. The good guys aren't always the happy ones either. The bad guys are very happy with how they succeed in their quintessential badness, and they glory in putting one over on the establishment. I knew that from the streets. They *love* to score points with the devil.

I even knew young guys who broke into houses and didn't think they did anything wrong because they didn't vandalize the places like their friends would have, like turning on the water taps and so on all over the house. They knew of a hundred things they could have done that were worse than breaking into a house and stealing jewelry from those who could afford it.

Sure I knew how they thought, and I knew how gullible and innocent the Christians were down at the Trinity Centre, feeling sorry for the street people, the druggies and their bad ways, and thinking they were all miserable. They weren't. The bad guys wouldn't even go to hell, if all were even, and the good guys were the ones who suffered with thoughts of sin and secret depravities, remorse and guilt. Wasn't fair, maybe, but we must put ourselves in the other's sandals and get the blinders the hell off our fair Caucasian Christian eyes. Life wasn't fair, and it wasn't Christian, and it wasn't like the Good Book said.

The foghorn sang me to sleep as the moon rode over the marina and to the other side, where I couldn't see it any more from my crisp white sheets.

Chapter Seventy-three

"You're certainly looking spiffy this morning, Miss Annie," Mark remarked as we walked to our table in the Lebanese diner. "I chose this establishment because I know you don't drink, and the Red Ox Inn is notorious for its drinks and drinkers."

"Besides," I said, checking my BlueBell phone, "This place is cheaper and you took nurse Molly Dewitt to the Red Ox Inn just last night."

"Oh, that hurts." Mark smacked his head with his hand. "It's also true, but that's not the reason we're here. I like Lebanese food, and I have a hangover this morning."

"You know the saying, a hair of the dog that bit you," I said. "My mother always said that."

"Not true. Tell me, dear," Mark slid a chair from beneath a table for me. There were no servers in sight and the cook was busy behind the bar. "Tell me, hun, are you jealous of Molly?"

"No," I said too quickly and sat with a flump in the sturdy wooden chair with the flowered cushions. "Not true."

"I think we should talk." Mark was serious. He sat next to me at the small table, elbows leaning on the plain white cloth, eyebrows drawn together and his mouth pursed.

"What about?"

It was true, I looked spiffy. I had looked at myself in the tall bathroom mirror this morning, and again coming into La Shish. My short curly hair bounced around a tanned face with startling violet eyes, my buck teeth didn't look so obvious after I'd carved out a nice cupid's bow on my lips with doll-pink lipstick, my new top said PINK on it in white letters and complemented my lipstick and my mousse foundation. The jeans fitted loose since I'd lost another ten pounds and were held up by a snazzy tan leather belt with a silver buckle. I was really looking good, dude, I thought.

I wasn't stupid. I knew what we had to talk about. Us.

"You know, I like Samir. I really do," Mark began. He continued to lean toward me and looked so serious I laughed.

Mistake to laugh at a dude. He looked hurt and drew back.

"Oh, I'm sorry," I said. "I wasn't laughing at what you said or even at you, Mark. I was laughing at how serious you look. Really, I can explain. But first I want you to know that I answered too quick, and yes, I'm jealous of Molly. I'm jealous of any woman you spend time with. Want to know why?"

"Guess I feel the same way about Samir," he said. "For the same reason."

"That is…?"

Neither of us wanted to say it. We were attracted to each other. That's the truth. It was… it was electricity. Like walking into a room after a thunderstorm, all drenched and snapping with ozone. Like a party where you're half lit and having the time of your life, even when you leave, even when you go home, you're dancing together with golden boots and diamonds in your eyes. I told you, I aced drama in high school.

I didn't say all that, of course. I just sat there and stared into Mark's eyes, that weren't ice at all, I noticed, but deep and so blue that the summer sky must be jealous of them.

"Have you ever… you know… with Samir?" he asked. I grinned and shook my head.

"No."

Mark sighed and leaned back in his chair.

"That's a relief," he said.

"Never," I said. "With anyone." I grinned inside my head.

"Really?"

"You?"

"Yes, of course, but not with Molly or anyone on this island. Not with anyone for a very long time."

"Were you ever married?" I just guessed, thinking that he seemed lost in thought, perhaps with someone long ago and far away.

"Bingo," he said.

I didn't ask what happened. I just sat there and waited, eyebrows raised, my hands clasped in front of me.

"Yes. To a wonderful girl I'd known since Grade Five. She thought I was wonderful, too, until... she wanted children."

"Yes?"

"I... I can't have children. I didn't want to adopt. Too risky, I thought, to adopt an unknown set of genes or pregnancy, maybe alcohol abuse or a developmental disease with premature death, maybe mental illness, I was so pig headed and obstinate about it, and she... she left me finally."

"Because you didn't want children?"

"Not that I didn't want them. I just thought we should have our own and I couldn't so we had no language in common anymore."

"Is it so important to have children?"

"She thought so. She would have loved to stay home, have a passel of kids, cook for me."

"Sounds old-fashioned and stultifying, if you ask me, if you don't mind my saying so, Mark." I sort of leaned back in my chair, away from him, a bit stunned by this revelation and by the fact that he had been married and apparently chosen someone so different from me. I was jealous of this unknown woman. Jealous of her apparent hold on him after all these years. "How many years ago did she leave you?"

"Oh, we were young, I was twenty. So fifteen years ago."

"No sex since then, is that what you're saying?" He grinned.

"No, that's not what I'm saying."

"I'm not going to ask you any more questions about *that*."

"And you, never with Samir or anyone else?"

"Nope."

"How old are you, Miss Anne?" The Lebanese server was hovering at the table. He moved away, then back again, with his order book in his hand. We took a look at the menu and I chose the falafel plate. Mark ordered malfouf (stuffed cabbage with meat and rice). He said he liked cabbage rolls and this was what he preferred from the menu.

"I'm a conservative guy," he said. I would have to teach him something different.

"You know how old I am," I said.

"It was a rhetorical question."

"Remember the two dozen plus one roses?"

"Yes."

"Those were the first roses anybody ever bought me," I said as the waiter arrived with a basket of warm pita bread and something he said was eggplant, that looked like hummus. When I questioned the waiter, he told me what it was called in Lebanese. Baba ghanouj. I tried to remember that. Sophisticated women knew how to act in any setting.

I grinned again. Electricity coursed through the air between Mark and me. We were talking about roses but really something much deeper and better than roses was happening between us.

"You gave one to me for my buttonhole."

"Yes, I thought there were enough to spare one."

"Usually they cut one off." He spread some baba ghanouj on a piece of pita. I did the same, not knowing any better.

"I didn't know that," I said. "Mmm, this is good."

"You've never had ghanouj?"

"Of course I have." I grinned and shook my head.

"My gosh, you need an older fellow like me to take you out more, little miss innocent."

"Yes."

I agreed. I needed to go out more, and I needed to do it with Mark. Hee, hee.

Chapter Seventy-four

Samir understood about Mark and me the next time I talked to him. I'd gone to the Powolskis to look him up and have the talk that I thought we should have, since talking seemed the order of the day. It was good to see Meredith and Henry again. After a half hour of fruit juice and cookies, I excused myself and went upstairs to see Samir, where he was lying in bed watching his big screen HDTV. He looked over when I walked in the room but he didn't get up.

"Oh, hi, Angel," was all he said. There was a soccer game on between Brazil and Great Britain. I knew Samir would cheer for Brazil. I waited a bit then sat down on the bed opposite.

"Where's Pepsi?" I asked.

"I don't know. He went out this morning." Samir didn't take his beautiful brown eyes off the screen. "I know why you're here, doll."

"Why?" Surely he hadn't figured me out that well. I wasn't that transparent. Was I?

"Yeah. It's about your detective lover boy."

"Oh my gosh, Samir. You're so smart."

"It's about time we got it out on the savannah in the open, so to speak. I'm not blind, I'm not crazy, and I'm not stupid. Also, I don't care."

"You don't?"

"Nah. You and me are just friends, doll. I knew that all along."

"Really?"

"Yeah. We shared this room for eight months and nothing happened. What does that show you?"

"Either I'm a lesbian or you're pretty damn understanding."

"Yeah, well, you're not a lesbian. I'm not that understanding, either. The chemistry just isn't there."

"Oh." I felt like my stomach had hit my shoes and I'd stuck my head in a toilet. "I thought different for a while."

"Did you? We did have a few good times, some hugs, shared a kiss, I remember. Maybe more than that."

Is that all there is? I wished Pepsi would come back. "No big deal, right?"

"Right." He continued to watch the soccer game.

"Nothing to talk about then?"

"Not really. Go ahead and have a good life, angel pie."

"Are we still friends?"

He looked over at me and his eyes widened. His mouth sort of twisted and made an O, and I thought he was going to laugh at me. I wasn't sure what he would say. I'd thought we were friends. I'd always thought so. I'd thought we were more than friends until Mark came along. I'd spent months being torn between the two of them. Now it was over, with Samir, just like this, as though nothing had ever happened. He seemed so disinterested. I was really hurt.

"Of course we're still friends," he said. "Goofy." Then he did something remarkable. He got up off his bed and reached for his crutches. The walking cast clunked on the floor as he crossed the space between us in a couple of long strides. Then he leaned over and hugged me. As his face touched mine I swear his cheeks were wet with tears. I didn't know what to say or do. When he straightened up he was smiling at me, very soft and gentle, like I'd never seen him before.

"Good luck," he whispered. Then he clunked back to his bed and turned the TV louder.

He ignored me from then on. I reached over and squeezed his hand. He smiled, still with his eyes on the screen, and I choked, "Thank you."

Mrs. P was stumping up the stairs and I thought it was time to go.

Chapter Seventy-five

The Mounties were getting pretty antsy about finding a suspect for the murder at City Hall. The new mayor and her aldermen were putting pressure on the cops because the voting public was putting pressure on the mayor. I couldn't figure out why they hadn't arrested Lorne yet but then thought he probably had an alibi I didn't know about. Or he knew somebody important who was taking the pressure off him.

Then they arrested him.

I found out about it the next day when Mark phoned to tell me the news. "It's because of the incident at the float house," he said. "I told them what you told me about the gun and shooting at you and everything… his drinking, which a lot of people don't know about. He had the opportunity and a motive for blowing away Hizhonnor. I told them how close you and I came to arresting him at his office, and how Samir's situation put Lorne on a back burner for a while."

"You're not so sure about Samir anymore?"

"No, I'm not. I don't like to think it was personal. I'm a pro, baby. But I'm not convinced now that either Samir or Pepsi did it. They sort of covered each other, which is suspicious, and I'm not entirely sure Samir didn't take the drugs and the cash and limp away with it, and the fact the poker was missing also seems pretty damning."

"Why don't we arrest them, too?"

"We tried, you'll remember that. Samir threatened to sue us for false arrest and racial prejudice, and Constable Tom and Sergeant Ross weren't ready to take that on in this little town. What we could do is take him to Victoria and put him in the city buckets there. We don't have enough on Pepsi to arrest him, although Firewall Eddie Raven seems to have collapsed as an alibi. He'd still need a motive. Maybe the fact that he tried to protect his cousin would damn him? I don't know. The case isn't simple."

"You're new at this, aren't you, Mark? Why did Erna send you?"

"No, I'm not new in law enforcement. I was put on a desk because I told you, I hurt my leg and can't be on the beat anymore."

I chewed on my nails and then clenched my hand on the phone. Time to confront my lover boy with his apparent lack of professionalism. I had a job to do, after all, and couldn't let personal feelings interfere with getting that job done. Some hard questions had to be asked. "No specific training for a promotion?"

"I don't know what you're getting at. This isn't like you, hun."

"I'm just saying, this case should have been closed months ago. We keep letting suspects slip through our fingers."

"We can't arrest someone just because we need a suspect. We have to have solid evidence or we'll look like fools." Mark's voice inched up an octave. I had to smile a bit. I was getting to him.

"We're looking like fools, anyway. How long do you think the media will be happy to be closed out of the case, and what we're doing about it?"

"They'll be happy as long as I darn well say they should be," he said.

"This is a high profile case. I think we need more help than the Mounties tied up at City Hall with the mayor's murder, and you and the local cops here. And me."

"Yes, and you. Maybe you don't want to work with me anymore, Annie?"

I thought, *I'm a mean little witch and I'm enjoying this.* I didn't feel good about myself anymore. "It's not that, Mark, you know that. Maybe we're too close to the situation. Maybe we've been working on it too long. Maybe we should take a step back."

"Think out of the box?" he asked. "I think we should step back and distance ourselves a bit. I think that's a great idea. You and me, Annie, we've got to keep this professional. We've been letting our feelings for each other get the best of us."

"Yes." It was out in the open. Our personal feelings were interfering with getting our jobs done.

"When's the last time you counted?" he asked.

"You know about that?" My fingers started to fly. "I didn't know you knew about it."

"You told me you were OCD. I know something about it. My wife was like that, she counted, too."

Oh, shit. "Your wife?"

"Yes. Sandi."

"Sandi Snow? Nice."

"She kept her name. Her name was Sandi Elizabeth Carter-Snow."

"Nice." I was stuck. Couldn't think of anything to say except *nice*. Why had he told me this? I didn't want to know.

Maybe he wanted a relationship that was based on truth. Oddly enough, I didn't think I could handle a relationship based on truth.

Just then the voices began again.

Chapter Seventy-six

I went down to the NA meeting at the bookstore early the next Monday and saw Leroy and Firewall Eddie there with a small group of addicts. They were there pretty well every meeting, I could depend on that. I wanted to talk to Eddie and find out what he knew about the night the mayor got blown away, and the night old Doc Hubert met his grisly end. It wasn't the first time I'd talked to Leroy and Eddie. They sort of rolled their eyes when they saw me.

"You know Lorne's in jail," I started out, buttonholing pore Eddie as he stood near the coffee urn talking to Calvin. "Samir's on probation, released on his own recognizance simply because they felt sorry for him just out of the hospital, I think, also because he threatened to sue." Firewall Eddie chuckled. "The public and the cops are crazy to get this case wrapped up and they're going to do it one way or the other. Now how can you help me, Firewall Eddie? What do you know? We've got two lives at stake here, Lorne and Samir, maybe Pepsi, and I don't really believe any of them did it. But who did? What do you know?"

I was squeezing him for information, calling on old favors, anything to get this case over and done with. I didn't care really if Lorne was in jail, the fat old SOB, and I didn't care if Samir was out on bail because I thought he could beat any rap, and I didn't think they had a strong enough case against Pepsi. But I did think it was possible any or all of my friends could be railroaded by a Crown Prosecutor who wanted to wrap up the case and make the public and City Hall happy. So I was kind of desperate, too, to find out what I could about what really happened there that night at Doc's clinic in November, and later in City Hall.

"I don't know nothin'," Eddie said, not surprising me, but then he looked kind of puzzled, screwed up his eyes a bit and squinted, and said, "You know, Annie, I lost my gun at ol' Doc's place a couple of nights before he got his brains drilled out of his head. Beats me where it is now. I didn't get a chance to go back to get it. It wasn't there last time I looked. Cops didn't say nothin' about it. It couldn't have been the murder weapon? It wasn't important, was it?"

I thought maybe it was. "What kind of gun was it, Eddie?" I asked, knowing the answer already.

"It was a regulation issue SIG Pro semi-automatic pistol."

"*That* was your gun? Why didn't you report it missing?"

"So much went on, by the time I got back to looking for it, I was afraid I'd be charged with the murder," he said. "Fear kept me from asking about it. But it looks like I'm off the hook now, except, what *did* happen to my gun?"

"I think it's in Victoria at the forensics lab," I said. *This is big news, you little witch*, my voices whispered. *They all hate you. You kept this news from the Mounties and they're going to arrest you, Annie Fanny big fat Fanny.* "No," I said. "I didn't know you'd lost your gun."

"How could you have known?" Firewall Eddie asked. It was time for the meeting to start and he sat down. I sat next to him with a Styrofoam cup of lukewarm tea in my hand.

You stupid woman. You don't let on you hear voices, do you, or they'll take you away, ha, ha, yes, they'll come and take you away.

I started to sweat.

"What were you doing at Doc's clinic and why'd you bring your gun?" I whispered.

Firewall Eddie whispered back, "Shhh. Meeting's started."

The chairperson asked for silence. Firewall Eddie and I smiled and focused on the meeting. They asked me to talk, as a guest.

After the meeting, Eddie took me out for coffee at the Golden Arches. All the recovering addicts were there, or most of them, at the 'meeting after the meeting'. I can't say any more than that. I shouldn't say that much.

"I got drugs, okay, from Doc," Eddie confided. "He gave them out pretty free, bennies and stuff, not just methadone, not ol' Doc. You had to pay for them if you could, but he was a soft touch, too, and not everybody could pay. I got this habit, you know that. I was just off work so had my SIG Pro with me on my belt. I took it out to show Doc. He was interested in the regulation weapon. He knew something about firearms, seemed to, turned it over in his big beefy hands and laid it down on the counter. Someone came in just then and I left before they recognized me."

"What time was this?" I asked. "Did you see who came in?"

"About eleven at night. No, I didn't see who it was before the door opened. It was the door in the back, maybe one of Doc's lady friends. I didn't want anybody on the street to see me there, so I bolted. I thought maybe it was the law, too, you never know in a clinic like that. The constable would sometimes come in to check things out. Doc was always in a bit of trouble with the law but he was smart enough get out of it. Until the end, of course. Somebody got to him or somebody got him."

"Yes, they did for sure. Thanks. That's very helpful." He did it, stupid, I thought. He wouldn't leave his gun there in plain sight with the Doc who had all kinds of low life at his clinic. He blew the Doc away, admit it. You have no friends. Your friends are all winos and thugs. Annie, you're a loser. Arrest this guy. You'll be a hero.

"They got Lorne down at the station and Samir better be real careful," Firewall Eddie whispered. The others in the room began to stare.

My hands flew under the table, counting the tiles on the wall.

Chapter Seventy-seven

Mark drove me to the pharmacy two days later for my injection. I went into the back room because I had to bend over and expose my butt. Mark wouldn't be ready for that yet, nor would the other customers in the store. I sort of grinned at the image. After the injection, I was free of the voices for quite a while.

"I do like tall, blond men," I murmured as we left the drugstore. "You in particular." I put my hand through his arm.

Old Mrs. Antoine stared as we left the store arm in arm. I smiled at her and lifted my eyebrows, then lifted a hand in greeting to her husband, about a hundred years old, who shuffled beside her with a walker.

"I have a plan." Mark patted my hand. "You've never seen my place, have you?"

"No."

"Would you like to see my fancy little apartment?" He veered to the side when we left the store. "It's right up this street."

"Really? Shouldn't we take the car?"

"If you insist. But it's only two blocks away."

"You live in the Heights?"

"Yes. I can afford it. Single and all. Detective's salary."

"I'm impressed."

He grinned. "That's the idea, hun."

"This isn't like a come on, is it?" I asked, getting in his silver SUV.

"No, of course not, Annie. I just want to show you my place. I've been to yours a number of times. I want you to see how I live." He drove slowly down the street and stopped in front of a concrete and glass high rise.

"I didn't know people actually lived here. This is a brand new apartment building and expensive as hell," I said. "It just went up a year ago."

"I leased it for six months. Come on, let's go up and I'll show you the glass elevator."

"It's at least ten stories. Wow. Like a big city building. Nice view?"

"The best. It's getting late but it doesn't get dark until after ten. When it gets dark we'll open the drapes and see the lights of downtown Serendipity."

"Wow."

He was right, it was a glass elevator. It went up swiftly and smoothly to the top floor. I *was* impressed until I walked into his place.

What a mess. That's what I thought when I first walked in. Then I realized everything had a place and everything meant something to my friend Mark.

It was a small studio apartment, crammed with computer equipment and photographic equipment, cameras, tripods, a huge plasma TV, a forty-inch computer monitor at least, what looked like a little darkroom. In the corner behind a rosewood partition was a single bed with a leopard print quilt on it and about six pillows, all brown and gold. The galley kitchen was neat and clean, the counters bare, apparently any coffee pots or microwaves were under the counters or in the cupboards or drawers. A utility cart was against one wall and that explained some of the space available, as it was full of shining copper pots, a Mr. Coffee, and a toaster oven. No microwave I could see and maybe he didn't have one. Then I noticed the toaster and canisters against one wall behind a little divider on the middle counter.

"Everything has a place," I said. "Very nice."

"Yes," he said. "I have to be efficient in a place this small. And with this much *stuff.*"

"You are," I said. "Very nice." I looked at some original paintings on the wall by unknown artists, all impressionist or post-modern cubist. A giclée digital print of Vancouver's skyline hung on the wall over a cream leather loveseat.

"Have a seat," Mark said, taking off his jacket and tie. "May I get you some juice or coffee?"

"Orange juice, please," I said, and plunked myself into a stark black leather chair. I'd taken my shoes off and my toes sunk into a white shag area rug. The rest of the floor was shining hardwood.

"Very nice," I repeated.

"Of course, it's not mine," he said. My heart sank. All this gorgeous stuff wasn't *his*?

"No, of course not." I realized then that he was only here for six months. He'd have no use for all this fine furniture and paintings, it wouldn't make sense to sink his cash into furnishings.

"I'm renting it," he said.

"Oh." My heart went back up. He was renting all this neat stuff. He'd picked it out.

"The owner spends half the year in Afghanistan," Mark continued. "This belongs to him."

"All of it?" I asked, hoping at least the leather sofa or the bed belonged to Mark.

"Yes. It just made sense to rent."

"It's very nice," I said for the third time. "You chose well. Your friend has good taste."

"He's not my friend. He's a guy I found on Craig's list, looking for somebody to rent his condo for part of the year. Just to look after things while he's gone."

"Oh. That must mean the rent is cheap."

"Very."

"You're full of surprises, Mark."

He handed me a generous portion of cold orange juice with a little umbrella on top flirting with the glass.

"I really am hopeless at decorating," he said. "But I have good taste."

"I like it. It doesn't look exactly like you, though. I'm not surprised it's not really yours."

"It needs a woman's touch," he said. He winked at me and sat on the leather loveseat, pushing a large James Dean cushion out of the way. "I can't change it but when the owner gets back I'll have to find my own place and presumably decorate it somehow."

I sipped at my juice through a red straw. "Are you going to be here on the island that long?"

"I didn't tell you, but I've been given a transfer. I asked for it. I like it here and it's good training. I'll be stationed with the sergeant and Tom, I can use a little office there, and I'll report to Erna in Victoria. When this case is cleared up, of course. Until then, I'm working pretty close with the Mounties at City Hall, and with you, Annie."

"You're going to *live* here?"

"That is, unless you have any objections."

"No, but it's a surprise. I thought I'd have to move to Victoria to be with you."

Mark flicked on the TV and we watched as he surfed the channels, some looking pretty good. I only watched movies on my computer. This was a *huge* improvement. "We could discuss that. But I like the small town atmosphere here and the quiet island living."

"Quiet?"

"It was until someone blew the mayor's balls away," he said.

"I would like it if you stayed. Does that mean you're my boss?"

"I don't know. Erna wasn't clear on that."

"Does that mean you're getting a demotion?"

"It looks like that, but it's what I asked for," Mark said, and switched off the TV, leaving the room silent.

"Why?"

"Why what?" he asked. He grinned. I grinned back at him. Fire flickered in my veins, through the room, through our guts. Power beyond all measure. It was raw. The silence quaked with hidden meanings, with secret vendettas, with promise. We could be Doc and have a hole the size of a ping pong ball drilled in our skulls, our brains spilled out in a wet heap beside the bodies, our sex exposed.

"Wow," I said.

"Wow," he said, and reached out for me. Lightning flashed between us.

Chapter Seventy-eight

I sat in my kitchen that day late in May and pondered what I'd seen on the Doc's memory stick. The lists, the client names, the hints of what had happened that night in November last year.

Now the cops had the computer and the memory stick, too.

Not before I'd copied it onto my laptop. Ha.

As I leafed through the files and the Word pages, the Excel sheets, the data entries, I noticed something a bit odd.

All the entries that were clues to who had an appointment at Doc's clinic that night were unique to that particular Saturday. No other week had those entries. No other week made any mention of an MS or a Maser. The client lists were open and not always coded in every instance except that Saturday when Doc Hubert...

That seemed odd. Then I started digging a bit deeper. *What are you doing, dummy Annie? You'll never find it.* The voices sounded a bit desperate. Was I onto something?

Every single one of the entries that indicated a client by initial or code name on that date had been entered later. I could tell by the dates on the entries. They were entered after midnight on November seventeenth. After Doc had been killed.

Very interesting. And who would have had access to these entries?

I couldn't imagine it would have been Samir, computer illiterate, or Firewall Eddie, though it could have been Firewall Eddie. Lorne might have been capable of it but when would he have had the time to fiddle with the files? I didn't think the cops who had the hard drive and memory stick now might have noticed what I just did, because they wouldn't have had the thoughts I did. I knew now what I should have known in November, what was obvious to me then.

Someone meant for me to see the original files and didn't think I'd be smart enough to figure out they'd been doctored. So to speak, heh heh.

It was the world's biggest type of kipper made from dried, smoked, and salted fish.

In other words, a disambiguation. A piece of information intended to be misleading. It was here in front of me all the time, and I'd missed it.

By the time Mark Snow got here, I was marking dates on the calendar, figuring things out, I noticed that night would be a full moon and that meant lots of light if there was no cloud cover. I checked the forecast and put my head outside the door to see for myself. A clear day and I could see forever. It would be a clear night.

"Mark," I said.

"Annie." He grinned. I told him what I'd figured out. He was appropriately blown away.

"You don't know for certain," he warned.

"No, I'll have to check it out," I said.

"How?"

"I have my ways."

Mark was sure I had my ways and smirked when he put a hand on my left breast to prove it. That felt sort of too good to be ignored. I shut my laptop because there was nothing I could do until later tonight, around eleven or later.

Until then, though, there was lots we could do. We climbed the ladder-like stairs up to the creaking second floor and fell together on the spare white bed where Samir and Pepsi had cracked jokes until early morning, that winter. It seemed so long ago, and so innocent.

Chapter Seventy-nine

I went over to the cop shop around four and peeked in on Lorne, who was sitting in a cell looking very angry and sad at the same time. Constable Tom dangled the keys in front of the door and slid a coffee under the bars.

"Thanks for that," I said, but Lorne didn't get up or reach for it. I didn't blame him. He didn't belong here but I couldn't do anything to help him right now. Maybe later. Almost certainly later. I asked Tom about Samir's case.

"So far Samir and Pepsi have kept to the terms of their probation order. It's a non-reporting probation. They're very lucky to have had a liberal JP that morning. They're lucky not to be sharing a cell with your friend Lorne here."

"When is he scheduled to be transferred to Victoria?"

"Not for any time soon. We're still investigating the murder weapon at the forensics lab and the Doc's client list as it shows up on the memory stick. Lots of it in code, it's taking our guys a while to figure it out. The murder weapon's been wiped clean of prints, we're looking for bullet matches. All takes time, and we're not the only murder case the lab's working on."

"What about the memory stick?" I asked. "Is there anything new on that?"

"Annie." Tom strode to the coffee machine and poured us both a very strong and very black cup of java. "We both know you would have copied the thumb drive onto your laptop." Wow, he's smarter than you thought. Smarter than the ordinary gumshoe like Mark...

"My friend Mark," I said.

"What?"

"Nothing," I said, and sat in the ragged chair opposite the constable. I could see Sergeant Ross doing paperwork in the other office. Mark wasn't anywhere around, I thought perhaps I'd left him at the float house thinking things over, and going through my BlueBell phone records and the files on my computer. I'd told him he could do that. Mia casa your casa or something like that.

"I'll never get used to crazy Annie and her voices," Tom commented. "No offense, darling, but you talk to yourself. Out loud. In front of other people. I've no way of telling if you're talking to me or talking to your dang voices."

I felt the usual twinge of guilt for being crazy. "I know." *We're right here. We won't leave you, Annie.*

I was afraid of that. That the voices wouldn't leave me. All that bother about the new injection and it looked like I might need another Zyprexa on top of what I took, or an increase in the Flupenthixol. I really didn't want to do that. I was doing so well figuring things out, too. The stress of it was pushing me over the edge again. Dang.

"You and Samir getting along okay?" Tom seemed to be making conversation rather than genuinely interested, so I brushed him off with a brief, "Sure."

"I've got a favor to ask of you and Sergeant Ross," I said.

"Anything within reason." Tom hooked his thumbs over his suspenders and tapped his fingers on his broad expanse of stomach. The sergeant looked up from the other room. These guys were maybe small town or small island cops, but nothing really got by them. Except maybe this; what I'd discovered.

"I want a search warrant," I said. "I need it for tonight."

"We'll have to see what the circuit judge says about that," Tom said. The sergeant nodded.

"Or the Justice of Peace," Ross commented. "He'd be able to get you one."

"Where is he?" I asked, pretending to be so cool. Tom was admiring my PINK shirt, I could tell, and maybe the cleavage it exposed. I felt so cool to be finally attractive to men and it didn't matter, it might be superficial and trite, but I was finally a *real woman.*

"Shut up," I said, but the voices hadn't said anything.

It turned out the JP was at home eating dinner. He came to the cop shop and gave me what I wanted as soon as he finished his pork chops and pumpkin pie. I left the station all gleeful, the warrant tucked in my pocket. Mark didn't know exactly what I was up to that night or he might have insisted he go with me, but I wasn't entirely sure what I'd find or where I'd find it.

All I knew was I was sure I was right. It would work out all right as long as I didn't get caught and maybe murdered like the Doc was. Or blown away like the mayor. Because I was pretty convinced that one person had done both dastardly deeds, so to speak, as my mother would have said.

I was going to dig for the evidence tonight, under the full moon, without a flashlight to draw attention to myself. The full moon cast shadows in a small town, where there wasn't a lot of light. Something a city girl or boy wouldn't know. Somebody like Mark, who was waiting for me at home at the float house.

I'd have to lie to him.

Chapter Eighty

Mark had left by the time I got back to my place. Must have used the key in the window box. I saw evidence he'd been there, a bouquet of spring flowers smiling on my counter, probably picked from the perimeter of the parking lot up on the hill (they looked very familiar); the dishes were done and stacked on the drain board, the floor had been swept. Little stuff I didn't have time to do anymore.

I was really my mother's daughter in that regard, too, my mother who had spent her life painting and writing, not on housework or cleaning up. She'd been a good cook, though, but she was a good cook only because she was interested in the flavors and appearances of various foods brought together, an artistic concept rather than mundane, such as it was to me. I took advantage of her cookbooks and tried to create culinary masterpieces like she had done, but it was all a bit beyond me. I did have a reason now to impress a good man, though. Mrs. P had cooked very well for Samir and me. I never went near the kitchen back then. Samir didn't know at that time that I even knew how to poach an egg.

Mark had made himself handy and useful. First man I ever met who was adept in the kitchen, and brought me flowers, too. He was a gem, and I learned more about him and more surprises the more time we spent together. That was a lot lately.

I was surprised he'd gone home but pleased, too. I had plans for tonight and they would involve Mark but not now.

That's why I was so disappointed when the door swung open around six o'clock and Samir limped in. I thought we'd made it plain last time at the Powolskis that we were through, but friends. *Yes, friends, you moron, he's here to ask a favor of you as a friend. Now listen up, Annie fat Fanny.*

"What?" I said as he closed the door and leaned against it. He was using a cane now with his walking cast.

"I need a favor, angel pie." He was out of breath, had probably slid down the hill from the parking lot. Pepsi must be up there in his blue Mercury, waiting for his blood brother cuz to finish down here at my place. He didn't come around very often anymore. I wondered why and then thought he and Samir would have talked, Pepsi was more sensitive maybe to moods, also he and I had never been close.

I thought about Eddie as well as Pepsi's job. No alibi. They were both wide open to arrest at any time. I would work on that and if I had my way, this case would be closed, King, by tomorrow morning.

Meantime, Samir had a favor to ask of me.

"What?" I said.

"I need to go to the Campbell River clinic tomorrow," he said. He clumped over to the settee he seemed to like so much. He sank onto the cushions with a sigh. I took a deep breath myself. It seemed easier to do him the favor than to argue. I was feeling weak that way tonight, anxious to be by myself and get the job over with that I had in mind. The search warrant was crumpled in my pocket. I took it out and straightened it, careful not to let Samir see it.

"You were wondering if I could go with you?" I asked. "You're not supposed to leave the island by yourself."

"That's right," he said.

"That won't last too much longer," I said. "But yes, I'll go with you if it's in the afternoon tomorrow." *You won't be finished in a day, stupid.*

"Yes, I will," I murmured to the voices and started to count with my hands thrust in my pockets. I counted to thirty then, for good luck, counted to thirty again. That should appease them. Who? Why, the powers that be, like my mother always said. Should appease the crazies gods in the universe who poured their thoughts into my brain. Should appease the voices. *Ha, ha, nothing can appease us.*

"I know."

"What?" Samir asked.

"Why didn't you call?" I asked.

"I couldn't get through."

"Oh. My phone is probably dead." I checked and yes, it was. I plugged it in, put the search warrant back in my pocket, and patted Samir on the shoulder.

"Don't worry," I said. "I'm here for you, pal. I'll cover your back." *He'll need it.* Shut up.

"It could be, though," I added, "that I won't be able to get away tomorrow. You may not be able to get away, either. It's about the ferry." I was careful. "It's possible they won't let anyone leave the island."

"What about the ferry? It runs from six a.m. to ten."

"I know. I'm just thinking something might change that."

"What, you crazy woman?"

"Me. I might change my mind about going with you. So don't count on it for tomorrow. Maybe another day. Or the ferry might be stopped. It's been known to happen."

I was being secretive, I knew, and probably worried him. He'd think I wasn't taking my meds again.

The evening was getting darker now, it was coming on to ten o'clock and Samir had to go. I had things to do and the moon was coming up all silver and grey over the eastern hills. The lighthouse was beginning to swing its lamps through my window and throw shadow pictures on my walls. The foghorn wasn't operative tonight. The night was very clear. I could tell it was a good night to do what I'd planned.

Samir finally left. *You're such a bitch, Annie,* the voices whispered.

I know. My fingers flew, in the pockets of my denim capris with the orange stripe down the side. I was nothing if not stylish.

Chapter Eighty-one

The full moon shone like a Chinese lantern on the job I had to do. Again on a Saturday. Everything significant happened on a Saturday. Tonight was May twenty-fifth and the moon cast shadows on Molly (Margaret Schneider) De-witt's back yard as I bent my back and searched for what I knew would be there, a mound of fresh earth. I'd seen it from Molly's living room last year, the pretty garden and the spade leaning against the garden shed.

Spade in hand, I searched with the blade for what I knew was there, a box beneath the soil. No luck the first time I tried it, just bulbs newly planted. Under the bulbs, I struck something hard.

The evidence was there. I turned the soil carefully and dug deep. The edge of the box caught on the spade and lifted. I leaned over and cradled it in my arms, brushing the dirt away and the mud of winter. The wooden crate was sealed with tape and staples. I grunted as I worked at them. A light came on from Molly's kitchen. I slunk into a corner where shadows hid me and carried the box to the gate. I slipped out the side of Molly's little yard and made my way to the scooter parked down the street. The box fit in the scooter's trunk and I wobbled down the street until I got my wheels firm underneath and turning.

When I got home I set the crate on my kitchen table and called Mark.

"What do you think is in it?" he asked over the phone. The distance between us buzzed. I felt giddy. Mark was asking me something I already knew and I told him.

"Cold cash and drugs," I said. "Why she did it."

"Why she did what?"

I sighed. Mark could be so thick sometimes. "Hit the Doc over the head with the flat of her karate hand several times, drilled a hole in his head the size of a ping pong ball, and fixed his computer records to reflect a red herring."

"Red herring? Like Maser and MS?"

"Exactly. She knew it would drive me crazy trying to figure it out. That's why she gave me the memory stick in the first place. She wanted to throw suspicion off herself."

"But her initials are MS, too. Molly Marilyn Schneider." His voice sounded animated. I'd struck gold dust and he knew it.

"Yes, that must have made her chuckle to throw me off like that. She's pretty clever," I said.

"Why would she take the drugs and cash when she worked there? She'd have the opportunity to put her hands on drugs or cash any time she wanted."

"Molly had a drug habit and the Doc refused to supply her anymore. She lost her job, nobody knew, the Doc told her that night and in a fit of rage she karate chopped him on the back of his head and drilled a hole in his skull to make the murder look like a madman had done it. Or a homeless person. Or someone with a paramedic background, like Samir."

There was silence on the line for a moment. "Did she know that?"

"Molly knew most of the people in this town. She knew Doc's patients and Samir had come in more than once for drugs to ease the pain in his leg. Molly knew that and also knew about the women who came from the reserve. She was mad with jealousy and burning for revenge when the Doc waited for her that night after hours and gave the little nurse her walking papers and a final stash of drugs, that she paid for. Then he put her cash in his wallet. She took it all to throw suspicion off her and make it look like a burglary, and she took the drugs."

"So it wasn't Samir after all." Mark sighed. "You know, I'm almost glad of that."

"No, it wasn't Samir," I said. "If you search her house you'll find cash and more drugs in a bookcase. I noticed the night I was there that a book was out of order. She had them all filed by alphabetical order but a large volume of Aristotle was out of place. She'd evidently put it back in a hurry when she heard the scooter drive up. If you take a look you'll find either it's a hollow book made to hide cash and valuables, or behind it is a hole in the wall."

"How do you know all this?"

"I have the crate from her backyard on my kitchen table. I had the memory stick from the computer copied onto my laptop. I have brains enough to wait until I'm sure by the process of elimination that it had to be the nurse in the clinic with the brown belt."

Mark was ever the cautious cop. I heard him sigh. "Did you have a search warrant?"

"I did. I went to the station earlier today and got one. Tom and the sergeant were interested but didn't believe I'd come up with anything. However, I got my search warrant on reasonable evidence when I explained what I knew."

"Didn't they want to go with you?"

"Nah. Constable Tom and the sergeant know me from way back. They know Annie can take care of herself. I have respect in this town, Mark."

He was silent. "With good reason. I'm coming over."

I tapped the crate. "Good idea. I don't want to open this by myself."

He was there in less than an hour.

"Why didn't you call me?" he asked. "It's awful late to be going out like that by yourself. Don't you know any better than to go out without backup?"

"I had to prove to myself I was right. I had to be very quiet and almost invisible. I didn't want to expose you to any danger, Mark. Or myself. As it is, I think she saw me. She'll be alerted. She's a clever little fox, is Margaret Schneider."

"No more clever than our Annie," he said. "Let's open this box and find out if you're right. It could be a buried dead cat for all we know."

"Or a severed head." I laughed. "But I don't think so."

"Let's do it."

Chapter Eighty-two

Mark and I stared at the crate on my kitchen table that had come from nurse Molly's garden. I pried at it with a knife and it sprang open.

"A light went on in her kitchen just as I was leaving the garden," I said. "I think she saw me. We'll have to confront her before she leaves the Island."

Mark scooped up the little vials of white powder and the multicolored pills that nestled in bags in the crate. "I don't even know what this stuff is, but the white powder is almost certainly an opioid, and I can guess at the pretty candy here. It's ecstasy and something else that's common on the street. I can guess she would try to sell it in Victoria or go into the big city on the mainland and barter it there."

"The next ferry leaves at six a.m.," I said. "You're right about the drugs but I think she may have meant them to feed her own drug habit. She'd have to have money to get away to the mainland and start another life under an assumed name, as she almost certainly did last time she moved."

"Let's go back there," Mark said. "We might need some help."

"Are you skilled in martial arts?" I asked.

"I know some jujitsu," he said. "Got it in training. I'll bring my semi-automatic with us. I think you should stay here, Annie."

"No way," I said. "I'm in this up to my neck in alligators now. I'm coming with you. We'll need to search her house. Maybe we should bring some men with us."

"I doubt that she's home now," he said.

"She has no place to go until six." I checked my BlueBell phone. "It's almost four now."

"Let's go," Mark said. He loosened his gun in its holster and made sure we locked the door as we left. He didn't have to tell me. I had a couple million in drugs sitting there on my kitchen table.

"Wait," I said.

"What?"

I opened the door and stepped over the gap to the alcove. The crate was wide open. I slipped it under the settee where it wasn't too obvious, then joined Mark on the dock.

"Lock the door," he said. "Here, I'll put the key back in the window box."

"Hot damn," I said, "Everyone knows about the key. Speaking of locking the door, thanks for the flowers you left, you cat burglar. You're a good house-keeper, too, Mark." He laughed.

We took Mark's SUV and parked half a block from nurse Molly's little house. We could see the light on in the kitchen as we walked with quiet feet around the perimeter of her property. The For Sale sign was still up.

"Guess she'll have to leave without selling it," I said. "Regretful, isn't it?"

"Yeah," Mark grinned. "Poor Molly."

We knocked on the door and Mark shouted, "Police. Open the door."

"Of course," Molly said, as she stood in the doorway. "What do you want this early?" She looked wide awake and was dressed. I could see a suitcase behind her in the hall.

"Going somewhere?" Mark asked.

Molly didn't answer.

"Game's over," Mark said. "You might as well admit it, Margaret Schneider. I've been doing some checking in your old hometown. Seems like you have a drug habit, Molly. Anything to do with Doc's murder? We think so." He stepped into the house, brushed past Molly, and closed the door. I stood just behind him inside the kitchen, near the bookshelves. I reached out and grasped *Aristotle*. Sure enough, there was a safe in the wall behind it.

"What's the combination, Molly?" I asked.

"Don't be stupid," she said and laughed. She was wearing jeans and a pressed orange shirt. Her face looked scrubbed and her lipstick was fresh.

"You look like you're going somewhere," I said. "I bet the safe is empty, am I right?" I gestured toward her suitcases.

"Bugger off," she said and threw herself at Mark, chopping him just below the jaw with a vicious blow which sent him reeling. Before she could launch herself at me, I ducked and covered Mark with my body. He drew his pistol and shouted.

"I'll shoot! This is your only warning, Molly Schneider."

She kicked the gun from his hand, but Mark was as quick as her blow. He reached for the gun and aimed it at Molly's head. She ducked as he shot at close range. The bullet went over her head and lodged in the wall.

"Damn you, cop," she screamed and slumped against the bookshelves. "I can still take you both if I wanted to."

"You don't want to, do you, Molly?' I asked."You were all washed up when you found out your doctor friend was unfaithful. That took all the spunk out of you and now you don't care if we take you in. That right?"

Tears coursed down the nurse's face. "I gave him five of my finest years," she sobbed."I couldn't understand what he saw in those whores he entertained after hours. When I found out about it, something snapped. He was unfaithful, he wasn't going to supply me with drugs anymore, he fired me." She continued to sob. "I have chronic pain. I need the drugs and Doc would prescribe them at first, then he started to give them to me. I was grateful but before I knew it, I couldn't do without them or the quantity he gave me. Then he cut me off. I went crazy."

"You used karate to chop him on the head. That's why the police couldn't find a blunt instrument. Your hand was the blunt instrument."

"Yes," she cried. "Yes, I killed him, my would-be lover. I'm glad it's over. It was too much to keep running."

"Thank you, Molly," I said. "I'm truly sorry."

Mark was silent, holding his gun hand steady.

"What about the mayor?" I asked.

"Spacey was a friend of Doc's. He came in just after I left," Molly said. "But he must have seen me and what happened to Bill. Spacey called me the next day, threatened to blackmail me. I had to make it look like a lunatic or a homeless person blew him away, too. I knew Firewall Eddie was too stoned to show up at work at City Hall that evening. I know the guys on the street. They came to the clinic all the time. I took a chance, went to the mayor's office, he let me in, thinking I had money and drugs. I didn't. I'd taken Firewall Eddie's gun from the Doc's cupboard. I blew Spacey away, then simply melted out the door and went home."

"You're glad it's over," I repeated. Her tears continued to course down her cheeks.

Mark said, "You must have known it had to end this way, Margaret."

That's when Molly lunged again, kicked the gun out of Mark's hand, struck him a vicious blow on the bridge of his nose, kicked him again on a muscle on the side of his thigh, and ran out the door. I heard her car start up and knew she was heading for the ferry.

I didn't move. She hadn't threatened me and Mark needed me right then. He was doubled over, blood pouring from his nose. His gun had skidded yards into a corner of the kitchen. I dashed over and picked it up.

"Got my cell," I said, and called the station. "Pick her up," I instructed, "and bring lots of reinforcements. Bring the dogs and be careful. She's a human weapon and she probably has a gun. She used Firewall Eddie's gun to blow away the mayor. We heard her confession. But she cried and ran."

The voice on the other end was deep and comforting. "Don't worry, Annie," Tom said. "We'll look after it, and Lorne's a free man. How's Mark?"

"He'll be all right," I said. "I'll drive him to Emergency so they can check for broken bones and maybe set his nose."

"Clean him up first," the ever-practical Tom said.

I did that, then we got into Mark's SUV and I adjusted the seat to make him more comfortable. He reached over to touch my hand.

"Well, King." Mark smiled. "This case is closed."

Chapter Eighty-three

I heard they picked up Molly at the ferry just as it was pulling in. Did I tell you I was good at drama? This nurse was even better. In the past she seemed acquiescent and even helpful to the police and me. What a clever cover. I almost admired her. The RCMP had martial arts training but Molly was good, she was real good for such a badass. It took four cops and three guns to restrain her when they took her in before the ferry pulled out.

Mark and Samir stretched their legs in my tiny living room. Pepsi slouched in the wicker chair in the kitchen. I turned the dial to an Oldies station. I wanted to make my place more inviting now I had friends over.

A delicious aroma of shrimp and melted cheese casserole wafted from the oven. My scones hadn't improved, though. Some things take more time to learn than others. Maybe by next Christmas the scones wouldn't taste like raspberry air freshener.

Mark rubbed a tanned hand over his blond head and grinned. "Two weeks' personal leave and I'm having a good time right here, Miss Anne."

"Does that mean you're not going back to Victoria?" I asked.

"I thought I'd spend my holidays here," he said. "With you."

Samir nodded and started to sing along with the music.

"That's all right with us." Pepsi drummed his fingers on the table. "It's all right, mama."

I grabbed Mark's hand, he stood, and we danced. Clumsy and hot, my heart pounded like the rhythm of my feet, and Mark smiled down at me from all of his six feet two. As he bent to kiss me, I felt the bristles on his chin, and touched the rough fabric of his plaid shirt, he enveloped me in fresh soap smell and a faint whiff of peppermint on his breath, his lips brushed my cheek and time stopped.

Through the bay window we watched a ribbon of orange stretch across the bay and settle on the purple disc of the horizon. Across the distance from my heart to eternity the foghorn moaned. A searchlight like a second moon sent fingers piercing ships at sea.

Samir was watching us. I didn't care. There was only the swaying room, the moan of an alpenhorn, and Mark's warm body next to mine.

I forgot to count.

About The Author

Kenna McKinnon is the author of *Short Circuit and Other Geek Stories; Space-Hive*, a middle grade sci-fi/fantasy novel; *BIGFOOT BOY: Lost on Earth*, published by Mockingbird Lane Press, a traditional small press. A children's **Chapter** book, *Benjamin & Rumblechum*, will be published by Mockingbird Lane Press in late 2014. *The Insanity Machine*, a self-published memoir with co-author Austin Mardon, PhD, CM; and *DISCOVERY – A Collection of Poetry*, were released by CreateSpace in 2012. Her books are available in eBook and paperback worldwide on Amazon, Smashwords, Barnes & Noble, etc., and in selected bookstores and public libraries.

Her interests / hobbies include fitness and health, volunteering, reading, writing, music, and walking. She lives in a high-rise bachelor suite in the trendy neighborhood of Oliver in the City of Edmonton. Her most memorable years were spent at the University of Alberta, where she graduated with Distinction with a degree in Anthropology (1975). She has lived successfully with schizophrenia for many years and is a member of the Writers' Guild of Alberta and the Canadian Authors Association. She has three wonderful children and three grandsons.

Message from the Author

Dear Reader,

I hope you've enjoyed the journey of a young lady who suffers from a sometimes delightful and often misunderstood mental illness. In 1978 I was diagnosed with paranoid schizophrenia and spent the next thirty-six years alternately struggling with it and rejoicing in any small victories. My university professors and others at the University of Alberta are to be credited with recognizing and attempting to deal with the illness as far back as 1975. Dr. Robert Fischer attempted to reconcile my wildness with the gentleness of spirit and love he saw in me, and I salute his memory and the expertise and compassion he brought to my therapy. My children, family, and friends suffered with me through no fault of their own, and to them I bring my heartfelt congratulations and gratitude for the 'long walk' we all have sustained.

I have attempted in *Blood Sister* to present a very human yet vulnerable young protagonist, Annie Hansen, who finds love after all, and a success perhaps not applauded by the world at large, an understanding of her illness, and a likely ending to her search for meaning and success in a field that is well suited to the vagaries of imagination that schizophrenia presents. We have many opportunities. I have met so many (Phil who travels on trains, and Don, hello!) who make the most of their handicap, but it is not a disability.

I wish you friendship, love and success, no matter how you measure it, in life and any romance that may, with the rest of humanity, make you happy or not. It's up to you, my friends, enjoy what God has given you, and don't let anyone tell you that you are less than the best of humanity. Though a cliché, 'there but for the grace of God go I.'

Namaste.

References

- Her author's blog: http://KennaMcKinnonAuthor.com/

- Facebook: https://www.facebook.com/KennaMcKinnonAuthor

- Twitter: http://www.twitter.com/KennaMcKinnon

- Goodreads: https://www.goodreads.com/author/show /6480104.Kenna_McKinnon

- LinkedIn: http://www.linkedin.com/in/kennamckinnon

- Google+: https://plus.google.com/118297240319245529549/posts

http://www.AuthorsForACause.com/ - The charity that promotes reading in young adults and published this digital book for Ms. McKinnon.

Lightning Source UK Ltd.
Milton Keynes UK
UKHW010452250820
368775UK00006B/217